The Satellites of Jupiter

Also by Kathleen Kenny

Poetry:

Sex and Death (Diamond Twig, 2000)

Goose Tales and Other Flights (Koo Press, 2007)

Firesprung (Red Squirrel Press, 2008)

Keening with Spital Tongues (Red Squirrel Press, 2009)

Sandblasting the Cave (Flarestack, 2009)

Hole (Smokestack Books, 2009)

Travelling Like Eggs (Red Squirrel Press, 2011)

Kathleen Kenny

THE SATELLITES OF JUPITER

A Novel

First published in the United Kingdom in 2016 by
Postbox Press, an imprint of Red Squirrel Press
www.redsquirrelpress.com

Red Squirrel Press is distributed by Central Books Ltd.
and represented by Inpress Ltd.
www.inpressbooks.co.uk

Cover image © Pauline Kenny 2016

A CIP catalogue record is available from the British Library.

ISBN: 978 1 910437 28 5

Printed by Charlesworth Press.

In memory of

Rusty

and all our trusty pet companions

'In fiction something that did not happen has to happen. In memoir, something that happened has to happen all over again. And by making it happen all over again, of course, you somehow change it. So they're both tricky, but in different ways.'

- Dermot Healy

Contents

Prologue

———— ◦ ◉ ◦ ————

It is early in my life.

In the kitchen behind Dad, gripping the knees of his thick wide trouser-legs, trying to stay in step. *Behave*, he says, unpicking my fingers as we move forward through the passage to his coat over the banisters. His legs shuffle, flap, try to shake me off, but I keep tight hold, my arms his leg irons, stopping him leaving the house.

Better than working my own legs, I like standing on his toes moving backwards. My stocking-feet on the feet of his hard black boots, my face through his baggy knees.

Walking backwards to arrive, so much to work out.

My late Victorian father, boy soldier of the first war; lying wounded in no man's land, holes shot through his wrist and thigh.

Younger by seventeen years, a nun tugs at her habit, caught in a moving staircase in Paris. My mother, an Irish novice, heads for Mussolini's Italy, picks lemons in the convent orchard.

Marble Arch at the start of the second war: Lyons Corner House. My parents' first chance meeting, short courtship and marriage; their hasty retreat from the blitzed Anderson shelters of Barking to settle in Newcastle.

1941. Their first born, my brother. A small boy playing by the Tyne, watching water rush his friend downriver to drown.

A year on from him, my sister with the squint arrives. A runaway, recaptured, put under with ether: forced to have straightened eyes.

1947, the post-war baby boom brings my next sister in: the budding artist, drawing lives. The one who is bought three new dresses and a dolls' house, simply for having her tonsils out.

Then me, child of the 50s, and last in line: little skin and blister, *the bairn* with short sight.

Here we are, six of us, plus cats: Jupiter, the star we revolve around.

It is early in my life.

All names are changed except for the cats.

Part One

1957 - 1960

Warrington Road

Drowning

———— ◦ ◉ ◦ ————

Daddy blows on the saucer of scalding tea then lifts, slurps, and gulps. I start to tip my shaky teacup to copy but he puts his big hand in the way and says if I slop down my cardigan on my first day at school everyone will laugh at me.

Before I go I am having soft-boiled egg with soldiers laid criss-cross on the blue and white tea-plate. It's our only square plate and everyone's favourite, and is set at my place because my brother and sisters have already eaten and left.

'It looks funny.' I look at the funny egg.

'You can put the pet lip away.' Mammy slices the hat off and plonks it by my spoon.

'I don't want it. It's got spots.'

'Divvent be so fussy,' Daddy sucks up more tea. 'That'll set ye up for the day.'

Daddy never leaves early because he likes to have time to digest and he doesn't have to clock on or off like the men who work in the factories.

'By, she's being awkward today.' Mammy wipes her red hands on her apron and hurries to the scullery to splosh things about in the sink.

'That's a bantam egg,' Daddy says, 'them speckles are special.' He makes his mouth do a loud smack then puts a in a fresh tab and lights it with a match.

'It's got the measles.'

15

'That's a good egg, that. Got magic qualities.'

'*Bamtum?*'

'Aye. A bantam's a lucky hen. If yee eat that ye'll be lucky aal day.'

'The white and the yella?'

'Aye. If ye divvent eat it aal the luck doesn't work.'

When Mammy comes to clear the table she ticks Daddy off.

'Joe, for goodness sake, she's got egg yolk all over the place.'

'Wey, at least she's eaten it.'

'Still left the crusts though, even after I wasted time cutting them up.'

'Don't like them. They're hard.'

'Fusspot.' Mammy brushes the breadcrumbs and says if I don't start eating the crusts my ringlets will drop out, then swipes my face with a pongy dishcloth, until my mouth and chin are bright pink.

Mammy grips my hand hard all the way to Saint Michael's School then leads me into a hall that dips from the corridor. The slope makes my legs want to go fast, but I learn the first day running is not allowed, or entering the hall without permission. Inside, other children sit on long wooden forms. When Mammy leaves I press my knuckles into my eyelids and rub as hard as I can so no one else will see me being a softy. Miss Beckett, the head mistress, stands at the front. She is thin and has black plaits clipped up on her head. The smell from her dark dress reminds me of church and Mammy says I have seen her there, playing the organ. In church she is far up and tiny as a pin-tack, peering over the high rail. Here, her big watery eyes come close and her puffy cheeks twitch when she talks about the hard work and good behaviour she expects from us, her new pupils. I wonder if her plaits make her head ache as much as this tight ponytail scraped to the top of my head and tied in a white big bow.

My classroom teacher is the opposite of Miss Beckett. She is round and fat and has pink smudgy cheeks. Under her brown clothes Mrs Driver wears yellow knee-length bloomers, that make us all giggle. We only see them when she drops chalk and has to bend to pick it up, but she keeps pressing hard on the blackboard and keeps snapping it, so it happens a lot.

I tell Mammy I don't like school but she takes me again the next day, and the day after that. Whatever I say she keeps taking me back. She says now I am a pupil I have to do the same as everyone else. Pupils only have weekends and holidays to break up school days. Weekends and holidays are the only time off. I tell her about Mrs Driver's bloomers, and that makes her laugh. But she says even though Mrs Driver is fat and wears bloomers, she has still managed to catch a husband. Miss Beckett, on the other hand, is destined to be an old maid. Mammy says she has to be a head mistress and the church organist because she can't catch a man, poor soul.

I complain to my oldest sister, Meena, about the dints the tight ponytail has made in my hair and how sore and itchy my head is. But she says I have to have it tied back to stop me catching nits. She says if I catch nits all my hair will have to be cut off and then I will really have something to cry about. Since I took a lend of her camera without asking permission, Meena says I am not funny, and warns me, if I pinch it again, she will personally cut my thieving little fingers off, and I won't be able to go to school at all. She goes on about how much she had to save from her Saturday job, and how rolls of film and development cost too much money to waste on pictures of cats' ears and dolls' feet and the shed window ledge. She says she wouldn't mind if I had got the bodies in, or all the heads. But she still would.

My brother is one year older than Meena, and even worse for being bossy. If only I could make him forget I killed his goldfish. If I could make Joey forget about his goldfish then he might not treat me so mean. But he never believed me when I blamed the cat. Even though he knows fine well that cats like killing fish. Joey is as stubborn as a mule and thinks Jupiter is perfect and would never do something bad like that.

He never even believed I was only giving the fish a wash, which is what I said next, after blaming the cat. I don't know why, because it was wash day, and after ages watching Mammy soaping, scrubbing and rinsing, I knew exactly what to do and only wanted to clean something for myself.

He says I deliberately tortured it then drowned it. But I was bored, and Mammy wouldn't let me help her wash the clothes, and I never knew fish couldn't breathe outside water. It was wide awake when I first grabbed it out the bowl, slithering about and leaping off while it was being soaped. It still wriggled a bit when I rinsed it, but by the time I wrung it out and dried it on the tea-towel and put it back, well, by then it just floated about.

My other sister, Teresa, says it's no wonder I am hated, and if Joey slapped me for murdering his pet, I deserved what I got. She says Joey wouldn't hurt a fly except if it had my face, and then he would stamp it to death.

Ambition

———— ● ◉ ● ————

Wor Bob said to your Bob, if your Bob doesn't give wor Bob one bob,
then wor Bob is ganna give your Bob a punch in the gob.

A bob is worth a shilling, or two tanners, or four thru'pences, or twelve pennies, or twenty-four ha'pennies: learning from Dad is miles better than school but he is a landlord and has to look after lots of tenants so hasn't got time to teach me everything. The old green tobacco tin in his drawer is full of shiny shillings saved for tenants who want change for their gas meters and every Saturday he gives me one to spend at Maynard's.

When Mammy and Daddy first got married and came to live in Newcastle during the war, He only had one house, and now he has twelve, that's a dozen counting in eggs. We live in one and the rest are divided into rooms and let out. There are so many houses to look after he has no time for any other job. He says when he has made enough from renting out rooms he is going to build us a house in the country and we are going to move out of town and live among the big knobs and join the idle rich.

Gee jaw, bull's snoot, you're in and I'm oot. There upon the
mantelpiece shone a silver thru'penny piece, gee jaw, bull's snoot, I'm in,
you're oot.

Since I started school, Saturday is the only day of the

week I am left in peace and don't have to go to the infants or go to church. My sister, Teresa's favourite Saturday pastime is lazing beside our kitchen fire and mine is copying her. The fire is always kept lit to heat water and keep the range hot, and sometimes we lie on the floor and cut-out pictures from clothes catalogues left by tenants who have done moonlight flits. Teresa is four years older than me so is good at cutting along the lines and not chopping off heads. We cut out girls until our fingers are numb and our thumbs have dints. Last week someone left a set of Children's Britannica, brand new and still in the box. I sniff all the shiny pictures of animals and flags until my nose is as fat as a bagpipe.

Me and Teresa love Saturdays because we get pocket money to buy pop and sweets while our sister Meena has to go out and earn money laying fires and preparing meals for the family across the street; because she is old enough to work now and Jews can't do work on a Saturday. Every week before she goes, Dad says slaving for auld Goldstein will never make her rich and every week before she goes Mammy tells him off for saying it.

'Holy Mary, I'm pooped.' Meena flops on the kitchen chair, forces off her black lace-ups and sticks her feet straight out in front.

'Pooh, put those back on, pal-ease.' Teresa raises her head up from her drawing book and flares her nostrils. It's the first time she's looked up from the table for ages. If she gets a Big Top writing pad and a new pencil that's the last anyone knows for hours.

'What's wrong with you?' Meena wafts her ankles up and down then round and round.

'Your feet!'

'For Heaven's sake, you whinger. I've been at work.'

'They pong.'

Meena looks at her squashed toes and wiggles them about even more.

'You should try it.'

'What?'

'Work.'

'Not old enough. Anyway I'm learning to be an artist so I won't have to.'

'If I could choose, I would be a Jewess.' Meena lets her feet plump down onto the lino.

'Why's that?'

'Cos I wouldn't have to lift a finger, that's why.'

'On Saturdays. What about the other days?'

'Don't know, do I? I only go over on a Saturday.'

'Will you keep going over after you leave school?'

'You kidding? This time next year I'll have a proper job. I'll put a good word in for you though, lazy bones. By then you should be able to lay a fire and peel a few spuds.'

Meena turns from looking at her feet to staring at her fingernails and Teresa goes back to training to be a really good drawer.

Daddy says if Teresa had lived in the olden days she would be the perfect size to be a chimney sweep. He says in Victorian times loads of ten-year-olds worked full-time up chimney flues or down the pits. One way and another Teresa is lucky this is the nineteen fifties and she can lie about so much.

Mammy never lies about. She was brought up in the country and raised animals that had to be fed and milked. She can hardly wait to live in the fresh air again and put the washing out without it getting covered in soot. She says she is never finished cleaning because of all the filth from the chimneys and the muck belched up from Scotswood Road's factories where thousands of men work. She must love cleaning things more than anything else because she cleans church as well as our house, and even cleans the outside step. She will have nothing to do when we move to the country and there is no soot and no smoke, and our socks stay white and our shoes never get scuffed, and there are no tide marks on our necks to scrub, and our only animals are cats.

Eye

———— ◦ ◉ ◦ ————

I pour tea onto my saucer and lap it up like a cat.

'Not like that.' Dad says, picking his saucer up with one hand and sipping it. 'Ah divvent knaa lad, nee decorum. Noo watch.' He puts his empty saucer back on the table and pours more tea. 'Here, look, Ah'll show ye one more time.'

After Mam brings the dishcloth, gives me one last warning and cleans up my spilled tea, Dad explains that jackdaws are his favourite bird because they are clever and can talk and he knew someone once who kept one as a pet. There's a drawing in Volume J of my new set of books and I ask him to read out the words.

'Nee time the neet. Haway, lad, put those away.'

Dad was brought up in Ireland until he was seven then came to England and learned to be a Geordie. He says if he hadn't learned fast he would've got filled in. Now he is a broad Geordie and calls everyone lad, even me.

'Can we get one, Dad? Can we have a jackdaw and teach it how to talk?'

'Now you've started her off.' Mam hurries to get tidied because its bonfire night and everyone is in a dash.

'Where would Ah find a jackdaw at this time of neet?' He scratches his head.

'Tomorrow then?'

'Give over pestering, and get the rest of that tea doon yer

neck before it gans stone cold.'

When the dishes are being cleared and everyone is out of sight I kneel up on my chair, hold back my hair, and give my saucer one last lick so as not to waste a drop.

On Guy Fawkes' night the bonfires stand like wigwams. There is one at the top of our lane, one at the bottom, and ours, the biggest, in the middle. The big boys take turns to stand guard against sabotage, then after tea everybody meets out the back. I hop about in the dark, but soon my fingers freeze and my nose holes get soaked. Joey nails the Catherine wheels to our back door then puts the rockets in the clean milk bottles ready to be set off. Bangers, jumpy jacks, Roman candles and silver streams are all lined up.

'Don't go near them,' Joey wags a finger in front of my face. He is growing a long fringe called a quiff and keeps flicking it back so he can see.

'If you touch anything you'll be for it.' It flops forward again.

Joey has left school to be a shipyard apprentice and says Blast it, and Blooming heck, whenever he likes, and doesn't care that his hair annoys Dad, who thinks men should have short, back, and sides.

'I got some fireworks.'

'Sparklers?'

'A whole packet.'

'Good. Because if you touch or loosen any of these, one

might fly off and hit you in the eye and blind you like that lad from Kenilworth Road. Right?'

'A Catherine wheel?'

'It flew off a back door and took his eye clean out like a cork.' Joey sucks a finger and pops his cheek really loud.

When everything is ready the bonfire is set alight. Smoke and flames crackle, and wind whips through the sparks. The guy is given a shuggy-boat, swung backwards and forwards, then chucked on top. Everybody cheers. Bangers are thrown and my ears crack. I try not to scream but an ugly mush from the next street, who wolf-whistles at our Meena, aims one at me and a noise flies out.

'Don't be a softy or you're going back in the house,' Joey warns.

'Joey, those lads just said you were a...'

All at once a whizz and a whoosh whitens the sky then a Jumpy Jack twists and turns and latches on to me.

I start to run fast but it follows my feet even when I zigzag. If it catches up it will blow my legs off. I fly down the lane, until it fizzes out at my toes.

By the time I get back, Joey is lighting Roman candles and Meena is setting off the Catherine wheels and trying to stop our Teresa from striking all the matches. I make sure I stand well back in case my eyes blow out. Then a million rainbows and gold threads and silver stars spout and spin, and a shower of rockets head to the moon. Oohs! and ahhs! lift to the sky all the way up and down the lane, and all over Elswick.

On my way to school next day, straggles of smoke curls over heaps of ash and dead fireworks, itching my nose, and making me sneeze. Mam takes out a hanky and swishes it round my face then shoves it back in her coat. She pulls her blue headscarf forward, tucking in a loose bit of hair that has fallen out of its curl. Up every murky lane I imagine Ugly Mush and his friends chanting: *your Joey is a killer. Your Joey is a killer.* Suddenly, the sound of a horn blasts up from the river and Mam jumps out of her skin.

'What's wrong, Mammy?'

'Nothing, luv,' she says, glancing down to the water and squeezing my hand too tight in her silky glove. 'Just a cold shiver.'

Orphans

———— ● ● ● ————

Blue, lemon, pink, cream? We wait for Mrs Driver to drop her chalk then twist our necks to see the colour of her bloomers.

'Green!' Pamela Ferry is the first to shout out and we all giggle.

'Pay attention class,' Mrs Driver says, straightening up. Pamela has to put her hand over her mouth. 'Be quiet!'

No giggling is allowed. We are learning how to read the clock, and learning the clock is very difficult.

On the last school day before Christmas, Miss Beckett makes the whole school stop having lessons and come to the hall for assembly and sit cross-legged on the polished floor. Pamela Ferry squashes right up next to me and starts sucking in snots from her runny nose then licking her lips. I have a folded hanky up my sleeve but I am not letting her see it in case she asks for a lend. Mam makes us all carry hankies. Mine has a pink B embroidered on the corner. Even Mam has a hanky with her initial sewn on. Mam's has M for Mam and for Mary, both her names.

'Fold your arms, and keep quiet,' Miss Beckett says, 'otherwise there'll be no surprise.'

The teachers sit on big chairs round the edges of the hall. Miss Beckett stands at the front in her shiny black dress, with the row of white beads that look like baby teeth and says she is very pleased with our work this term, and also, because we have raised lots of money for the African Mission, she is going to give each child a present, donated from the people of the parish. We all smile and jiggle.

One of the few things I like about school is bringing pennies so my black baby can climb the cardboard ladder. The babies are real orphans who live in Africa and everyone in class starts with a picture of their baby's head placed on the bottom rung. Every time pennies are brought in, that person's baby moves up. When my baby reaches the top she will be christened with the name I have picked. I can call her anything I like, so long as it is a saint's name. I have picked Barbara because it is the same as my doll.

'The Canon and I are very pleased to able to send off such a large amount to Africa,' she says. 'And Canon Connell will say a thanksgiving Mass when we return in the New Year.' We keep smiling, but lose our jiggles. Mass takes ages and makes me yawn more than anything else.

When two of the teachers go up to the front and pull away the sheets covering the pile of toys, all her words go into a big lump that bung my ears. They are piled like a new bonfire. Everybody is staring to see what is there, but Teddy and I have already locked eyes. My heart bangs like a drum as all the pupils with surnames beginning A to J get to pick one toy each before me. If it went by first names, my name, Bernadette would be near the front but K for Keenan means I have to wait. I pray that Jesus will make all the others take the fire engine, the pram, the jigsaw, anything except the teddy. Michael Cunningham chooses a train, Pamela Ferry a doll. My chest flies up and down as each person in front of me runs forward.

At last, it is me. He is still there. I race to him. Teddy, my teddy, rescued forever. I have never had or loved a teddy, until now.

Mam is really pleased about Teddy, but when I tell her he looks hungry, she warns me not to try to feed him like I did with the dolls. Because a teddy's fur doesn't clean up like a doll's face does.

'Mam?'

'Mmm?'

'You know how you and Dad are both orphans?'

'Yes.'

'Does that mean a stranger picked your names?'

'What?'

'Well, this baby I'm buying a name for, she's nearly at the top of the ladder, and...'

'That's different, Bernadette. We weren't born in Africa.'

'But when she gets to the top she'll be called Barbara for ever and ever.'

'If that's the name you've chosen.'

'I know, but do you think she'll like being called Barbara? I'm not even sure Doll Barbara likes it that much.'

'Why don't you give her two names then if she doesn't like one she can use the other. I stopped using my first name,

Cecelia, because I didn't like it.'

'Cecilia?'

'Cecilia Mary.'

'It might cost more for two names though.'

Rat-a-tat-tat!

'Dad man!'

'Ye hear that?'

As soon as Dad gets home for tea he hangs his jacket in the passage, comes and stands right in front of the fire then lets off, really loud.

'Machine gun fire, everybody lie doon flat.'

Rat-a-tat-tat!

'That was you!' I pinch my nose and get ready for the pong.

'Nah! There it gans again. Enemy fire.'

'Da!!' Teresa has been trying to listen to the wireless. 'That's horrible.

'Hold the lines while Ah gan te the netty,' he says, rushing out.

When he comes back I tell him about my black baby and how I have nearly paid enough pennies to give her a name. He takes his cap off and rakes his head with his long hard nails and says it's not just in Africa where people live on charity; he says Auntie Agnes and her brood live on his charity. Mam says to take no notice of anything Dad says.

Mam likes Auntie Agnes because she is Irish like Mam, and is her sister. And anyway, Mam says Auntie Agnes is getting a new council house with a gas fire soon, and she won't need to stay in Dad's rooms any more or send the children down with the big pram to borrow coal.

Dad says if Mam hadn't kept sending letters over to her sisters in Ireland they wouldn't know where we live, and Agnes would never have landed on him, with her work-shy man and her huge brood. Mam says Uncle Pat isn't well enough for work but would if he could. And dad says tenement rooms are not meant for families, and are no good for kids, and if he wasn't so soft he would maintain that the best principle in life is: self first, self second, and if there's owt left over, self again.

I wonder if Auntie Agnes has a name she doesn't use, like Mam does? If she does it must be pretty awful to be worse than Agnes. Until today I never even knew Mam had a name I have never heard of. And, apart from that, our Meena's proper name is Philomena, which doesn't even start with the right letter. Then Dad and Joey are both Joseph, but my brother Joseph is Joey, and my dad Joseph is Joe. Sharing Joseph between them, I bet they hate that. I would hate to share my name. I wonder if that's why they don't like each other.

Jupiter

Breaking up for Christmas makes it snow. I scrape a cat's face on the ice inside the sash window and look through the eyes, catching sight of Joey who has sneaked out back, quiet as a mouse. I see him break an icicle off the shed door, wrap it in a hanky then slide it in his pocket. For the first time this winter he has been buttering the runners of his sledge, skidding it past his frozen boiler suits hanging on the line, then racing off. I jump down and run to get my coat and hat.

'Joey, give iz a go.' Our Teresa is already out and first in the queue. Joey never minds sharing when it's her. She sits on while he steers. At the bottom of the lane she lies flat on her front and he pulls her all the way back up.

'My turn, my turn.' I try to get on.

'Wait.' Teresa takes ages getting off, points her *I dare you* look, and gives me a shove.

'Please Joey, please.'

'Right! I'll give you a ride if you pull me along first.' Joey grins at Teresa and she grins back, joining up with each other to be spiteful. Meena used to stick up for me, but hardly plays out lately, because, even though she is a year younger than Joey she acts more grown up.

'Alright.' Joey sits on and hands me the rope.

'Pull!'

I pull as hard as I can but can't make it budge.

'Come on Bernadette, pull, harder than that. You're not even trying.'

'I can't make it go. You better get off.' My lips start to shake.

'All right, you baby. Don't start to bubble for heck's sake.' Joey gets up and lets me take his place.

'You spoil sport,' Teresa says, glaring at me. 'You've always got to ruin things and get your own way.'

'Haway then.' Joey pulls the sledge and whizzes me around, making it go so fast my heart thumps.

'Right, off. That's your lot,' he orders.

'But she's getting more goes than me.'

I see Teresa's pouty mouth and her arms folded like a teacher.

'It's not fair!' I yell, running in.

'Go on, get in and *tell your Mammy*. You big soft baby.'

'I don't say that now...I don't say any baby words, you, you...'

In the house I pull off my gloves with my teeth. My fingers are so cold and wet I can't unbutton my coat or stop my nose dribbling.

'Come here,' Mam says. 'Let me.' She grabs my hanky and squeezes my nose until it stings.

I tell her about Joey and Teresa leaving me out. But all she says it's no use crying over spilt milk, and she hopes this isn't how the whole school holidays are going to turn out.

When she leaves the room I try to shove Jupiter away from the hearth so I can sit over the fire but he grips the mat with his claws and makes his bum as heavy as lead and flops down again hogging the heat. I try to give him a nip but my fingers are too cold and weak. There is nothing left to do but sulk because no one in the whole house will take my side.

Before Christmas lots of things get done. Mam cleans everything in sight and gets the box of decorations out. She carries back bag-loads of groceries from town, including mountains of meat. Mam says we need meat to stay alive. But since our Teresa had her tonsils out and was force fed liver in the convalescent home, meat smells make her retch and Mam has a right job getting any down her neck.

Mr Power calls to empty the mission box Mam fills with all her spare change, and any she can cadge from Dad. Mr Power is a Brother of Saint Vincent de Paul, and a teacher at top school. He has a high squeaky voice and Joey says that when he gets mad he screeches like a monkey and the kids have to nip their own hands to stop themselves laughing and getting the strap. I thought he was really nice but Joey says he is only nice when he is not in school. Mam says it's because he wears different hats and gives Joey a *shut up* look.

In little school Miss Beckett has a head mistress hat and a church organist hat, and a dead fox she drapes round her neck for Mass. Its furry tail hangs down her back and its small pointy head over her chest. In place of eyes it has shiny jet stones. Meena says it has the stare of death and is so moth eaten she should be ashamed to wear it.

> *Christmas is coming, the goose is getting fat,*
> *Please put a penny in the old man's hat,*
> *If you haven't got a penny, a ha'penny will do,*
> *If you haven't got a ha'penny, God bless you.*

'He won't come until you are fast asleep,' Mam says. 'He knows when you're pretending.'

'If he sees your eyelids flicker he leaves nothing,' Teresa joins in as if she is a grown up.

'Someone could have flickery eyelids and still be asleep. How does Santa know?'

'He just does, now say your prayers and get into bed. I'll come back in a few minutes to put out the light.'

We get changed, kneel and race through our prayers, then dive in between the sheets. Joey and Meena have their own rooms but me and Teresa are youngest so have to share. A gale rushes down mine and Teddy's necks. It is so cold I don't even want to slide my legs to find the water bottle.

'Ahh! me feet are burning.' Teresa scalds her soles but can't resist the rubbery heat.

'Goodnight Teresa.'

'Goodnight, God bless Bernadette.'

'Goodnight, God bless, sweet dreams.'

'Goodnight, God bless, sweet dreams, see you in the

morning.'

'Goodnight, God bless, sweet dreams, see you in the morning. Don't have nightmares.'

'Goodnight, God bless, sweet dreams, see you in the morning. Don't have nightmares, and don't let the bed bugs bite.'

She has to have the last word no matter what.

After a tiny snooze, I wake up. Mam must have been because the light is off and the room is pitch dark. I hear Teresa's bedsprings squeak, as if she's moving about trying to get comfy.

'Teresa, are you asleep?' I whisper.

'No. Are you?' She whispers back.

'No. I can't sleep. I've got pains down me legs. Has Santa Claus been yet?'

'No. I've got pains in my legs as well.'

'What sort of pains have you got?'

'Sciatica pains.'

'What's that?'

'It's called sciatica, and it's what you get when you're excited.'

'Shh! What's that? Listen!'

'Quick, get to sleep.'

My legs twitch and jump but I try to make them stay calm. The door knob turns, and the floorboards creak. It's him! Santa is in our room. I must keep my eyelids still.

For ages after the rustles stop neither of us move.

'Teresa! Are you asleep?'

'No.'

'Has he been?'

'Yes.'

'Can we get up now and put the light on.'

'Who's going to put it on, you or me?'

'You're nearest.'

'You're youngest.'

'I'm scared.'

'Oh, for pity's sake.'

When New Year comes in Mam and Dad let us stay up past midnight so we can go to the front door and hear all the boats on the river blowing their horns. Mam comes to the doorstep but as soon as the ships start to hoot she pulls her cardi up round her neck, shivers and goes back in. Dad wraps a few nuggets of coal in newspaper and steps to the end of the path, then turns round and brings it back. Bringing coal means we will have good luck. Dad always does this and is always our first foot. To bring the best luck first foots have to be tall dark and handsome. So that's why, according to Dad, it is always him.

Eye

———— ● ◉ ● ————

Mam is in the middle of spring cleaning: changing blankets and curtains and washing windows, so we have been warned to keep out of her road. Teresa's friend Susan is round to play and I say I want to explore in the cupboard under the stairs but as usual, Teresa follows Joey, so up to the landing we go. Teresa disappears into the big wall cupboard to snoop about, and Joey decides it will be funny to lock the door, flipping the catch and laughing himself hoarse. From inside the dark she gives a long scream. We all laugh then, but suddenly she stops and we go silent. A blade pokes through the crack: Teresa has found a knife and is trying to flip the lock. Joey darts forward to set her free but, too late, she staggers like a stuntman, the knife stuck above her eyes. Joey grabs the handle and howks it out. Then like stuffed dummies we stand and stare at the split in her skin, filling with a spit of red then a trickle, then a big spurt gushing like a teapot spout.

Before the day turns back to being quiet there is a lot more noise. Susan is sent home, Joey vanishes, and I sit by the kitchen fire with Jupiter on my knee. Mam takes Teresa to hospital with her head coiled in bandages as fat as Mr Singh's turban.

Mr Singh is Susan's dad and he is a Sikh, so never cuts his hair. Neither does Susan. I close my eyes and count to twenty over and over again and think of the thick black plaits

41

she sometimes takes out and redoes while we count and clap. Even though her hair is right down her back, her hands are so fast we never get to more than twenty. And twenty is my top number, off by heart.

Susan's house is exactly the same as ours, except the front room has no chairs and the adults sit cross-legged on the floor. On Susan's birthday Mrs Singh made trays full of sweets and invited me and Teresa in:

'Come girls, help yourselves to anything you like.' Her armful of golden bangles clinked and her blue and silver scarf kept falling off her rope of black hair.

The sweets looked even better than Maynard's but the first one tasted like marsh mellow, and the second not like a sweet at all, gooey and chewy with yukky flavours.

'Are you having a nice time, girls?'

'Yes thank you.' Teresa said, trying to push me off from gripping her skirt.

'You're not eating very much, come on now, don't be shy, have some more.' More platters of pretty sweeties were placed before our eyes.

'Mmm, they're really lovely,' Teresa lied.

I stroke Jup's warm fur and wonder if Susan is getting wrong for being at the stabbing. She did laugh at first but it was all Joey's fault. If only we had explored in the cupboard under the stairs, none of this would have happened. There is more air in there, and much more room, and no knives sitting about. We could have unfurled the massive Union Jack that Mam and Dad flew from an upstairs window when we won the war. We could have stomped about like soldiers, marched and saluted. The sort of game I like best, but no one listens to me, and now my sister is scarred for life.

Teresa and Joey would rather clart with the stuff he keeps under his bed that I am never allowed to touch. His secret treasure trove: the dagger, the bayonet, the model war planes and armies of tiny cowboys and Indians; his precious old toffee tin full of foreign coins. Who knows, in all this fuss, it could be the best time to go and have a proper nose about.

Joey's bedroom is the smallest in the house. Apart from his bed there is only space for one chair, looped with the snake-clasp of his belt, and a tall cupboard hooked with a boiler suit. I creep in. The tinge of metal tangs the air, and a whiff of Meppo wafts from the blankets. A half bottle of methylated spirit sits in the light on the window sill, pretty enough to swig if it weren't for the stink. Meena's room always smells of nail varnish and remover and scent, kind of the same but kind of different.

I get down on my hunkers and root about: a bag of marbles. Brilliant. I tip them out and inspect. Joey's marbles have taken years to collect and he never lets me play with them. I put the milky white one down as a target and flick the one he calls Sapphire along the carpet.

'Missed! Not far enough.'

The brightest green one is bigger than the rest so I try that.

'This time. Hit! Yes!'

Jupiter has followed me in and leaps at the balls, scattering them.

'Oh no, don't do that. You idiot.' I chase him off but Sapphire has disappeared and I have to lie flat and get my head under the bed to see where it's rolled to.

'Uh ho!' A noise. I try to get up quick but bang my nut on the metal leg.

'What are you doing in my room? Get out!' Joey bounds in from nowhere, shouting. 'Get out now, you little swine.'

'But I was only having a look.' I try to suck in my cheeks because the toffee I found is big and bulging at the sides.

'You're going to get a good wallop.'

'One measly Harrogate toffee, that's all I took.' A dribble of juice runs down my chin when I try to speak.

'Blasted thief!'

'I didn't think you'd miss it.'

'Get out,' I've been saving them in the Billy-can all Lent. Get out, before I kill you.'

'I'll tell Mam on you, if you touch me.' Diving for the door I take a slap on the arm and another one on the back of my head. His slaps are really hard and sting like blazes.

I hide in the bathroom until I hear Mam and Teresa come back from the hospital. They have been away for hours and Teresa has a black line of stitches sewn in her brow. Mam says it's a miracle she didn't lose an eye, and tells our Joey he is old enough to have more sense. I think our Joey should be ashamed of himself, locking his favourite sister in a dark scary place like that. If she had lost an eye I bet he would have given *her* his green marble without any complaints. One green marble in place of one green eye. I can just picture it.

Rituals

— ● ◉ ● —

Mam is tired after shopping and has a good excuse not to go to church but she never seems to want a night off to put her feet up.

'Come on, I need to get ready and get away.' She is in a hurry and Dad clears the dinner things off the table so she can get the mirror out and put on her make-up.

'I've washed the pans. Can I leave you to dry and put away?'

'Wey aye. What's yer hurry, is the Pope coming?'

'There's a Legion of Mary meeting and I want to use the meal table to get ready.'

'Gan on, make yerself beautified. Ah'll sort this lot.'

'Thanks, Joe.' Mam tips all the things out of her bag and sets the cracked mirror up against the sugar bowl.

'If yee were as good looking as me you wouldn't have to bother with that clart.' Dad is always saying things that make Mam laugh.

I sit on my chair and watch what she does.

'Can I put some rouge on?' The rouge is in a small cardboard tub and I want to stick my finger in.

'No.' She pulls it away, dabs a circle on each cheek then spreads it until her skin is only faintly pink. Next she makes a sweet smelling cloud float up from the powder puff. Last of all she pulls her lips into a tight line and draws the bright red lipstick on.

'Please, Mam, let iz have a go.' I try to make her notice my sad look.

'No, I said. No means no.'

When it is all done she puts her glasses back, returns the things, checks her teeth then smacks her lips, and snaps the handbag shut.

The last thing she does is fasten her coat and tie the blue headscarf in a knot under her chin. Mam never goes out without a headscarf or a hat, and Dad always wears his cap, whether he's inside or out. In church it is a sin for a man to wear a hat and a sin for a woman not to wear a hat: two opposite things, but two the same sins.

At Easter me and our Teresa change out of winter clothes into white ankle socks and sandals. We have new lemon dotted dresses and navy blazers, and straw bonnets that tie with satin ribbons. The big brim shades Teresa's scar which Dad says is just as well so people won't think we've been trying to do her in.

At the railway station coming back from the seaside masses of people try to squeeze on the train. We manage a seat, but I have to sit on Dad's knee. I have eaten my whole stick of minty rock and am squashed, but the clickedy-clack and the heat send me to sleep. Dad's Sunday jacket smells of the sun and I like the feel of his big hand round my tum. But Mam leans across and wipes my sticky mouth with a hanky she has just spat on and suddenly I wake up feeling sick.

After Church on Easter Sunday, Mam presents me and Teresa with the Easter eggs I bought with the stolen pound note. When I pinched it her purse was so fat I never thought she would miss one measly little pound. But as soon as I sneaked back from the shop with the two huge chocolate eggs there she was, waiting behind the wavy glass, her hand raised, ready to give me a good clout. I told her straight away, only one was meant for me, but it made no difference. She took them away and said she would make sure they were the only ones me and Teresa got, full stop.

Receiving her one and only egg reminds my sister to be furious all over again. She takes my arm and twists it and twists it: a Chinese burn that stays red raw and kills for ages.

'Ow! What's that for?'

She moves in for more.

'That's for nothing and this is a nip and a punch for the first of the month.'

'But...it's not...'

She nips my other arm, then punches hard with her knuckles.

'Well then,' I get my breath back, 'a nip and a kick for being so quick.' I try to catch her with my foot but she trips me up and I land on the floor. I shout for Mam but know she will have no sympathy because I am a little thief, and I will be wasting my time. I wish now I had never bothered stealing one for Teresa. She has no gratitude at all.

Loony Bin

— • ◦ • —

Mad as a March hare,' Dad says when Stan-the-stiff-legged-Pole is carted off to the loony bin.

'Only a daft bugger like him would let a dead dog rot away in the hoose. It'll bring rats. Better get the cats' teeth sharpened quick, kidda.'

Mam saws at her chop while the cats drool on yard windowsill and stare in at us eating.

'The three wise monkeys.' Dad nods at them and our Joey nearly forgets he doesn't speak to Dad and almost laughs. Corky and Tibby are old and scraggy with rubbery teeth. No one is sure how old Jupiter is but he has never even caught a mouse since he came to live with us. Joey says Jupiter is a pass-a-fist, which means he refuses to use violence. Joey says they are both *pacifists*, except where it comes to me, then they have to make an exception.

After dinner our Meena cools a tray of cinder toffee and tells us all about the people in the white coats who carted Stan-the-stiff-legged-Pole away.

'Apparently the stink was so bad two of the men in white coats sicked up green slime in the street.'

I pull my best disgusted mouth.

'Honestly?' Teresa says.

'Uh-huh. It's true.' Meena rolls her eyes up until the green bits almost disappear.

'That's awful,' Teresa says, staring at the golden tray and sniffing up the golden sweetness. 'Is this cinder toffee ready to eat yet?'

'Patience is a virtue,' Meena says. 'Wait till it's cool, then you can have some.'

'Being in the Girl Guides all that time made you a great cook, Meena. If I wasn't so busy learning to be an artist I would join.'

'Flattery will get you nowhere...Oh well, go on, you can have one bit each. That's all. Here, hold your hands out.' She plops a sticky square on each palm. 'And don't forget to say an extra prayer for Stan-the-stiff-legged-Pole tonight.' We pop the lovely gooey toffee in and give a little hum.

Meena is really nice about Stan-the-stiff-legged-Pole, even though he swears under his breath, and goes out the front in braces and a dirty vest and makes me hold my breath when I pass because he pongs so much. She tells us Stan-the-stiff-legged-Pole is Polish, and he was a Polish soldier, and that he had his leg blown off fighting in the war. When she is being nice, having Meena for a sister is great because apart from making cinder toffee she tells me and our Teresa loads of things we would never find out from anyone else.

'What prayer should we say?'

'Say, Dear God, please make Stan-the-stiff-legged-Pole come back from being gone in the head. And let him get a new dog that's not going to die and spend three months stinking out the house.'

'Alright, Meena,' I say.

'Alright, Meena,' our Teresa says, licking her lips and eyeing up the toffee still left stuck on to the tray.

I say a prayer for Stan-the-stiff-legged-Pole not to be gone in the head, but miss out the bit about the new dog, because I hate dogs, especially his snarly, slavery, growly one: the massive dead Alsatian whose two front teeth were as big and white as my legs.

Luckily, all the talk about Stan-the-stiff-legged-Pole takes Mam's mind off being mad with me. I wore her best watch to school and thought I could get it back before she noticed it was missing from her drawer, but she was waiting by the railings at playtime and pulled it off my hand, and nipped my wrist in the stretchy bracelet. It really stung, and all the kids in the yard saw, and knew then that it was pinched, and knew I had only been pretending I could read the time.

She's still a bit furious when she comes with me for my school medical and hardly talks at all. The hall has been changed to look like a hospital, with green screens and the stink of disinfectant. Most of my classmates are with their mothers as well, and all of them are stripped to knickers and vests and sit on rows of chairs that have been set out especially. Only Mam ever sees my underwear, and I go hot and cold and sweaty when a nurse says we have to take off our vests. There are boys looking, and my bare legs stick like putty. I droop my shoulders and wish I could disappear. Mam is next to me but won't see my eyes, or do anything to rescue me.

On the other side of the screens, a line of strangers in white coats sit behind tables, and move us along from one to the next, Mam answering questions, me being examined:

'Say ah!' A piece of wood forces my tongue flat.

'Ahh!'

'Again.'

'Ahh!' The wood is making the wobbly thing in my throat want to be sick.

'That's fine. Next!'

By the time we get home we have changed places. Mam has forgotten about the watch but I am in a huff because she never stopped the people from looking at my bare top.

I think she has moved her mood with me onto Dad because he fixed a shelf and it broke again and she is muttering: 'Jack of all trades, master of none,' and, 'if you want something doing, do it yourself.' When she fills the kettle she makes it sound like she's flooding the house.

I find Dad in the yard, sawing firewood. He looks hot and smells of turps and paint, but not stinky like Stan-the-stiff-legged-Pole. I wonder if the men in white coats in school today were the same ones who took Stan-the-stiff-legged-Pole away.

'Can I have a go, Dad?' He has one foot on the plank across the sawing chair, and wheezes as he straightens up. He takes off his cap and wipes the shine from his forehead, then pulls it back down to his eyebrows.

'Aye, alreet.' His eyes look sore and red and are nearly shut against the dust.

'Can I try your cap on?'

'Divvent start acting the goat.'

'Please?'

'Stop your nonsense.'

Last week he let me drill holes in the sawing chair, so now it looks like cartoon cheese.

'Can I do more holes then?'

'If yee drill any more holes in there, there'll be nee chair left,' he coughs.

I start sawing but the saw bends and jerks. It is so much harder than Dad makes it seem. I play with the shavings that have fallen into curly piles under the seat, stacking them into little heaps and patting them into pyramids. Then Dad splits wood into small stakes with the chopping axe. Another cigarette burns in the corner of his mouth, making his eyes wince and water as the smoke crawls up his cheeks.

'Yer making a lovely mess,' he says.

Town Bull

Dad stands about for ages in the front street talking to Mr Singh, telling him all about Stan-the-stiff-legged-Pole being gone in the head and getting carted off by the men in white coats, and about the dog being dead. Mr Singh's mouth flaps like a letter box and I clutch Dad's sleeve and wait in case I miss anything, but my legs start to wiggle for the toilet and dad notices and says I better run in before I wet myself. Then he sees Mister Towers cross over the road towards them and decides it's time he came in as well. He says Mister Towers is an old windbag but Mam says that sounds a bit like the pot calling the kettle black.

Me and Dad are out of the doghouse and he lets me go with him to the hardware shop to buy some new tools. On the way I roll my fingers along the railings we pass, then walk on the walls, hopping over the iron stumps sawn off in the war. On the higher walls Dad holds my hand in case I fall.

'Divvent want ye putting any dints in them stones,' he says.

Joey once chipped his front tooth falling from the park rocks and another time broke his arm crashing off a wall: two things that have to be a lesson to us all.

From every shop on Elswick Road different smells float: the fish shop's seaweed and salt, the butcher's sawdust and blood, the cobbler's leather and glue, and the hardware's metal and wood.

The hardware shop is squashed full of brushes, ladders

and nails, and Dad takes so long to decide what he wants I think he loves it nearly as much as I love Maynard's. Maynard's: vanilla and mint.

On the way home Dad says 'Aye, aye' to everyone we pass: Mrs Towers outside the paper shop, the man from the milk depot at the top of our street, and Mr Goldstein with his black spaniel who carries the newspaper in its slavvery chops. Mr Goldstein tips his hat to Dad, and Dad says, 'Clever dog that,' and touches his cap.

During the day news spreads like wildfire. A bull escaped from the cattle market at Marlborough Crescent and is heading up Gloucester Street to Elswick. Angela is playing in her front path across the road and must be warned. Since her mam has been busy with the new baby with the cleft palate and hair lip, Angela is being left to play out a lot. It's up to me.

'Angela, Angela, have you heard about the escaped bull?'

'What do you mean?' Her bottom lip turns down and pokes out.

'Heading this way.' I run over to her as fast as my legs will go.

'No, no, it's not.'

'It's true. They tried to catch it, but it was too strong and they've just made it really mad. The man on the wireless says: stay in till it's caught.' Her pet lip is really shaking now. I feel like Mighty God and decide to wait a bit before I tell her it has already been recaptured.

'Look, there at the bottom of the street. I think I can hear it. Listen.'

'I want to go in.'

'Did you know they love red, Angela? Did you know that your ribbons would be very attracting to a bull?'

'I'm going in to tell me Mam.' Angela's whole face is like pink blancmange.

'No, don't do that.' I try to give her a hug but she wipes some snots on my dress and I have to push her away.

'Oops-a-daisy,' I say, as her bangs her knee.

'I'm scared. I'm going in.' Big bubbles start blubbing in and out of her nose as if she is blowing gum.

'Don't tell your Mam, Angela.'

'Mam! Mam!' She races in.

'I was just kidding, Angela. They only eat boys, Angela. They don't like girls.'

I don't think she's heard because she makes such a fuss that her mam and my mam have to talk about it, then I have to stay in for rest of the day, looking at the silver snot trail on my frock, and examining my conscience. On top of that, I know Angela's Mam won't like me any more; but at least I won't have to pretend that Angela's new brother is lovely to look at.

Country Bull

After breakfast Dad puts the brush, silver razor, and stick of speckled soap on the table then pours steamy water from the kettle into the white basin with the blue rim. I copy everything, creaming my face, nipping and pulling my nose from side to side then scraping away stubble with my pretend razor. When he's finished he licks and sticks a torn off bit of newspaper on his chin.

'Bliddy blood,' I say, and Dad laughs. Normally I get told off for saying bliddy, and bloody, but it really is bliddy blood, so I'm allowed.

'Can I have some, Dad? Look, I've cut my chin.'

Dad rips off another bit, licks it, and sticks it on my cheek.

'Urgh!'

'There. It'll soon dry up.'

At Sunday Mass Mam buys the Universe from the back of church. Dad gets the People and Pictorial, the weekend papers everybody really loves. On weekdays it's the Chronicle, sometimes Reveille or Titbits. Mam says she has no interest but reads them inside out. Teresa likes Joey's comics about cowboys and Indians and wars. She makes on she likes them because she wishes she had been a boy, and even wants a haversack, same as Joey. Meena's comics are Romeo and Valentine. They have drawings of handsome men and good-looking girls who say soppy things and sometimes end up kissing. Mam says Meena is filling her head with rubbish but if Meena's supply of Romeo and Valentine dried up, I think the men in white coats would have to come and cart *her* off.

Joey has accidentally cut his finger and holds it like a candle while Mam bandages. Dad tells her it's 'Nee mere than a graze,' and says, 'Nee wonder he's so soft. Hurry yourself up or we'll miss the bus.'

Most Summer Sundays Mam and Dad take us out. These days Joey and Meena stay home and slouch, while me and Teresa are dressed, ready for the off. Sometimes we go to the seaside but this afternoon it's Corbridge. Corbridge is the country, and means a train ride and a bus.

On the way we see fields of horses, sheep and cows. Walking over the bridge to the village we pass a farmyard of geese sleeping on one leg. The sight reminds Dad of his factory work in the war: winding the waist of his boiler suit in a vice so he could sleep standing up.

'Ah just leaned back, let mesel go. The gaffers never twigged.' He grins.

'Trust you to find a way to get your beauty sleep, Joe.'

'Wey aye! Ten straight night shifts, man. Ye had to be resilient.'

We all laugh. Then in the café Mam and Dad have scones and tea, and me and Teresa have lemonade and squishy jam cake.

'There's nowt like a bit of fresh air,' Dad says, lighting a tab to have with his last dregs of tea. 'Good to leave the toon behind' His chin shines like a new pin and his cheeks are ruddy.

'You can't beat the countryside,' Mam agrees. 'I was brought up on it.'

'Can I have an ice-cream, Dad?' Teresa asks.

'Can I have an ice-cream as well?' I hate to be left out.

'Will youse two go and play for a bit and let me and your dad talk for once.'

On the other side of the window we put our noses to the glass, steaming it up so Teresa can draw smiley faces and I can dot the eyes.

'What should we do now?' I ask.

'Do you want to play I Spy?'

'Alright, but let me win one first.'

On the way back to the station Dad decides to take a short cut over a field. We follow, watching our feet in case there are any big cow pats dolloped on the grass.

'Country smells,' Mam smiles, sniffing up the stink as if it's nice.

My legs are sore from walking and even though he says I am too big for it, I manage to nag Dad into giving me a piggy back. Teresa plucks bits of grass, giving me sulky eyes, then whistles through a long blade.

Up high I am taller than everyone else. I bounce, and have the best view, and reach to touch the blue sky. One hand, two hands. Look at me.

All of a sudden Dad's slow feet begin to race and his knees rattle like machine guns. I try to hang onto his head, but my hands fall over his eyes as we trot.

'Bull!' Dad shouts at the top of his voice.

'Bull!' We race for the nearest fence and scramble out, Mam pulling Teresa by the arm, and tearing big holes in her stockings, both legs.

I have never seen anything with such a big head, or neck.

'So much for the countryside.' Mam puffs and gasps.

'A close call, that was.' Dad is out of breath, mopping sweat from his lathered brow.

'How did you know it was a bull?' Teresa asks. 'I thought it was a cow.'

'Bulls are aalways black.' Dad says, swinging me back to the ground, and my real size.

'Really? Are they Dad?'

'Have ye ever seen a black coo?'

'No...'

'Wey then...'

'Come on,' Mam says, laughing herself beetroot. 'Let's get to the station and get back into town.' She is so relieved we are still alive that she has started seeing the funny side.

The train ride home is rocky and sends me to sleep. We take a lurch and my head flops off Dad's sleeve back onto the seat, leaving a wet patch on the arm of his beige Mac. We are almost back into Central Station and I have missed a Big Conversation that Teresa has no doubt been putting her oar in. I am only in time to catch the tail end of what's being said: Dad making plans, telling Mam and Teresa about building a house for us all in the countryside, and deciding whereabouts he will buy a plot of land.

Loony Bin

———— ● ◉ ● ————

The day after upsetting Little Angela I was put on best behaviour and sent out to play. No sign of her, or any of my friends, so I found a twig and sat poking moss from the kerb stones, waiting. The spongy strips were luscious, and I didn't notice the lanky drip from bottom of the street creep up. He shouted a joke to some big lads standing near Angela's lamppost, about a girl called Fuckaharder. I knew it was rude so laughed along, until Lanky's knobbly knees stopped beside my head, and he hockled a gob of spit right next to my feet.

'There's nowt to do in this street,' he said, jerking about and scratching himself. 'A few of us are going down the river, you wanna come?'

I stayed on my hunkers, and told the boy's knees I would get killed if I did.

The river is even more dangerous than the park rocks or high walls and I have been warned about those.

'Oh aye, that's reet, since that kid drooned yer ma doesn't let yer gan near, doesn't she not?'

I wanted to poke his stupid legs, and his stupid mouth, but kept digging with my stick until his loony laugh dripped away. Then I made a circle of damp moss on the pavement slab and laid sun-rays coming off.

When Angela did come out she wouldn't even speak, so I sloped off behind the hedge in front of our house and picked a brown leaf, peeling it back to find a bright green caterpillar wriggling, waiting its chance to turn into a butterfly.

'Lead me not into temptation. Lead me not into temptation.'

Now I've got a bug and am in bed bad. Either I caught it after one of Teresa's red hot pokers twisting my arm or from the lanky lad breathing germs on my head. One or the other. I'm not sure which.

Having tonsillitis gives me loads of time to consider Life Everlasting which I am learning about at school. There is Heaven and Hell, and Purgatory, and Limbo, where dead people go if they are not baptised. They float about forever and can never get out. There is no pain, like in the Fires of Hell, but it is endless. Purgatory is painful like Hell but people can get out once they pay for their sins. Alive people say prayers for their souls and gain Indulgences to get them out quick. So Purgatory is definitely better than Limbo, even though souls in Limbo never suffer.

Eternity and the Afterlife make my stomach swish. Jupiter is under the blanket, purring. He couldn't care less about not having a soul the same as me. Mam says there is a special heaven for animals, but I want us to go to the same heaven. It will be really boring without any animals.

'Eee, are yee still in that bed, lad?'

When the cat hears Dad's voice he dives out from under the blankets and gallops downstairs.

The best thing about being poorly is the sound of Dad's heavy boots on the landing and knowing I'm in for a treat. He has bad knees and only climbs the stairs to go to bed or use the lavvy. Mam says his knees were destroyed in the trenches. His knees make him swear, and are a million years old: thousands older than the rest of him.

'Hello, Dad.' I croak.

'What yee deein in bed during the day?' He throws a brown paper bag onto the eiderdown then shows me the bottle of Lucozade tucked in his armpit.

'I'm bad, Dad. I've gorra sore throat.' I open my mouth and lift my head up. 'Look.'

'Playing the wag.' he says, taking no notice.

I give a sore cough to show him I'm not making it up.

The Lucozade is wrapped in yellow crinkly paper the same as the paper inside Watson's shop window that stops the sun fading their displays. The bag is twisted at each side like cats' ears. I undo the twists and find four massive oranges.

'Oranges!' The biggest fattest, orangest, oranges, I have ever seen.

'Ahh thanks Dad.'

'Noo divvent eat them aal at once.' He warns.

'I won't...Will ye peel one for iz?' I try to copy the way he talks.

'Aye, gan on, give iz one here.' He takes one of the oranges and digs his long hard thumb nail into the top then slowly peels off the thick skin. It never breaks once and the peel left in his hand stays in an orange shape that he pats like a yo-yo.

Dad knows a lot about oranges. He says we don't know how lucky we are because in the second war they were rare as gold, and in the first war he knew men who could peel oranges in their pockets. Dad knows a lot about oranges, and a lot about wars.

Teresa hates sharing a bedroom, especially when I am feeling bad. She says if any of my germs blow across to her bed I will wish I was dead. Dead as a doornail, she says.

Mam and Dad share as well, but Joey has the box room to himself because he is eldest, and the only boy. Our Meena has the back room because she wears a bra and has suspenders and nylons and never has to be bothered by anyone else. She reads her stars to find out what the future holds, and can never be interrupted. And if she loses her temper, watch out, because she has very long pointed nails.

Teresa says when Joey and Meena come of age and move out, she will have first bogzies on which room she takes. I'm glad the house is squashed. If I never had Teresa to ask questions and pester it would be lonely at bedtime and even more scary thinking about Eternity all by myself.

'Will you keep your mouth shut and stop breathing germs everywhere?'

Once we are curled up she starts playing war about my cough. I try to ask her my saved up questions about Eternity but she is being a right bossy boots.

'But is it really forever and ever?'

'Yes, for ever, and ever, and ever.

'How long is that, ever and ever?

'It never stops, it goes on, and on, and on, like you.'

'Even after thousands and thousands of years?'

'Yes.'

'Even after millions and billions and trillions?'

'Yippidy, yes.'

'But will we be happy there?'

'Well nobody will have tonsillitis.'

'What will we do all day?'

'I don't know. We'll be in Heaven, in Paradise with God and all the angels and saints.'

'But what will we do all day?'

'Just float about.'

'Float about?

'Float about, yes. Now stop breathing through your mouth, and making all that noise. Goodnight.'

'Goodnight, God Bless, sweet dreams.'

'Goodnight, God Bless, sweet dreams.'

I toss and turn, worrying, and not being able to breathe. I pull a few feathers out through my pillow and stash them underneath. I kick the blankets off to cool down then get so tired I drift off into a dream. Meena is wearing a scarf tied at the back like a gypsy's, and has a feathery fan and big loopy earrings, and is looking into a crystal ball. We are all in a mansion with a hundred white rooms, and I need a wee, so run to find the toilet.

I get to the middle of a long corridor and suddenly my feet start to leave the ground. I feel a bit gone in the head, so turn round to ask Meena if I've been carted off to the loony bin, but she disappears, and a stranger in a white coat comes walking in.

'Is this the loony bin?' I ask the man.

He nods up and down then pulls a fat orange from his pocket and bites into the skin.

'Did you see me float?' I ask him.

'Yes, I did,' the man says, dribbling juice down his chin.

He pulls a funny face and grins, and coughs some germs across the top of my head.

'Was I really floating?' I say again.

'Yes,' he says, 'you were really floating, both feet off the ground.'

Orphan

— ● ◉ ● —

Every day I'm in bed sick, Dad comes up to see me and brings a gift. Today he fetches a bar of Cadbury's and shows me how to circle my thumbs round and round without touching. Something to do to keep myself occupied.

'When ye get bored with deein it that way, then switch and dee it the other.'

He sits on the tufty bedspread and does it forwards, really fast.

'See, clockwise, then anticlockwise, first this way, then that.'

'But my thumbs keep catching each other.'

'Look, concentrate. Ah'll demonstrate one more time. He does it backwards really fast.

He says if I ever get bored in school I can do this under the desk without the teacher ever knowing. I give it a another test.

Being sick is almost worth it, everybody is that nice. It's the first day of me being better and Mam is singing Irish songs and has on her happy voice.

Kathleen, mavourneen, awake from thy slumbers...

'Do you know what I'm going to tell you?' She smiles, wiping the table. 'Mrs Ritson says you are invited out with them for a ride in their car.' It could hardly be better news if she had been asked to go herself.

The Ritsons live one up from the Singhs on our side and are the only family in the street who have a car and a television set. Their daughter, Rose Ritson is my best friend.

'Hop in the back.' Mr Ritson opens the car door. The long seat is as soft as a couch and me and Rose spring about like rabbits. There is enough room for at least two more, so we spread out and dangle on the leather, while her mam and dad squeeze up in front.

With the turn of a key the engine starts, and outside an orange light pops up like an arm to show we are pulling off. Mr Ritson sucks a pipe and makes clouds that have a lovely scent, and while he drives Rose's mam props his trilby on the stomach of her big flowery dress. My first time in a car is truly brilliant.

The cobbles make the car bump about and the terraced houses pass by even faster than racing on Joey's sledge. Mister Towers stands at his usual corner near Watson's the chemist, and salutes when he sees us pass. I wave back like a princess.

Along the way we stop at a carpet shop and Mr and Mrs Ritson choose one with red smudges for their living room, and talk to a man in a blue suit about having it delivered.

We go for miles and miles and I see more streets than I ever have. I try to look at all the buildings, there and back, but the warmth inside the car rocks me and Rose to sleep and Mr Ritson has to shake our arms when we pull up at their house. I wipe slavver onto my sleeve from my chin but remember to thank him before I run in. I can hardly wait to tell everyone about where I've been. I can hardly wait to be invited out again.

When Robin Hood night comes I run to Rose's house as usual, and get asked in. A man who is not her Dad is sitting on the front room couch as if he is part of the family.

'You can't sit there,' she whispers, 'you're blocking David's view.'

I move to the other side of the telly.

'That's no good either. You'll have to go behind me and lie flat.'

He gives out a laugh, gets up and leaves the room.

'Who's that man?' I ask.

'My brother, if you must know.' Rose is using a haughty voice I haven't heard before.

'I didn't know you had a brother. How old is he?'

'He doesn't live here. He's just visiting. He's twenty-nine and has his own house. Not that it's any of your business. Now be quiet, I'm trying to watch *my* television set.'

Honestly, to think of all the games I have let her win, and the sulks I put up with, all for the sake of watching Robin Hood on her stupid telly. I would *give up*, like Mam always says, but if I missed an episode, I know it would be the one where Robin finally proposes to Maid Marion and they get married and the Sheriff of Nottingham can't do a thing.

When I tell Mam about the man, she says Rose Ritson has a brother as old as twenty-nine because she's adopted. He is not her real brother at all and that explains why Mr and Mrs Ritson are so old, and why Rose gets everything she wants, and why Mr and Mrs Ritson look at each other sometimes as if they wish they could change their minds and send her back.

Rituals

—— ● ◉ ● ——

No one comes to watch First Confessions and there's no dressing up, just a lot of examining of consciences and reciting prayers we have all learned off by heart so we know what to say in the confessional box. All Roman Catholics have to go to Confession or they get ex-communicated. Dad says doing Easter Duties once a year is enough for him. Mam says I have to go every two weeks.

My classmates slide along the polished benches and squash up. When it's time to go forward Miss Beckett pokes us out of the warm spaces we've made.

The Canon is as deaf as a post and makes people shout their sins, so everyone in church can hear. No one wants to go to him, even the adults. *Especially the adults,* Mam says.

'Forgive me Father, for I have sinned.' I kneel in the wooden box and make the sign of the cross.

'In the name of the Father, and of the Son, and of the Holy Ghost, Amen.' The purple curtain between me and the priest shakes a bit when he speaks.

'This is my First Confession.'

'Yes, my child?'

'Erm, I told a lie Father. And, I..I..' My inside head starts mashing up. I go blank and forget everything I've been taught...

'Who did you tell a lie to child?' The priest must have got

sick of the wait.

'Erm, erm... I can't remember, Father.'

'Was it a big lie, or a small lie?'

'Bi...Small.' The bones in my knees get pains from the hard kneeler, and start rocking about on the stiff wood.

'Is there anything else?' His voice sounds odd not having a face.

'No, that's all, Father.' I peep up quickly but can't see through the grill.

'Nothing else you would like to tell me about?'

'No.'

'All right. But you must try to be truthful. Will you promise me that you will always be truthful?

'Yes Father.'

'Good. Now, for your penance, I would like you say one Our Father, one Hail Mary, and one Glory Be.'

'Yes, Father.'

'Now, let me hear you make a good act of contrition.'

'Oh my God, because you are so good, I am ss..sorry I have sinned against you, and with the help of your grace, I will not ss..sin again.'

'Now, go in peace, God bless you, and absolve you from your sins. In nomine Patris, et Filii, et Spiritus Sancti, Amen.'

He must be making the sign of the cross so I do as well. Up off my knees I feel the blood start to come back. Pins and needles rush along my feet and I fumble back into the light.

I see Miss Beckett holding up her joined palms, glaring at me from her pew. I forgot about my hands and slap them together quick, fingertips upwards, thumbs crossed. Then I walk my holiest walk to the altar rail. The teachers will be watching as I kneel to say my penance. I get through The Hail Mary and the Our Father, but can't remember The Glory Be. I know it's short but it has disappeared from my head. I have to go home with only two of my three prayers said.

At bedtime Mam helps me recite it, so at last I have paid for my sins and can go to sleep.

'Glory Be to the Father, and to the Son, and to the Holy Ghost. As it was in the beginning, is now, and ever shall be, world without end. Amen.'

After First Confessions we get ready to make First Holy Communion so need to learn the Catechism, the most important book in school. It is full of questions about God and his earthly Church, which is built on Peter who was a rock.

'Who made you?' It starts with an easy one.

'God made me.'

'Why did God make you?' Another easy one.

'God made me to know him, love him, and serve him.'

After that I get stuck, but learning the answers will make me truly know everything about God and His church. Mam can answer every question without even looking hot. Her cheeks never go red except from rouge. She really does know everything about God. Before she got married she was a nun, so it was her job.

'Hands up anyone who can tell me about the priest's message at Mass?'

Every Monday morning the teacher asks us about the Sunday sermon. No one raises a hand.

'Come on, come on, someone must remember. It was only yesterday.'

I go all hot prickles, in case I get picked out. I never know what the priest is talking about.

The Mass is in Latin, which is foreign, and the priest keeps his back turned so no one sees his mouth. Mam is the only one who knows what he says but she has a big black Missal with ribbons she moves from page to page, following the prayers. She speaks all the Latin words and knows all the Latin hymns. She talks and sings all the answers. She says when she was a novice she sang in the choir. She must have sounded much better when she was young than she does now.

'In nomine Patris, et Filii, et Spiritus Sancti, Amen.' This is the priest's blessing before he comes off the altar. It means, one, two, three, four: *the end*, and is the only Latin I know off by heart.

The sermon is in English but is always boring, especially when the Canon does it. When he climbs into the pulpit every person in every pew sighs.

Orphans

———— ● ● ● ————

Even though I tell her I haven't done any new sins, two weeks after making my First Confession Mam makes me go again. Dad walks with us as far as the bottom of the street, then crosses at Watson's and heads over the cobbles towards the bus stop.

'Dad, I thought you were coming with us this time.'

'Later on. Ah've just got t' gan and quench this thirst first.'

He hurries round the corner with his hands clasped behind his back and disappears.

'But why do I have to go to Confession when Dad doesn't?'

'He'll go before Easter.'

'Easter's miles away.'

'He has town to go to.'

'Why can't I wait until Easter?'

'Give me your hand, and stop acting yourself.'

Mam grabs my wrist and yanks me all the way to church.

When I get home Teresa is copying girls from an old catalogue onto her Big Top drawing pad.

'Why didn't you come to Confession?' I slide in at the kitchen table beside her.

'Stop squashing me.' She elbows my ribs. 'Budge.'

'Ow! It's not fair.'

'If you must know, the priest came to my school to take confessions so I went then instead.'

'I wish I was at big school.'

'You won't be saying that when you get there.' Joey has spilled a bit of milk and is letting Jupiter lick some off his hand. 'When you get to top school they give the strap for the least little thing.'

'Did you have it Joey?'

'Hell yes. Loads of times.' Joey nods his head so fast his fringe flops up and down. 'Those teachers don't think twice about giving the belt.'

I fold my arms on the table and rest my head. When Joey leaves the kitchen the cat starts scratching at the door, trying to follow. I think cats are lucky they don't have to go to school. I wish I didn't, and wish I didn't ever have to move up from infants to juniors.

'What the hell you doing?' Teresa nudges my chair, scraping it along the lino. 'Get out of my way will you? I can hardly move my arm you're sitting so close.'

'Eee, you'll get wrong for swearing.'

'Don't be stupid. Joey says *hell* all the time. Hell's not swearing.

'Bet Mam says it is.'

When she's drawing girls Teresa goes into a dream and hates being disturbed. Her mouth drops open and a whiff of pear drops wafts up my nose.

'What you eating?'

'Never mind.'

'Greeding our Joey's sweets eh?'

She won't look up but tries to stab the back of my hand with her pencil point.

'Har, missed!'

'Where there's a will there's a way.' She has another go, sticking out the tip of her tongue so I can see the clear white sweet on her pink pimples. Then she brings her face right up and blows out the aniseed scent, before snapping her lips shut and turning her back.

A knock at the door brings Mam through from the scullery drying her hands.

'That door never stops,' she mutters. 'And no doubt it'll be for your dad.'

Loads of people knock at our door, wanting Dad because he is a landlord. Most of them are men looking for rooms, some with accents I don't understand: Irish navvies and labourers. This knock is Mrs Ritson all crooked in her worn down zippy slippers. Her fat ankles swelled right up as she blocks the path.

'I had my suspicions from the start,' her arms are flying about.

'What's that supposed to mean?' Mam folds hers to keep them calm. Mrs Ritson is making her mad.

'Your daughter, Bernadette has been stealing from my house.'

'What?'

'I'm not certain about the other things that disappeared, but the day our Rose let her in to watch TV a necklace went from the mantelpiece, and has gone from the house.'

'You can't come to someone's door and make accusations like that.' Mam's voice wobbles about.

'No one else could have taken it except her.'

'Oh, now I've heard enough. Bernadette, Bernadette.'

I am dragged to the front of Mam's skirt.

'Bernadette, did you take a necklace or anything else from Mrs Ritson's house while you were there?'

'No, Mam. I never did.' My heart feels stabbed and clatters like spoons.

'Did you take anything at any time?'

'No, Mam. I never did.'

'Answer me honestly.'

'I never took nothing!' Quiet tears pop up and out. 'I never saw a necklace. I never.' The tears get heavier and I can hardly breathe.

'See what you've done to this child?' Mam stares at Mrs Ritson as if she has committed a mortal sin.

Mrs Ritson stops raving or saying anything, but looks even older than she normally does.

'I hope you are satisfied with yourself.' Mam closes the door and we come back in.

Bernadette Keenan is no good, chop her up for firewood. When she's dead boil her head, make her into ginger bread.

Rose Ritson's knocking is much quieter than her mother's, and her talking is as well.

'So, your mother couldn't come and tell me that herself?' Mam is as cool as a cucumber now.

'No Mrs Keenan, she's not feeling very well.'

'I'm not surprised,' Mam closes the door again, but softly. She says she can't understand why people their age want to go about adopting, especially as they've already got children grown-up.

My eyes are swollen from all the sobs and I feel too worn out to properly enjoy this turn about.

'That kid's got rings run round those two, she has.'

When Dad comes back in Mam tells him everything that's gone on. 'I knew that bliddy necklace would be in the same place it was lost.' She enjoys swearing even though she'll have to tell the priest when she goes to Confession. 'They never even looked properly before they came here accusing us. What a surprise eh? Their own kid all the time.'

Dad nods and says 'Aye' and 'Ah Naah' even more times than he normally does. They have a fresh pot of tea and talk loads and loads.

'There's no fools like old fools.' Dad slurps from the saucer because the tea is too hot. Him and Mam have sayings for everything that happens, and the ones they are bringing out for this puts Mam in a right good mood.

'That's it mind, Bernadette. You are forbidden to ever cross their threshold again.'

'What about Robin...?' I start to plead but it's no good. I know I can never go back, not even for Robin Hood. For now all I care about is the big headache I've got from the millions of tears and snots.

'Never again. I mean it.'

I bet that little pest Rose Ritson planned all this out, so that she would be able to have her own stupid telly back all to herself. Let her stew in it then. That's what Mam says and I think so as well.

Rose Ritson is an orphan same as Mam and Dad. Dad says in their day orphans were farmed out to any relative who would put a roof over their heads, not adopted. That's why he was sent to be raised with his mother's family in Limerick after she died. And that's why he stayed there until his Da found a new wife in England and brought him back.

Rose is the first person I know who is officially adopted. And being accused of stealing by Mrs Ritson is the first time I've ever had an adult say I was a thief: an adult from outside my house that is.

Apart from my own Mam and Dad, and brother and sisters, I would never steal from anybody ever, not ever in the whole wide world.

Eye

——— ● ◉ ● ———

Meena is superstitious and never walks under ladders or crosses knives, or spills salt without throwing some over her left shoulder for luck. She has learned to read tea-leaves, and palms, and can tell fortunes, which is amazing considering she never had a magic wand, or magic dice, or any kind of magic set.

Since Meena left school and got a proper job, her and her best friend, Audrey, go to the pictures in town every Saturday night. I heard them talking about a film called Frankenstein, that has a monster who kills people. Our Meena caught me ear-wigging and said I had better not breathe a word about her going to see an X. I would never do anything to vex Meena because she might get a voodoo doll and stick pins in it and condemn me to death.

In the middle of Sunday afternoon Teresa finds caterpillars in the front hedge and lets them crawl on her hands. She says they tickle but I hate crawlies on me and I don't want to draw one either and I don't think they are a beautiful colour.

I examine the scar from the wart I got when I was forced to hold hands with Michael Cunningham in dance lesson: his podgy fingers scrubbing scratchy lumps on my hand. Meena rubbed on a chunk of raw meat then buried it under the hedge so the cats couldn't sniff it and dig it up. It worked like magic, just this faint mark left. She offered to do the same to stop our Joey getting sties but he said if she came near his eyes with a lump of dead cow she would get it slapped across her head. Him and our Teresa, those two are a right ungrateful pair and no mistake.

It's only a few weeks since the last sty was removed and now another one's been taken off. Joey has a pirate's patch taped over one eye, but white instead of black. If only he had let our Meena do the magic I bet it wouldn't have come back. I feel sorry for him but think it serves him right.

'Come and get your hands and face wiped.' Mam comes to the front step and commands us in. I can't believe she is stopping me and Teresa playing and making us go with her to Benediction. Benediction lasts quarter of an hour, which sounds short, but apart from Confession, and Mass, it is the worst thing about church.

Getting wiped with the cold wet flannel is like getting slapped with snot. I would much rather have a proper wash.

'Do I have to go?'

'Yes, you do.'

'Why? our Joey doesn't even go to Mass any more.'

'Never mind about what your brother does or doesn't do.'

'But I'm looking at these caterpillars.'

'No buts. Come on, in now. If you come right this minute I'll buy you a bar of chocolate on the way back.'

Mam is devout, our Teresa says, but has *no compassion.* our Teresa knows loads of words like that.

I have on my cardi but still shiver. Church is so cold the Blessed Sacrament must be freezing, sitting in the middle of the golden prongs. At Benediction we venerate the Blessed Sacrament: the Body of Christ in a round piece of bread. No one eats Him at Benediction, just reveres. I'm glad because He tastes cardboard and once the priest puts Him on your tongue you can't move your mouth or touch Him with your teeth, and He always sticks, and unless you poke Him down He takes ages to melt.

Incense hangs in the quiet air and calms people with its smell. We walk down the aisle in a holy line. Mam never goes to church without her big black missal with the shiny ribbons that keep her place. It is full of prayer cards for dead people: the souls of the faithful departed she says. I know none of the Benediction prayers and never want to learn. She knows all of them.

I kneel down and place the palms of my hands together and think of the promised chocolate bar they will soon hold.

Mam says we should keep them until we get home. But I want mine straight away, and can hardly wait to rip the paper off.

'Mam, what's venerate?'

'Praise.'

'What's revere?'

'Revere's praise as well.'

'Is it alright to venerate Caramacs?'

'Don't be silly.'

'Revere them then, is that alright?'

'Just gannin for a couple of jars,' Dad tells Mam when we get back. He wipes the end of his nose with a hanky then sticks it in his coat. Dad's hankies are the biggest in the house, but his nose isn't that much bigger than anyone else's.

'Never in a month of Sundays,' Mam says, in a sarky voice. She takes her headscarf off, starts singing The Mountains of Mourne and goes to fill up the kettle.

'You shouldn't go out when you've got cold, Dad.'

'Sniffle, that's aal.' He sniffs, then a sneeze explodes like gunshot.

'Da, man!'

'What's the marra wi' ye?'

'Germs!'

'Nee germs from this snout I'll have you know. A Roman nose: roaming aal ower me face.' Dad laughs at his own joke as if it's the funniest thing he's heard all day. He told us once that when he was young he went to see a music hall act that farted tunes. We thought that was disgusting, but it makes him laugh to this day.

Cakes

———— ◦ ◉ ◦ ————

At top school there is a Christmas party and Mam lets me choose six cakes from Davies bread shop to take.

'Any ones I want?' I peer through the glass case at all the luscious things.

'Six of what ever you think will be nice.'

I have never been allowed six cakes in one go before. They sparkle with cream and jam and icing and sugar sprinkles, and oh....

'Errm? Errm?' I examine the line of cakes behind the glass: along, back, along, back.

'Come on, make your mind up.'

'Mmm?'

'Come on Bernadette, you're holding every body up.'

'It's all right, hinny, lerra take her time.' The woman behind the counter is really kind.

'I'll have two strawberry tarts, and errm, a chocolate éclair, and that cream thing?'

'Cream horn?'

'Yes, that. And, can I have a pink cream slice, and a white cream slice, I mean vanilla, and...'

'That'll do. That's enough.'

'Oophs, lost count.'

The woman in the white apron brings out a flat piece of

cardboard and makes it into a box, then carefully places the cakes in, and ties it up with shiny red ribbon.

'Be careful now. Hold it by the loop on the top.'

'Thank you.' I take it softly in my hands. I am starving for cake, and dying to get to school for the feast of my life.

At playtime we get our milk from the crates then go outside to play for an extra long time. When we come back everyone is freezing and excited. All the desks have been put together to make a long table piled with food. I see my cakes have been put on a plate. There's a dash for places and, from where I get to sit, they are so far away I can't reach.

'Where do you think you are going Bernadette Keenan?'

'I was going to change my place Miss.'

'Sit down girl.'

'But...'

'Sit down, and eat.'

'Bu...' I can't believe it.

She glares over to the drawer where the strap is kept.

'Yes, Miss.' I slap down onto the seat.

In the blink of an eye all my cakes vanish from sight. They are the best cakes on the table. They are the best cakes in the entire universe. The only things within reach are jam-rolls, rich teas, and some thin iced biscuits. My fresh cream cakes and all their sugar sprinkles are plastered on the greedy beaks at the far end of the form. The only time I have ever been allowed six delicious cream cakes in a single go, and I never got one miserable measly taste. I never want to have a Christmas feast in school again. Everything our Joey said about top school was correct.

'Ah was fighting a war at his age,' Dad reminds Mam when Joey complains about having to run messages. Mam relies on him to carry heavy things like taties, but I am old enough to go for light groceries now and am being sent to the Co-op, so memorise our number for the dividend. 55251.

'Hand me the note, hinny?' A woman in pink leans across the counter. Her hair is sticking out of her hat and clags to her face like lemon curd. This is the first time I've run a message to the Co-op. 55251.

I hand over the scrumpled list and the pound note. 55251. She takes the empty bag then slices bacon on the silver machine, folding thin strips onto grease proof paper, weighing and wrapping it, then taking the hunk of bacon and replacing it with cooked ham. 55251. When she's finished she gives me the bag and change, some tickets, and the list with the meat crossed off. 55251. I wait at another counter for butter to be cut from a slab, then sugar is weighed into a thick purple bag. 55251. Everything takes ages. I see the broken biscuit jar, but Mam only buys whole biscuits and they're not on the list. I get more dividend tickets. 55251.

At the kerb I swing the bag and try to stop the number. 55251. I have done the messages but it keeps going. 55251. I try to think about what Mam will make when I get back. 55251. Then a car stops right beside me and a man leans across.

'Hello' he opens the door. 'Where are you off to?'

'Nowhere.' I say, wondering why he asks. 55251.

'Nowhere. Well, would you like to come for a ride?'

'I have to go home.'

'You can have sweets. Would you like some sweets?' He opens his hand and shows me a sparkly jelly stuck in the centre of his palm.

'Hop in pet, I won't bite. Hop in and I'll give you a lift.'

The leather smell of the car is floating out, reminding me of the day I went to buy a carpet with the Ritsons. My only ever car ride.

'Hello Bernadette, you all right?' I didn't see Mister Towers leaning by the butcher's wall, 'Emm...' I'm mixed up. The weight of the shopping bag is pulling my arm out.

Mister Towers bends down to the driver who slams his car door and roars off.

'Come on Bernadette, give me your hand and I'll take you across the road.' I don't like holding his hand. It's hot and sweaty even though it's cold, but I do as I am told. Sometimes I play with out with his daughter, Marie, who has sweaty hands like her dad. He leads me over the road then lets me run ahead, watching all the way, until we are back in our street. It's a relief to get home, without sweets, or broken biscuits, but at last the number has shot out of my head, and I still have the shopping bag.

'What in the world?' Mam looks fed up, talking to Mister Towers for ages on the front step but not asking him in. I think she's embarrassed because she has a load of silver hair curlers in.

'That's the first and last time you go up to Elswick Road on your own, Bernadette.'

'Cannit let them out of yer sight.' Mister Towers says.

Dad looks even more sick when he comes home, and is told about the man in the car, and about Mister Tower's good deed.

'Just as well Mister appeared.'

'Aye,' Dad says, nipping the end of his nose then scratching his chin.

'I dread to think what might have happened if he hadn't shown up.' Mam keeps on singing his praises.

'He misses nowt, that bloke.'

'What a relief, anyway. We can thank our lucky stars she wasn't abducted, and we can thank Mister for having nothing better to do all day but stand about minding other people's business.'

'That's it.' Dad shakes his head and sighs. 'That man's never done a day's work in years.'

Marie is the only person in the world who doesn't call her dad Mister Towers. Even Mrs Towers, his wife, calls him Mister, and never uses his first name. Marie is half-way in age between me and Teresa, and is an only child because Mrs Towers was too old to have any more. If there is no one else out we let her play, but she's another right softy, and always running in to tell her mam when she doesn't get her own way.

Dad hates Mister Towers being my rescuer because now he will have to stop and chat when he sees him keeping sentry on the corner. Mister won't work nor want, Dad says, and that's why they are hard up and have to rent. It's funny though, because Marie has a piano in her front room and once a week a proper piano teacher comes. Their front room is full of fancy plates and glass ornaments and has a grandfather clock. I know they get coke not best coal, and Puro milk, and margarine instead of butter, but still, we don't even have a mouth organ or a tambourine let alone a piano, so they can't be as poor as all that.

Meena

— ● ● ● —

These days our Meena is forever fiddling with her face and hair. If that sausage curl comes out of its curler wonky there's hell to pay. Every time Audrey calls for her they spend ages examining themselves in the mirror, then reading each other's stars, or tea leaves, or palms, before they go out. Getting dressed up is Meena's favourite occupation and listening to records is her second. The minute Mam leaves the room she takes Max Bygraves off the turntable and puts Paul Anka back on. She has a job as a waitress and bought his song, Diana, with her wages, and plays it every chance she gets.

'It's a wonder there's any grooves left on this, you play it that much.' Mam is through from the scullery and frowning at Meena's song.

'I thought you were cooking?'

'I'm having a cup of tea while the meat's stewing. Put Tap your Sabots on while I get warmed.'

Mam raises her skirt and backs her bot towards the kitchen range. She gets as close as she can without burning, then rubs her hands round and round. The scullery is always freezing and nobody likes being in it, but Mam has to cook so has no choice.

Tap your Sabots is about Saint Bernadette scraping away mud to make the grotto at Lourdes. It has a nice tune and says my name a lot. It's sung by a priest, and reminds Mam of being a nun in France. She travelled through on her way to Italy, stopping in Paris to sight-see even though she was a nun and wasn't supposed to be interested in sights. She went along the Seine and saw the bridges Eartha Kitt sings about; growling like a cat in Under the Bridges of Paris.

If school was as easy as learning songs my brain would be stuffed to the brim. Some of the things I have to learn in school are impossible. I know loads of words to songs though and even Mam knows some, and in a good mood will sing along. She sings Bimbo to the cats, even though none of them are called that. I ask if we can get a cat and call it Bimbo, but she tells me to stop acting myself.

Bimbo, Bimbo, where ya gonna go-e-o?
Bimbo, Bimbo, whatcha gonna do-e-o?
Bimbo, Bimbo, does your mommy know
That you're goin' down the road to see a little girleo?

Friday nights after tea are the best time to catch Dad for sweets and stories, especially if most of his tenants have paid their rent. Even better if the fish has been nice, because he enjoys the taste of fish even though it's a penance to go without proper meat.

'Did Ah ever tell yeese aboot the time I joined the French Foreign Legion?'

'Dad, man! You did not.' Teresa thinks she knows everything.

'Aye, it's true, seven years; me and Errol Flynn both signed the same day.'

'Did you Dad? What's the French Foreign Legion?'

'Top secret. Carried out secret missions aal ower the world, me and Errol.'

'But what did you do?'

'Sworn to secrecy.'

'Arrh, man. Tell me, I won't tell anybody else.'

'Haway, which one of yeese wants to run up to the paper shop and get me a packet of Woodbines?'

'Mam says we can't.' Teresa sighs as if she wants to go, when she really does not.

'Oh, aye. Ah forgot.'

From now on me and our Teresa have to stay in the street. Joey is *livered* because he thought he was getting rid of the job of going to the shops.

Ever since he got bashed in by some lads from Kennilworth Road, he hates being seen going up the street with the tatie bag. He got a black eye and the shopping money was pinched and Dad said Joey let them take the cash out of his hand. Dad said he could do with toughening up instead of hiding behind his mother's apron strings, as if *his mother* was a different woman, and had nothing to do with our Mam.

'Meena, isn't it time *you* went for the messages?' Joey flicks his fringe and glowers at Mam's note. Meena has been to work and is getting ready to go out and that takes hours. Our Joey doesn't work on a Saturday so this is bound to end in a row.

'What's up with you?' She says, blowing dust off her

nail file, and perching her bottle of red varnish on the arm of the couch.

'Nothing, but I'm always the one to go.'

'So? I've been to work.'

'You're not the only one who goes to work. I'd like to see you get up at six-o-clock and traipse all the way to the shipyards.'

'Not today though?'

'No, but I work more hours than you the other days.'

'You want me to lift a stone and a half of taties after I've been on me feet all day, running up and down stairs carrying trays of dishes?'

'Look how much time you waste painting your nails.'

'Hey, I have to be presentable for my job. It's alright for you, you just turn up in a boiler suit and no one cares.' Meena frowns at Joey's bitten down nails, sharpening hers into daggers. 'I have to spend time on my appearance, I wouldn't dare show my face if my nails looked like that.'

'Get knotted.' Joey scowls, tucking his hands up his sleeves then spitting a fresh bit of raggy fingernail at the hearth.

When he gets back Meena has her legs curled the opposite way, but apart from that has hardly moved.

'Charming. You haven't budged one inch since I left.' He plonks the shopping bag on the corner of the settee and wipes his top lip with his sleeve.

'Put a sock in it Joey.' Meena holds both arms out and examines her nails, then brings them back, shakes and blows on the wet nail varnish, as if she is playing a harmonica.

'Oh no, look what you've done.' She notices a smudge and pulls a horrified face.

'Don't blame me.' Joey drags the bag out to the kitchen.

'Now I'll have to repair this all over again. Bernadette, petal, can you pass the varnish remover?'

I push myself up off the cushion, give the orange liquid a good sniff then pass it across, my eyes whirling as she wipes the pearly varnish off.

'Meena, did you know Dad was once in the French Foreign Legion?'

She stops what she's doing for a sec and looks up.

'And he rode cattle ships to South America where they make corned beef.'

Meena lets her eyes drop, puffs and blows and sets to work again.

'Are you sure? He told me it was his da who did that.'

'His da, who he calls *the auld chep*?' I'm confused.

'His da, our grandfather, yes.'

'Dad's dad went to South America?' I try to get it straight.

'Yep.'

'Our Teresa says he makes it up.'

'Some of it he does. But I think that one is true, and I know he fell off a jaunting car in Ireland and nearly lost a leg.'

'Did he? He never told me that.'

'He said it was hanging by a thread and a team of Ireland's

101

finest surgeons took hours to stitch it back in place. They did such a good job he doesn't even have a limp.'

Joey comes back from the kitchen and flops, raising his eyebrows and fluttering his lips when he realises the subject. Meena carefully pats the rollers in her sausage fringe and goes back to getting ready.

Let Sleeping Dogs Lie

Dad makes shadows dance on the wall. In the right light he can make any animal come alive: dogs, rabbits, birds, even elephants. I ask Joey if he ever did picture shows for him but he just grunts and yawns, as if Dad is a tiresome subject.

Frankie is the only man who comes in our house who everybody likes. I like him because I can call him by his first name and Mam likes him because he has an allotment where he grows flowers and cabbages and rhubarb, bringing some to Mam between church and Sunday dinner. They talk about the flowers she is going to grow when Dad builds our new house and we move to the country. With Frankie she smiles and looks relaxed, the opposite of how she is with most people.

Frankie is Dad's odd-job man and does repairs to his houses so Dad likes him for that, but grumbles about the cost.

'Joe, who are you complaining about now?' Mam catches him in the act.

'The price he's charged for fixing that roof, and the first bit of wind blows three tiles off. Ah might as well have climbed the bliddy ladders and done it mesel.'

'Frankie again? When I left you five minutes ago it was the rent collector you were moaning about.'

'Him anaal. Useless buggers, the pair of them.'

Since Dad bought more houses and got more tenants, he

has so much to do, and so many bad payers, he has to employ Mr Coyle to help him get the money in. At least Frankie wears a cap and speaks Geordie. Mr Coyle though, he wears a trilby and talks posh. Dad is his boss but you would never think so.

A bit after Dad's grumble about money I overhear him talking to Mam at the kitchen table, quiet but loud enough for me to hear.

'Better the divil you know, than the divil you don't.'

'You're right there, kidda.' Dad is chewing a plateful of corned beef slices with best butter and bread. He must love corned beef because of his da being on the cattle ships.

'It's a long time ago, Joe, and he paid the price.'

I am behind the door peeping in through the crack.

'Never interested in women though. It was aalways lads...'

'Still, there's no harm in him. And prison's a hard lesson.'

It's Frankie they are talking about.

I find Meena and tell her everything.

'Frankie! A child molester! Don't be daft.' Meena scoffs.

I never heard of child molesters before the man in the car who offered me sweets. But it wasn't him Mam and Dad were talking about, it was definitely Dad's handyman, Frankie.

'But I heard Mam and Dad saying he'd been to prison.'

'And?' Meena is sitting at her dressing table giving big false sighs. 'Tell me something I don't know.'

'You knew?'

'Course.'

'Dad said he was a *Nancy boy*, and something about young lads.'

'Being a Nancy boy doesn't mean he molests children.'

'Does he not then?'

'*No.*' She says in serious tone.

'What does it mean then?'

Meena has on her black dress and reaches for the white apron hanging from the wardrobe.

'Don't let anybody hear you repeating any of that.' She gives me a look and ties a bow behind her back.

'I won't.'

'He's alright, Frankie is. He's nice.' She fluffs the frills and turns into a waitress.

'I know. I think he's nice as well, except for the whistling.'

'What whistling?'

'He whistles all the time.'

'I never noticed.'

'It doesn't even make a proper tune.'

'Well, I feel sorry for him. I remember once he fetched his friend...brought him round... his...his frien...Oh, never mind.'

'Did he whistle as well?'

'Who?'

'His friend.'

'No, he was younger.'

'Too young to whistle?'

'What?'

'Is it just old men who whistle?'

'Frankie isn't that old. Well, not ancient. But old enough to carry the can.'

'What can?'

'Oh, it's a law...It doesn't matter now. Look, I have to go to work. Don't you be repeating any of this, mind.'

'I said I won't.'

'Well, just make sure you don't. Here, can you reach the top of my dress and do the hook and eye up?'

Meena flashes her claws, turns her heels and clonks out. I'm surprised she's got the nerve to be wearing high heels after the fuss Dad made about the stiletto holes. He says the whole kitchen floor looks machine-gunned. She might appear skinny and have an eighteen inch waist but my sister must have put some weight into making those dints in the lino.

Cakes

It's rent collecting day and Dad is full of beans. Last Friday he called Mr Coyle a bull's knacker, but this week he must have collected loads of rent because Dad is frisky as a two-year-old, carrying on and telling us jokes.

'What did the big chimney say to the little chimney?' One of his riddles.

'You're too young to smoke.' Teresa jumps in.

'Let me answer one Dad?' I plead. 'Me, me, me!'

Dad is washing down his food with tea before he goes to the pub. Fish and chips are delicious but the smell they leave is yuk.

'Alreet, noo listen. What gans up the chimney doon but not doon the chimney up?'

'Erm!'

'I know Dad, I know!' Teresa again.

'Give the bairn a chance, see if she can get it.' Dad waits for me to say the answer but my brain starts to buzz and I can't think.

'Erm...'

'Gan on then, tell her.'

'An umbrella, you nit!' Teresa is over the moon with herself.

'An umbrella? That's daft.'

'Alreet. This is yer last chance: what's black and white and red all ower?'

'Erm...?'

'Err...A...A...?'

'A newspaper! I divvent knaa, lad! Too slow to catch cold.'

He drains his cup, stands up, then starts looking for his coat. Time to act.

'Dad can we have sweets?'

'It's not pocket money day until the morra.'

'Just one little bag...Pleeease.' I give him my pitiful look.

'Alreet. Two ounces or a quarter, what would ye rather have?'

'Two ounces.'

'No, Dad, a quarter.' Teresa butts in.

'You, lad! You're getting too clever fer yer own good.' Dad holds out his coat. 'Here, feel the weight of that.'

Teresa tries to hold it up but her arms collapse.

'Haway then, get yer coats.' He heaves his over his shoulder and jerks his arms down the sleeves. 'Yeese can come doon the shop with iz before I get the bus if ye can answer this.'

'Thanks, Dad!'

'Reet. Fatty and Skinny went up in a balloon. Fatty farted and Skinny fell doon...'

'Arr, Dad!

'Hang on a minute. The question is, which one of yeese two is Fatty?'

'I'm Skinny.'

'No, I'm Skinny.'

'Me!'

'No. Me, Dad, me!'

Dad chuckles away at the sight of us squabbling, as if it's the height of amusement.

Mam blames all the sweets and cakes for the state of my teeth. She says we get far too much sugar, and the dentist agrees.

'Don't worry pet, it's only one.'

She repeats what the dentist says.

'We'll give you some gas to send you to sleep and when you wake up the tooth will be gone and you won't feel a thing.' The dentist's flabby face smiles as he pushes a rubber bit in my mouth and covers it with a heavy mask. The smell is sweet and sickly and there is no escape from the hiss of gas.

I wake on a black leather couch in a different room, wind whistling in the fire grate. Mam helps push me into coat sleeves as my gums bubble with blood. She puts a white pad over my mouth and ties a woollen scarf tight round my head and chin. I can taste our old tablespoon.

'It's over now, pet,' she says. 'Come on, let's get you home.' She ties a knot in her headscarf and glances in the huge mirror as we pass along the hallway.

Walking out through the glass door, my knees give and she yanks my arm to keep me up. We pass the Big Lamp sweet shop without me, this once, pestering. On the trolley bus my sobs taste of watery salt and still the metal spoon.

'What's amiss with the bairn?' A woman leans over to ask.

'She's just had eight teeth out,' Mam says.

'Poor little blighter.'

Sobbing is my only noise. *Eight* my only thought.

Once we are home Mam tucks me up on the couch and starts cooking home-made broth. When I wake up she brings some in a cup but the raw holes in my mouth are full of jellied-blood that I can't bear anything to touch.

I wonder if the dentist is a Catholic and goes to Confession and tells the priest about lying: promising he would only take one tooth out, then putting me to sleep and pulling out eight.

Next day I am kept off school so try to cheer up and take a few sips of milk. Mam wraps a scarf round my chin again and takes me on the trolley to the big store in Benwell. I choose a Brer Rabbit colouring book and a new set of crayons, and start colouring in by the fire as soon as we get home. Cooking smells waft in, and when it's ready Mam serves me bread and butter pudding with Carnation milk. My stomach is growling but the gum holes wince, and I try to guess how long it would take to starve to death.

Mam warns me not to sit too close to the fire, but I take no notice and hog the heat until red and white rings appear on my legs and the tops of my feet. When Teresa comes in from school she explains corpuscles and chilblains and says I should never stick my feet over the flames.

Dad says as soon as I can eat properly he will buy me sweets and cakes and a big bottle of pop. Dad says, *eight teeth is nowt.* He got all his teeth out in one go and got the false set put straight in on the National Health. When he was young no one bothered with dentists, they just tied one end of string round the rotten tooth and the other end round a door handle then slam: that was it. The tooth was out.

Rents

Malvern Street is my favourite house because it has two front doors, one at the end of the long front path and another down some wonky steps. The rent collector, Mr Coyle, is on holiday and as a special treat Dad is letting me go with him to collect the rents. Being off school is fantastic.

In the front basement a woman with a grey bun keeps a caged canary that talks in her identical voice. She wears glasses that make her eyes look massive, and her mouth is a black space. She has a glass jar of sweets, as big as a jar in a sweet shop, and brings it down from the shelf just for me.

'Hello Mr Keenan, hello dear, come in.'

'Hello Mr Keenan, hello dear, come in,' the bird repeats.

She welcomes us like proper guests, bringing the rent and the rent book from the mantelpiece then giving me sticky bits of rock from the jar.

Dad says she has a cheap rent because the room is small. It's so small and dark there's hardly enough space for the cooker, table, chairs, cupboard, wardrobe and bed. All the things she has to have. Most of the rooms are taken by single men and I wonder if she has a husband or if she has lost one, or if she keeps one hidden in a secret passage or behind a secret wall.

'Canny wife, that,' Dad says. 'Did ye like the bord?' Back at ground level the gloom disappears. We go to the front door and blink at the sun and screw our eyes while Dad lights a Woodbine and takes five minutes rest.

'Does she ever let it out of the cage?'

'Pays her rent every Friday and never comes to borrow it back, not like that bloke in the next room.'

'Did she get rotten teeth from eating sticky rock?'

'What's wrang with her teeth?'

'They're black.'

'Gan on?'

'Dad! I'm not kidding. They are.'

'Ah well, ask the bord, next time ye gan in. That bord's clever, knaas aal the answers.'

There are no carpets in any of the houses and everywhere echoes. On the stairs Dad's feet and voice thunder, even though he never talks loud. Even my tiptoes clatter. On the first floor we knock at the front room door where an old couple Dad calls the Ladvians live.

'Alreet?'

They answer the door together, their haggard faces grinning over yellow stumps that look like they need pulling out. A lot of people in Dad's rooms come and go, but the Ladvians have been here ever since the war and seem right at home.

'Come, come,' they beckon us in to the red hot room. Fire blares up the chimney as if it isn't a warm day at all. The exact right money sits waiting on the table and Dad marks up the rent book, signs it then hands it back. Their room is the biggest in the house so they pay two pounds, one of the highest amounts.

I wonder how they get on at the shops when they can't talk the same language as everyone else but Dad says pointing is a universal language.

As usual there is a wardrobe, chest of drawers, table and cooker, and in another corner one big bed. By the window a huge pile of coal stretches from the floor right up to the ceiling. At first I expect this to make Dad mad, but he acts as if he hasn't even noticed.

The lady has on a massive headscarf, and an apron over a long flared skirt and her husband wears a round black hat and baggy corduroy trousers tucked into his boots, like people out of a world costume book.

'Dad, have you seen how much coal they've collected?' Back out on the landing I can't wait to ask.

'Aye. They're good payers,' he says.

'Da...ad?'

'Eh?'

'What *is* a *Ladvian*?'

'Refugees, from Latvia.'

'Where's Latvia?'

'Neewhere noo. It's aal part of Russia since Stalin took ower.'

'Da...ad? Why have they only got one bed?'

'Ah wish every body paid as prompt.' He says, starting to

look irritated.

Mam and Dad have a bed each and I thought sharing only happened in the olden days. Dad told me when he was brought back from Ireland as a child he had to share with three step-brothers who were practically strangers. Imagine four people in one bed? That must have been awful, twice as bad as for the Latvians.

At the door underneath the Latvians there is no answer. Dad says the tenant is a Polish refugee and he is definitely in because there is no padlock and no one goes out without locking their room. There's a funny smell, and I try to get Dad to come away but he says if he doesn't get the Pole's money today then it will be drunk and he'll be in arrears. When the man finally opens up he has on a mucky vest and no shirt and mutters under his breath and I can tell Dad doesn't like having to talk to him.

While dad counts the rent I inspect the ceiling in the corner where the pile of coal is. It's not sagging or black or stained, but the weight on the upstairs floorboards must be a strain and I try to figure how much more coal can be heaped up before the whole ceiling comes down with a crash and lands on the Polish man's bed.

After Malvern Street, it's nice to get out in the fresh air for a bit. We take our time walking to the next house, and Dad calls in at the hardware shop to get a broom shank. At Bentinck Crescent we head straight to the huge dusty kitchen. The shelves are full of cans and tins heaped with bolts, washers, nuts and screws. There are padlocks and paint, and sheets of used sandpaper and planks of wood and sacks of sand, and a broken chair with a split bag of pink plaster spilling on the floor like custard powder. Under the dark window a stained square sink drips green drips from a brass tap. A rusty toilet cistern is propped beside the old fireplace, and newspapers litter the concrete floor. The whole place is brilliant.

'De ye fancy a bit of clearing up?' Dad fixes the new shank on the big hard brush and leans it on the wall. I take the brush and sweep a cloud of dust up in the centre of the floor. We both cough.

'Never mind, let's gan up and have a look at the bathroom. Auld Bob's complaining the tap's ceased again.'

Upstairs the bath tub is full of yellow newspapers that look a hundred years old. Dad twists the sink taps. One gives, and water gushes out, but the other is stuck.

'Ah divvent knaa why he's complaining. This one's alreet.'

'What about the other one?'

'I'll have to put a new washer on. It'll wait. One works. That'll dee for now.'

'Can I use the toilet?'

'Aye, gan on, but hurry up.'

The toilet door has green and gold wavy glass that can be seen through. The lavvy bowl is stained dark brown and instead of a chain there's a piece of string hanging from the cistern and tied in a loop. The top is clean as straw but the bottom is black from all the tenants pulling it to flush.

I thought I wanted to go on, but I'm not in that much of a rush. I've been in ten houses full of strangers sharing one toilet, and never had a wee in one. In my house Mam keeps everything in our bathroom clean and white and scrubbed with bleach. Bleach goes down the plug-holes and toilet, also Dad uses it to clean his teeth.

Dad always steeps his teeth in a cup of Domestos overnight and Mam says if he doesn't stop doing it his stomach will rot.

'Ah rinse them first ye knaa, before I put them back.'

'Why do I waste my breath?' Mam says.

'Gives them a good shine, man,' he laughs.

Dad says his jaws are hard as rock and he can chew his way through any meat even if it's as tough as old boots.

'Why don't you wear the top ones, Dad?'

'Ah divvent like tee many teeth. Dee ye not think Ah'm good looking enough withoot having another set of choppers in me mooth?'

The upper set are kept in the middle drawer of the sideboard and he hardly ever wears them. They have a palate that fits inside the roof of his mouth and I wonder what it must feel like to wear false teeth. When I sneak them out and have a proper close up, the pink bits remind me of bacon and I think of trying them in. The closer they come to my face though, the more the idea makes me feel ill.

Runaway

———— ● ◉ ● ————

Sundays should be as good as Saturdays but aren't. Mornings are spoiled by church, though Sunday dinners are nice and the puddings that follow and the trips out in the afternoon, if the weather is decent.

Today is breezy so me and Teresa put on coats and wait at the front door while Mam and Dad lock up. Before our jaunt we have to call off to bring Meena back from Bristol Terrace, where she has run off to, and is stopping. Girl Guide badges and making cinder toffee seems ages ago. All Meena does these days is make Mam tear her hair out. Dad says it's all about lads.

Apart from Joey the only lads I ever see are drawings in Meena's Romeo and Valentine; handsome ones at least. Our Joey doesn't have any friends, none he would ever bring home for us to see. Real older lads are a mystery.

Splinters and dust fly about and sting my cheeks and the wind is blinding. We reach a scruffy door and Mam knocks. She knocks again, then again, then once more, but nobody answers.

'Curtain's just moved, kidda,' Dad says. 'She's in there alreet.'

'Philomena!' Mam shouts up in her loudest voice. It's Sunday and Meena is getting her Sunday name. My face is stiff, and my knee-bones knock. I've never heard Mam shouting outside before.

'There it gans again.' Dad keeps looking, staring up at the window.

Teresa shuffles her feet, and studies them.

'Philomena, you might as well come out now. We're not leaving without you.'

This time the sash flies up and Philomena pokes her head out.

'Go away,' she shouts. 'I'm not coming back, ever. I'm sixteen and you can't make me.'

'You will come home now or I'll call the police. You're not sixteen yet and they will make you come back.'

Doors in the street are opening and people are coming out onto their steps. Another head arrives at the window. It doesn't stick out but shouts, Fuck off!

Philomena goes back inside and the window slams.

It was a lad.

When we finally get to the proper outing part of the day and arrive in the park Dad gives Teresa money to buy lollies from the kiosk. We eat them by the lake, then at the bandstand we clash our hands pretending they're cymbals and there's music, like on days before Joey and Meena got too big to come with us. Everything is so quiet we can hear insects dive in and out of the bushes behind us, searching for things to eat. Mam and Dad turn round to watch a massive spider weave a web that joins everything together. I slide along the seat so it won't get any ideas about coming near my head.

When I get in from school next day Philomena is back, with a face as long as a fiddle. She is at the fireplace pulling kiss curls in front of her ears, her eyes glazed as glass. Her and Mam must have signed a truce, but the house is full of gloom, like a cloud of hail stones getting ready to pelt.

Jupiter is squashed on her knee beside her vanity case, which is a good sign, because Meena wouldn't go anywhere without that. When she opens it the cat squeals and jumps off and hair lacquer fumes fly out making us all cough.

'Sorry,' she apologises to the cat as he skulks off.

If she ever goes off again maybe she will leave me the vanity case so I can try all her make-up. While the cat's away the mice will play, and next time I will be ready.

By Friday things are calmed down and Philomena goes into town to see Dracula with Audrey and doesn't come back until well after me and Tress are in bed. Tress is Teresa's new name for herself. I don't think I like it.

Since Philomena came home she has been quiet as the grave, until now. The bedroom door creaks open and interrupts a big yawn. There she is with a stack of black hair dragged over her face.

'D R A C U L A....D R A C U L A!' She has her arms straight out and moves towards us, slowly getting nearer and nearer. We scream and stick our heads under the bed clothes, but she pulls back Teresa's blankets and trails the creepy haystack over her arms.

'I vant your blood. Give me your blood.'

'Arrgh, gerr off. Hee hee hee! Don't make iz laugh, gerr off iz, you lump.' She bounds from Teresa's bed and starts staggering closer and closer to me.

'Give me your blood young girl. Let me kiss your neck my dear.'

'Aahh! Stop, stop. Meena don't. Not tickles!'

'Meena, who is this Meena? You mistake me. I am the count. Count D R A C U L A!'

'Hee, hee, hee, don't tickle me...noooh!'

'Stop it. Don't, don't! Don't!'

Me and Teresa and Meena are all laughing like hyenas.

Having her back is so much fun. It's a pity there's nothing to be done with her.

Jupiter

————— ● ◉ ● —————

After one week of peace and quiet all hell breaks lose. But this time it's Joey who is charging out the kitchen and up the stairs as if his tail is on fire.

'That's Joey's cat.'

'We cannit keep aal three.'

Mam and Dad are sitting at the meal table having a Big Conversation.

'Last in, first oot.' Dad kicks at the cat. 'Aal these useless buggers. It's not like this blighter's ever even caught a moose.'

Jupiter is too fast and skids right under the table.

'Where's the pail?' Dad scowls. 'Ah'll get rid of this one.' He tries to kick again but still can't get his toecap to reach.

When Mam sees me she shushes him and pours tea.

'Dad, man! What you doing?'

'Listening in again.' Dad pulls his foot back and scratches his chin. 'Lugs like a bliddy elephant. Will ye gan and occupy yerself somewhere else? Tell her, kidda, will ye?'

'Bernadette, where did you spring from?'

It suddenly dawns on me that Jupiter is for the chop and that's why Joey raced out. I can't believe my ears. Time to swoop. Before another move is made I dive for the cat, scoop him up in my arms and run for it.

I manage to shove him in the tatie bag and pelt hell for leather up the street while he scrabbles to get out. His growls joggle up and down, high and low, soft and loud. This is the first time I have ever left home. That's me and our Meena now, both runaways. The first two to leave home and I have beat her by nine years.

And she came back.

I am never coming back.

I am going for good.

There's a taste of blood in my throat. I suck in streaming snots and wipe my face on my cardigan cuff. At the blue box a policeman grips a boy by the sleeves. The boy struggles and gets a wallop across the head. The policeman is so busy thumping him he misses seeing me. I stop to get my breath. The sun is bright and makes my eyes more wet. I squeeze the bag to make sure Jupiter is still alive. He scratches at the inside until one of his claws comes right through the leather. I prop against a wall, wondering what to do next when a hand on my shoulder makes me jump out of my skin.

It's Dad.

'I'm not coming back. You can't make me.' I grip the handles.

'Haway, ye cannit stand here aal day.' He wants me to move because people are gawping and he hates any fuss. He has lots of sayings about *saying nowt*, especially the three wise monkeys: see no evil, hear no evil, speak no evil. He does the hand actions for that.

'No, you're not gonna drown Jupiter. You're not. You're not!'

'Am not ganna droon the cat,' he says in a whisper.

'Never, ever, ever?'

'*I am not going to drown the cat.* Now come on, come back.'

I clutch the struggling bag to my chest. Jupiter's tiny pink nostrils flare, jutting through the zip so his whiskers are squashed flat.

'Ah was only kidding. Ah was in a bad mood. Ah wouldn't droon the cat.'

I don't know what else to do so swallow hard and run back down the street and into the house, rushing the cat upstairs to my room, where he leaps out like a maniac.

When Dad disappears the next week he doesn't take a suitcase, so no one knows he is gone. When he doesn't come home for dinner Mam checks the sideboard drawer, his shaving brush and razor are gone, same as last year, when he left without a word and went to France. I can't ever remember him not being here and never realised that me and Philomena inherited running away from Dad.

Mam doesn't seem mad, or in a bad mood at all. She just says he must have gone to visit the battlefields where he fought in the war. She says no one can imagine what hell it was. The shelling left deep craters that filled with water where men fell in and drowned. And the noise from the shells was so loud it made Dad deaf, so if anybody whispers he can't hear a sound.

After five days he comes back because it's rent day and he doesn't trust Mr Coyle to collect all the money or get the arrears in.

I was set never to speak to him again, after what happened with the cat, but when he comes in I'm so excited I can't help talking.

'Where did you go Dad?'

'Belgium, the Mennin Gate.'

'Belgium? Mam says you went to France.'

'Aye, France as well.'

Mam goes to the kitchen to wash up while Dad has an after dinner cigarette. I can tell the way she bounces about she is excited to see him as well.

'What's the Mennin Gate?'

'A memorial. A big memorial with the names of the war dead on.'

'Is that where the war was?'

'Aal around there, aye, Ypres.'

I'm not sure I should ask any more questions but he seems in a good mood so it's worth a try.

'How old were you when you were in the war?'

'Seventeen-year-auld.'

He draws to the bottom of his tab and chucks it to the back of the fire with few cold dregs of tea. The black coals go creamy for a minute and we listen to the sizzle.

'Seventeen, but...'

'That's enough of the questions. Ah'm away for a couple of jars.'

'Did you bring anything back, Dad?'

He goes inside his topcoat pocket and brings out a packet of Black Bullets.

'Here, stick yer hand in and get one.'

I pull out one of the sticky sweets. It's got flecks of white paper stuck on but I shove it in and suck. Black Bullets are all right if there's nothing else but I don't see why Dad loves them so much.

'Here, try the other pocket.' He turns his coat round.

'Oh yes, thank you. Thank you!'

Two tubes of Spangles, one each for me and our Teresa, a quarter of toffees to share, and a postcard of the Eiffel Tower. Brilliant.

I am so pleased Dad didn't run away for good.

Bon Means Good

Dad pats his head with one hand and circles the other over his belly.

'Ah bet yee cannit dee that?' He grins.

I start patting the top of my head, and set the other hand off in circles, but it starts patting as well, exactly like the head hand.

'I can't do it.'

'Look, Ah'll show ye again.' Dad does it again, slower.

Now both my hands are doing circles.

'The trouble is, yer not ambidextrous.'

'What does that mean?'

'Means ye can de owt with either hand.'

'Why can't I be *amfi-dextrous*, then.'

'Took a lot of learning that did.'

All this week Dad has been really nice and has been showing me tricks, and buying me extra sweets. He even called into the wet fish shop and got real fish heads with revolting eyes and told Mam to boil them up and give the cats an extra feed.

I want to ask more questions about being *amfi-dextrous* but Dad hates nosy parkers, and I don't want him to start thinking about drowning anything else. Mam says he learned to use either hand after he was shot in the first war. The bullet stopped in his hip after going through his wrist and it took him two years in a military hospital to learn to write with either hand.

Soon after the trip to France, Dad gets the trolley bus to town to sort out an argument over Meena's wages. Meena is never going back to the restaurant where she works so Dad has to talk to her boss and get the money she is owed. He brings me for company and we are going for pop and tea afterwards.

Being a waitress sounds nice and our Meena looks lovely in black, and they gave her a little white cap, and a little white apron with frilly ties at the back. I think Meena must be the loveliest waitress they ever had; with her small waist and beautiful legs and I bet she collected loads of tips from underneath the plates and saucers. Dad always leaves a sixpence under the plate when we have fish and chips at the seaside.

In the doorway of the Tatler Cinema on Northumberland Street we turn in and climb some steep stairs. Meena's restaurant is at the very top. It has posh tablecloths and big plants, nothing like the cafés Dad likes. A man in black clothes comes and talks to Dad, and Dad gives him the bag with Meena's caps and aprons in. They talk in low voices then the man goes off. Dad's cheeks twitch while we wait and two pink spots spring up under his eyes. We wait ages more before the man brings an envelope and hands it to Dad.

Back outside Dad mutters and calls the man some names

but doesn't explain anything. Walking to Mark Toney's I take hold of his hand, and my heart that had sunk rises slowly back up, and I know Dad's does as well.

There are loads of cafés near the bus station but Mark Toney's is best. Cafés always have tea and always have cake and Dad loves going into them. He is teaching me about France where cakes are called gateaux. Meena says she knows some French and tells me *bon* means good, but she can't repeat the other words. It's great that Meena and Dad are friends again after all the carry on over her stiletto holes in the lino and the running away. Her running away not Dad's. Joey hasn't talked to Dad since he nearly drowned the cat, but they never talked before that either, so nothing changed except Joey must hate Dad even more than he did. I keep secretly wishing they would start to speak but every week comes and goes without a single word exchanged.

Square Eyes

Two men carefully carry in the brand new television set and fix it to the wire that connects to the aerial they have put on the roof. At last the front room has a real purpose. Mam tells me to contain myself, but this is the most exciting thing since Christmas and my legs and arms can't stop flapping about. My prayers have been answered: we have a Ferguson telly with a shiny wooden table. Dad moans it cost hundreds of pounds and says the aerial cost more than the telly, and the telly is a useless item. Mam says getting HP has made him angry, but it cost too much money to buy cash. He says Prince Brothers Electricals are hooks and are never getting another penny out of him.

Bliss.

Now I can forget about Rosie Ritson and her stupid television with the stupid doors. This telly is 21 inches big. It's the biggest telly in the street, bigger than the Ritsons', and much bigger than the Towers', who have one the size of a cornflakes box. I will never wish to go to Rosie's house again. Welcome to our wonderful world of TV.

Come away, come away with William Tell, from the land, from the land, I love so well. come away, come away with William Tell. Tell... from Switzerland!

It was a miracle: Pope Pious the twelfth died and Mam changed her mind, and suddenly we got a television and are watching black smoke coming out of the Vatican chimney. We lie around for hours and hours waiting for the new pope to be picked.

'Why does it take so long to pick a pope?'

'The black smoke has to turn white.' Mam knows all about it.

'When will it happen?'

'When all the Cardinals agree on who he will be.' Mam keeps popping in and out, because even though it's continuous, she still has to do jobs and prepare meals.

'Are the Cardinals the red ones or the purple ones, or are they the ones in white?'

'Red,' Teresa says, 'now put a cork in it.' She thinks she knows all about popes because she's drawn a picture of the cross-keys and crown on the front of a school scrap book called: *A book about Pope Pious XII*. It *is* a dead good drawing, though she used a ruler to do it.

'Tedious.' Joey says, getting up off his armchair. 'Give iz a shout when dinner's out.' Joey likes watching the new telly but not waiting for the new pope. It's ages since he came to church, and the last time Mam said she'd *given up*, he said his father never went so why should he? Joey never calls Dad Dad, and says *father* in a sarcastic voice.

Me and Tress don't care how long it takes. We watch hours and hours of black smoke and wait, and wait and wait.

'Every country in the world has a cardinal and every cardinal has a vote so they all go in to the enclave and stay there until it's decided.' Mam likes explaining it. 'They keep having ballots until they all agree.'

'You mean they're not allowed out until they reach a verdict?'

'They're locked away from the outside world and can't emerge until they send up the white smoke signal saying they have elected a new Pontiff.'

'So when the white smoke comes someone unlocks the door and lets them out?'

'They do.'

'They must be sick and tired, imagine having no food and not being able to go to the toilet.'

'Mam, Mam, come quick, the smoke's turning white.' Teresa shouts through to the kitchen. 'Hurry, you'll miss it.'

'Hurray,' I say, 'at last.'

We run and fetch her then watch an old man come out onto the balcony and wave at all the people gathered in Saint Peter's Square. He looks little and fat and friendly.

'A typical Italian,' Mam says when she sees him.

His name is Pope John the twenty-third. It's not his real name but when you become pope you can call yourself anything you like. Pope John XXlll has five Roman numerals and is in charge of the entire world. We have a new pope. Mam is smiling and wiping her eyes on her paisley pinny. The new telly has made her really and truly happy, and us.

Since the telly came Teresa gets more ideas for drawing and for dressing up. Since the telly came life has completely changed. Me and Teresa watch everything, even the boring Black and White Minstrel Show, and loads of Eamon Andrews. There is no TV during Sunday day, but in the evening there's What's My Line? Where someone hides behind a screen and panellists ask questions then try and guess their job.

In This is Your Life, Eamon surprises someone every week with a red book about their lives. Sometimes it's a famous person, but sometimes it's only a good person who no one has ever heard of.

Teresa drapes an old net curtain over one shoulder and wraps one round her middle to be an Indian princess, then paints a red spot on her forehead like Susan Singh's mam.

'If Meena finds out you've used her lipstick she'll kill you.'

'What the eye doesn't see...'

'But she's bound to find out.'

'Not unless you tell her. Now do you want me to paint your lips on or not?'

'Yes. I was just warning you...'

'Shut your mouth and stretch your lips like this.' Teresa makes her mouth into an oblong.

'Eeee....' I copy the shape but it's hard to keep.

'Now, smack your lips together like this Mmmwah!'

'Mmmwah!'

'Perfect.'

Here comes the bride, fifty inches wide,
fifty stitches in her britches, here comes the bride.

'Princess Riz, this is your life.' I hand Teresa the pretend book.

'Thank you, Eamon. You have been so kind. Thank you.'

'Now, the family and friends gather round and pat you on the back. Should I pretend to be them?'

'No, don't bother. I'm bored with this game. Let's be someone else.'

'Well, I'm not being a man.'

'Ok, but let's get Dad's wide-brimmed hat. He never wears it. With that and our Meena's flared black skirt and patent belt we will be perfect cowgirls.'

Sneaking into Meena's wardrobe is dangerous. Last time she caught me there was blue murder.

'If you ever, ever, ever...' I closed my ears. When the slap came she caught me wrong and broke the top off a precious nail, a harder slap came, then she burst into tears and ran out. It is the one and only time I have ever beat our Meena. There is definitely something wrong with her.

If Music be the Food of Love

'Why does *Ching-gas-cook* like Hawkeye better than the other Indians?'

'Chingachgook! They're blood brothers.'

'That's what I said, *Ching-gas-cook.*'

Joey loves watching Hawkeye, and Davy Crockett, and *Ching-gas-cook.* He knew about the Wild West before the television set came because he's seen loads of cowboy and Indian films. I am learning about different tribes from Joey's book of tribal names and maps and headdresses. Teresa uses Mam's old fur hat for being Hawkeye and puts plaits in my hair and ties a ribbon round my forehead and calls me Young Brave then slaps me on the back. The Indian chiefs and braves always have to lose in the end so being a squaw or a cowgirl is more fun.

Since Meena went to see Jailhouse Rock she hardly stays in to watch any telly. Elvis is the only thing she thinks about. She and Audrey went to see X certificate films before they were even sixteen, and our Meena never worried about getting in because she wears high heels and make-up and, apart from not being allowed to run away from home does what she wants.

Let's rock; everybody, let's rock
Everybody in the whole cell block
Was dancin' to the Jailhouse Rock
Dancin' to the Jailhouse Rock

Any chance she gets the record player is out and she is dancing about like a loon. She is so gone on Elvis she buys anything that has pictures of him. She even bought a black and white stripy top because that's what he wears in the film.

> *One, Two, Three O'clock, Four O'clock rock,*
> *Five, Six, Seven O'clock, Eight O'clock rock.*
> *Nine, Ten, Eleven O'clock, Twelve O'clock rock,*
> *We're gonna rock around the clock tonight.*

Her second favourite is Bill Hailey. He has a nice smile and a kiss-curl, that she copies, but next to Elvis he is a dead loss, far too old and too fat to want to marry.

If only she had seen it coming in the tea-leaves, Meena might have listened to her Elvis records even more. I get the blame for what happens but it's not my fault. Nobody looks behind cushions before they sit down, because nobody thinks anybody would be daft enough to leave records lying on the couch. Her precious records that are so breakable and delicate. And I don't see why I am being shouted at.

'I didn't see them, they were completely hidden.'

'You stupid little kid. You stupid little...'

I wait for a hard slap, but she collapses into tears, and nobody can get her to stop.

'I'm sorry, Meena, I didn't see them.'

'I put...put...just put them down for a minute...' The sobs are huge, as if her life has collapsed.

'Well somebody must have thrown the cushion over them,

Teresa or Joey? I didn't know.'

'If you hadn't thrown yourself down like an elephant you wouldn't have broken so many.' Spitey-mouth Teresa has to join in blaming me.

'You shut up. I bet it was you who covered them.'

'Some money's worth there.' Joey pipes up. Since he started swaggering about in that zippy bomber jacket he thinks he's the bee's knees.

'She spent all her pay on them.' Teresa just can't keep her nose out.

We all stare at the pile of smashed records lying about like hard bits of liquorice. They can't be stuck back together and no one knows what to do next. Meena is curled on the chair behind a tangle of black hair, making wounded dog sounds.

'Look Meena, they're not all broke. This one's not.' I grab the one record that's untouched and hold it up.

She lifts her floppy head, parts the curtain and looks across. I wave it like a prize then hold it under her nose.

'Wh...what is it?' She wails.

'Paul Anka. It's a miracle.'

'Not Elvis?'

'Better. It's *Diana*. Diana's all right. Look, not even a scratch.'

If I could turn back time I would make Meena forget Elvis, forever and ever Amen. Then Paul Anka would be her one true love all over again:

I'm so young and you're so old,
this my darling I've been told.
I don't care just what they say...
Oh please stay by me Diana.

Ambition

———— ◦ ◉ ◦ ————

Meena is having an interview for a new job and spends ages putting on make-up because she is worried about her eyes looking puffed out. Dad says she has nowt to worry about, because waitress jobs are ten a penny and he could do it with both hands tied behind his back. This starts Mam reminiscing about being a waitress in London, between being a nun and getting married. There's more to silver service than people imagine, she says, while he slides the last bit of egg from the edge of his knife onto a piece of fried bread. Saturday breakfast is always fried and when the things are washed and dried Mam makes her usual trip to the Grainger Market to buy enough meat and vegetables to last the rest of the weekend.

It's a sunny day so me and Tress walk up to Elswick Road to meet her coming back from town. The fat wall at the bus stop is perfect for jumping on and off, until her trolley bus comes. At first she is pleased to see us but as soon as we start diving in the shopping bags she moans.

'There's no treats.'

'Arrr!'

'Will you stop ransacking things, the pair of you, and carry one of these bags?'

The bags bulge with food and are really heavy so we each take a handle of the lightest one and rock it home like a carry-cot.

In the afternoon me and Tress help with the housework, skating round the wooden floors with dusters tied to our feet. The smell from the round tin of purple wax makes our nostrils tingle with lavender.

'I thought I told you to polish the floor, not turn it into an ice rink.' Mam skids in to see what we are doing. The floor is one thing but the dining chairs are hard to polish and I keep bashing my knuckles on legs and struts. Housework is all right for a bit but it makes me feel itchy and hot and wish I was sitting down in front of the telly, stretched out and relaxed.

Since channel eight came we lounge about watching the wrestling and wait for Mam to check the pools coupons against the football scores. Last week she won thirty-seven-pounds-seventeen-and-six, her biggest win and the best thing to happen since finding out we are moving to the country as soon as Dad has built our new house. Nothing in the world beats that.

I have no room to lie flat because Joey has his legs stretched out and is taking up all the couch. I ask if he will teach me how to strengthen my arm muscles so I can build houses when I'm an adult. He thinks I'm trying to steal his place, so tells me to watch the telly and button up.

'If you lie on your hint end much longer you'll turn into a plate of blancmange.'

'And if you set your lip once more you will be laughing on the other side of that mush.'

I was never laughing in the first place, but decide not to

push my luck, and hush.

The only bad thing about channel eight is that the parish priest calls at the exact time the wrestling starts. If there's a knock on the door, we have a good guess who it is, and know exactly what he'll say when he strides in, pretending to have come about church things and not because he wants to watch the fights. Dad says the priest is trying to catch him out. He hates anyone prying into his whereabouts, especially priests.

'How was I to know he likes wrestling?' Normally Mam only talks to the priest about prayers but I can tell she likes him calling, and nagging Dad about going to Mass. To Mam, having a priest in the house is like having a star guest. Having a priest in the house is the next best thing to winning a pools dividend.

'Hello, Joe.'

'Alreet, Father?'

'Now, did I see you at church last Sunday at all?'

'Nah, nah, couldn't manage it last Sunday.'

'And will you be there next Sunday, Joe?'

'Definitely, Father.'

'So, I'll see you at the auld Mass on Sunday then?'

'Sunday, aye, Ah'll be there. Definite.'

'Good show now. Hello children,' he turns to us. 'How's tings going with the auld wrestling match?'

This is when Dad disappears to chop some wood and doesn't come back. Once Dad leaves the room Father is free to relax and watch the box. Mam give us the sit up straight look while she talks posh and makes him tea and smiles a lot, and he sprawls on our settee shouting at the wrestlers.

The very next Saturday is my first visit to the new house. Meena is doing work training and Joey stays behind to watch the wrestling, and wouldn't come anyway, or go anywhere with Dad. Me and Teresa don't mind missing the fights because going to see the new house is much more exciting, even though, when we get there it is only a field. Mam says, once the foundations and the drains are laid everything will start taking shape.

To get there, me, Teresa, Mam and Dad take the bus to town then a number five from the Haymarket to Ponteland. Passing the airport we see a yellow wind sock in full sail telling which way the wind blows, and as the roads narrow the trees get bigger, and branches attack the windows like whips: smack, smack, smack.

Oh the Deadwood Stage is a-rollin' on over the plains...

The village has a wooden café beside a stream and a wooden veranda we run around while Mam and Dad talk about building and shifting. The café is opposite our new parish church, Saint Matthews, but for once Mam thinks only about tea and not about Mass, thank Goodness.

At first I imagine our new house is going to be just outside the village but it's another three miles further on and when the tea and sandwiches are eaten we take the bus again. Our plot is site 7, lot 177, Edge Hill, Darras Hall, Ponteland. I love the field straight away, even without the house. Dad paid over four hundred pounds for it and I think the number seven is brilliant. 77 Sunset Strip is my favourite programme and Dad is going to build a detached house and garage and when it's finished we are moving to the country and being very rich. Though we must be rich already because Teresa overheard Dad say he had spent more money in the last two years than the Tsar of bloody Persia.

The Nun's Story

The new house is going to have a name. I want Kookie after Kookie in 77 Sunset Strip but Mam says heaven preserve us and starts talking about names of roses.

'Well, can we get a new cat and call it Kookie?'

'No, definitely not. No more cats.'

Since Tibby died we only have one cat left and I think Jupiter really doesn't like being the only pet. I sit him on my knee and tell him about our outing to the building site and about the new house and how brilliant living in the country is going to be but he doesn't seem impressed. Since that one time I tried to lift him by the tail he is always suspicious.

As the house grows it gets red bricks on the outside and bigger grey ones in. Lots of new wood get cut and frames are made. On weekdays other men come to help Dad brick-lay, but nobody works on Sundays, and from now on we only go to see its progress on Sunday afternoons. We climb ladders to the first floor then step onto planks. We see right up inside the roof and I feel dizzy on the narrow beams.

Dad warns us not to put our feet between the slats.

'What will happen?'

'Yee'll end up back doonstairs,' he laughs.

The whole place smells of sawdust and putty and fresh wood. All smells I love. Going up is easy, but my legs aren't long enough to get from the joists back onto the top rung of the ladder. I can't make them wide enough and Dad has to coax me until my feet find the steps. I need to be taller but I am learning a lot about building a house. Dad says it took him years to be a master builder and he had to do loads of labouring to build his muscles up first. I want to be a builder as well but Dad says before I can be a master builder like him, I need to start on the bottom rung: labouring first, lifting bricks and carrying a hod.

Before we go home he makes tea in the front shed, opening a tin of condensed milk and serving Mam hers in a tin cup with two fat dollops plopped in it. Mam says whatever we are doing about getting back we are going to have to make it fast because she needs the toilet and there is nowhere for miles. Dad says she can crouch down in the long grass round the back.

'Take a run and jump,' she says, 'There's no way I'm doing that.'

In all the excitement of the new house it's a pleasant surprise when Mam decides to take me and Teresa to the Haymarket to see The Nun's story: a film about a woman who decides to leave the convent and not to take her final vows. This story is exactly like Mam's real life, and she really wants to see it. The first time I have known her want to go to the pictures.

I cry at the hair chopping scene, but try to do it quietly. I think Teresa and Mam do too because they keep yanking hankies from their sleeves then stuffing them up again. When we come out I ask Mam about when she was a nun, and why she left. She says that being a nun is a vocation, like a priest or a teacher or a nurse, and not a job, like being a milkman or a waitress, or driving a bus.

'If you become a nun you devote your life to God, so you must die to everyone else, even your family.'

'Really die?'

'No, not really.' Mam is irritated now.

On Sunday night I take my bath in a vest to see what it's like. Mam says that when she was a nun she always bathed in her vest because nuns aren't allowed to see themselves without clothes. My vest is longer than my liberty bodice but still won't stretch far enough to hide my rudies; nuns' vests must have to go right down to their knees.

I make sure the door is locked, but keep checking in case our Teresa bursts in. I have never trusted her not to do that again, ever since the day she brought Susan Singh in to stare and laugh and point at my pink spots. That was one of the loudest screams I have ever done.

I am not sure what to do, so soap the vest up until it is really slimy then slap down into the water and swish about and pretend to swim. Some parts of the vest blow up like a balloon but other bits cling to my skin and make me shiver.

I wonder what the nuns in Africa do because it must be too hot there to wear vests. Maybe they have special underwear that they only use for bathing.

The vest sticks like a soggy flannel and clags to my head when I try to wriggle out of it. After a struggle I am free and chuck it on the floor with a slop. I throw it behind the door, then lie back and think of where I can hide it so no one will know. Once I am out I ring it in the sink then hop over the puddle its left on the lino and tiptoe downstairs. I check the passage and kitchen to make sure no one is about then plop it on the back shelf in the cupboard under the stairs and hope no one will ever find me out.

Holiday

'For goodness sake, wash your face. You look like a coal man.' Mam notices one measly smudge of dirt on my face. 'And don't blame me if the gravy's dry,' she says to Dad who is in late. Steam swirls from the tin lid as it's lifted, the meat is stuck on and has to be knocked back to the plate.

'Frazzled that.' Dad sneers, poking the dried meat. The first forkful scalds the roof of his mouth and is spit back onto the plate.

'Ow!' He blows it like a candle.

Dad was delayed watching workmen dig the road, and Mam is fuming because some new rent books are scribbled on, and he is blaming her.

'What's that to do with me?' She nods my way. 'It'll be this one here. Lock things away if you don't want them spoiled, I haven't time to watch her.'

'Aalreet, aalreet.' Dad sounds as if he is wishing he hadn't opened his mouth.'

'You can't expect me to watch everything they do. I've been awake since four-thirty this morning with this blessed headache.' Mam gives a massive yawn that almost sucks him in.

'Haway, kidda, divvent huff.' Once his belly is full Dad tries to make up. 'Dee yee knaa why it takes fower men to dig a hole?'

'I have no clue,' she puffs.

'Well listen, ye might learn. One labourer to shovel the muck, a charge hand to watch him shovelling, a foreman to watch the charge hand watch him shovelling, and a gaffa to watch the foreman watching the charge hand watch him shovelling.'

'You could do that job, Joe. The gaffa's I mean.'

'Aye, if Ah'd been born with a silver spoon in me mooth. Better still, Ah wouldn't mind being one of them night watchmen. Aal those buggers ever dee is light a fire and sit round a brazier aal night, grumbling.' Dad has caught the yawns and uses his elbows to stretch.

'Why do they have to stay all night?' Our Teresa asks.

'Wey, in case somebody tries to steal the hole.'

'Nobody would steal a hole,' She laughs. 'That's daft.'

I want to join in but keep quiet because drawing in the clean rent books has put me in the doghouse.

'Am telling ye, they'd steal owt roond here. They'd steal yee if ye stood still long enough. If Ah had a penny for every hole Ah've seen disappear Ah'd be a rich man. Ah would.'

'Where there's muck there's money.' Mam's suddenly drops her sulky mood and cheers up.

'Aye kidda, never a truer word said. A bit of ambition, that's what ye want.' Dad points his fork at me and sneers.

Dad complains about how much money is being spent building the new house so I never thought in a million years he would also pay for a holiday. It's our first holiday since the fortnight in Berwick when I was three. This caravan is opposite Amble's sand dunes, and is a proper modern one, not like the wonky old double-decker bus we had then.

Mam knits us new cardigans, and when they're nearly finished she takes us to town to buy matching summer dresses, white ankle socks and white t-strap sandals. Dad gives us extra pocket money and once we're there I buy a plastic shoulder bag and squash in a pound of green grapes from the village shop. Sweet *seedless* grapes are my discovery. I stuff the whole bunch into my red, white and blue spotty bag to keep them out of sight of borrowers. Grapes are ten times as delicious without pips and I want to keep them all for myself.

On the first sunny day me and Tress hide in a dune and take our cardies off. I feel the buckle on one of my new sandals snap and bend to look but drop Mam's camera. I open the back to and try to turn the film round but it grinds to a stop. Tress calls me stupid and makes me go back and confess to Mam, still in the caravan washing up breakfast cups, never even noticing I'd sneaked the camera out.

I have broken the camera and my sandal strap has snapped. And I have itchy arms from the sun that I have to scratch.

'You stupid child! Whatever next?' Mam is even more furious when she sees I've no cardigan. I run back but all the sand dunes look alike and it has vanished into thin air.

The holiday is alright but not half as good as the one we had in Berwick when I was small and the six of us were all together, before Joey and Philomena grew up and went off to do things on their own. The modern caravan looks nice but isn't a patch on the old green bus. I only did one thing wrong on that holiday, and that was feed the hens my crusts.

It's good to get home to the television set. I missed that even more than the cat.

Soon after we get back Mam has to go into hospital to have an operation, and Dad has to stop building the new house and *play nursemaid* and cater to all our whims, meaning *cook the dinner*. Dad's dinners are good for a change but soon get boring. I can't wait for Mam to come back and make us proper teas. But when she does come home she can't do anything, not even wash or iron or shop or clean up.

'Get out!' Mam might be weak but can still shout. She is sitting on a hard chair in her bedroom, with a basin of water at her feet, holding a flannel in one hand and a bar of soap in the other. There is a dressing gown around her shoulders and nothing underneath.

'I just came in to say...' My eyes swoop to the two big bells hanging under her neck and I can't stop staring or move them away.

'Get out! Get out now, and shut the door.'

A big sore scar from her operation flashes red raw.

I had no idea what was going on under her clothes and dread to think my flat pink spots might end up like those. The worst thing is, my Dad is sitting on his bed looking and talking in a normal, matter-of-fact voice. My Dad is conducting a conversation with my nude mother as if this is perfectly acceptable behaviour. My mother completely without clothes in front of my dad. Nun indeed!

Runaway

———— ◦ ● ◦ ————

When Philomena disappears again, *with* the vanity case, no one has a clue where she is until a post card from Blackpool arrives with a message saying she is having a lovely time. I overhear: *Age of consent* and *ward of court*, Mam and Dad talk and talk. They want to do something to stop her running off, but have no idea what.

Absence does *not* make the heart grow fonder because when she lands back there are more rows. Philomena says mountains are being made out of molehills; and she is entitled to a holiday the same as anyone else. She says she knew it was no good asking permission because *she* would never be allowed to have any fun. Mam says it's Philomena who is making her ill and one of these days she is going to kill her off. Dad says it's about time Philomena stopped gallivanting and found herself a decent lad with some cash who would take her off his hands. Philomena says she wouldn't bring a lad to this place if it was the last house on earth then storms out and Mam says that girl will be the death of her, and she and Dad look at each other as if a bomb has been dropped. And it has.

When Meena gets her pictures developed I find one of her sauntering along Blackpool Pleasure Beach linking a man. His beard is black and bushy and I can just make out his smiling mouth. He is a proper man, not a lad, but no one dare tell Dad. We all move around the house as if one false step might cause an explosion, and over the next few weeks I become an expert at hiding behind doors, my eyes and ears always on the hop, my fingers and toes wriggling.

Smack! Mam pulls up the front room sash and lets a breeze waft, blowing the cream curtains in and out like lungs. It licks over the top of Meena's vanity case as it stands on the polished table, and through the crack between the door and the frame I can just make out Philomena next to it.

'Please, Mam.'

'No, Philomena, it's no good asking. You will get the same answer every time.'

'But, Mam...'

A gust of wind knocks over the small flower vase and my heart stops. They carry on as if they never heard but I miss some of what's said. Did I catch Philomena say *in love?* She's *in love?* Fancy our Meena saying mush right out of the Romeo and Valentine. And she's talking about somebody real, not off the films, like Elvis.

'No good will come of it, mark my words.' Mam's voice is sharp as a tack.

'Pleease!'

'For goodness sake, you're only seventeen.'

'Pleease...Give your permission.'

'You're too young Philomena. Be sensible.

Dad always says Philomena has never been sensible in her

life, so there is not much chance of that.

Philomena gasps in air and tears, as if it's the end of the world. My heart is clattering but I can't move off.

'Right then, if that's all you have to say.'

I can see my sister's white knuckles and her tiger's eye ring glinting on the vanity case handle.

'Your Dad and I will not let you get married at your age and that's all there is to it.' Mam doesn't budge an inch.

'Right, well...You can't stop me. I'm old enough to do what I want.'

'You are not. You need our permission and you don't have it. And will not get it, full stop.'

Meena's tears burst out. She snatches up her vanity case and flees, flattening my nose against the wood as she goes.

For the rest of the morning Mam is flushed in the face and bent with the weight of all the world's woes.

I forget to count how long Meena stays away. It must be months, but when she does come home it happens so fast I think I've been shot.

'Coming back any minute.' Mam's words blow up in my ears. This family never tell me anything.

'Back any minute?' I rush and pick up the skirt I've been riding side-saddle down the banisters in, give it a shake hoping the creases will drop out. No good. My knees are like jelly, I am truly in for it. The rest of Philomena's clothes are in heaps upstairs; the pink skin-tight jumper with the white bobbles and three-quarter sleeves; the tickly mohair cardy; the black and white spotty skirt. The pompoms on her velvet mules are loose and one of the heels snapped, and her precious necklace is strewn across the floor in a hundred shiny bits.

I sit next to Joey biting my nails. His are so short they are practically gone. When he picks his nose I don't know how he manages.

As soon as Philomena comes through the door I know straight away I need never have worried. Everything has changed. She is with a man, and has a big fat belly covered in a green-checked smock. The first good news is I am going to be an auntie. The second good news is this man doesn't have a beard. And the third and best good news is our Meena has lost interest in nice clothes and jewellery, and being done up like a dog's dinner. I am completely out of trouble: she who laughs last, laughs longest.

Strangers are usually kept at the door and not brought into the house, so having one come to live with us is odd. Knees and hands tap. Everyone shuffles. Usually it's Jupiter who is jumpy but he takes to the man no problem and stays a picture of calm.

Things are shifted about so Meena and Vince can sleep in the bedroom that was Mam and Dad's. My sister and mother sit as stiff as pokers and we are all shy and polite.

'Would you like to take your things up to your room?' Mam addresses Meena as if she is a guest.

'Yes, please, that would be nice.'

'Then shall I make you both a cup of tea?'

'Yes, thank you very much.'

I wonder if they will stay like this forever, acting as if they have only just met. I wonder if they will ever go back to being normal, to being like they were before she left.

'Twenty-eight he is. Eleven years on her.' Mam and Dad are at the table having a new Big Conversation.

'Ah divvent like them sleeping together in this hoose either.' Dad pokes at the worms of bacon rind left on his plate.

'What can you do?' Mam's bacon rashers are untouched and have gone cold.

'They're not properly married, ye knaa?'

'You can't close the door after the horse has bolted, Joe.'

When Mam and Dad start like this, they bring loads of animals in. I eat my boiled egg and toast as quietly as I can, hardly munching, keeping my ears clear. It's two days since Meena came back with a husband and a tattoo and I don't want to miss anything that's said.

'Ah divvent like it, aal the same.'

'Well, they say they've been married in a civil ceremony.'

'Gretna bliddy Green! I divvent call that a decent...'

'Shh! Keep your voice down. They'll hear you.'

'Well, Ah divvent call eloping to Gretna Green being married, and Ah wouldn't trust him as far as Ah could chuck him.' Dad eyes the cold rashers of bacon at Mam's elbows and picks up his fork.

'He's agreed to get re-married in church before the baby comes, so we'll have to hope...'

'Divvent count yer chickens. Get them doon there, doon to the church as quick as ye can. Get it done, before he changes his mind. Ah divvent care what you say, kidda, he's a wrong-un, and a leopard doesn't change its spots.'

'Indeed, it does not.'

'Now, are yee ganna eat that bacon or what?'

Hoppings

———— ● ● ● ————

I start dreaming about animals nearly every night: sheep with six legs, goats with two heads, and unicorns. I've never seen a freak show but Joey's told me all about them. Every June at the hoppings fair: Siamese twins, the smallest man in the world, and a woman with a beard.

Since Meena came home with Vince these dreams float in my head. One comes again and again, the whole family running to climb the town moor stile, Dad's bad knees clicking like knitting needles, being drowned out by the noise of the rides. The smells of petrol and fried onions sailing over the zigzag path, straight up my nose. We pass cows calmly grazing as if they're deaf, then head towards the lights and funfair sounds.

'Cow pat, look out!' Philomena has on polished shoes and is watching her step.

'You don't need to tell me, I can smell it.' Joey turns his nose toward the aroma of hot food that makes our stomachs rumble.

'Dad let's go on some rides.' Meena tugs Dad's sleeve.

'Here, share this and gan on what ye like.'

He reaches into a pocket, and pulls out a big handful of coins, dishing out half-crowns and smiling at us all in turn, even Joey.

After rides and toffee apples we go to the tea tent, then eat chips as we pass the wrestling and boxing booths, the freak shows, and striptease.

Fighters in shiny shorts and dressing coats bop about on stage, thrusting bandaged hands, eyeing the crowd, waving them in. The wrestlers wear masks and glare from slits and grunt through holes.

'Come and show what you're made of.' The compère wears a sleek jacket and holds a big silver microphone. 'Any man still standing after a two minute round will be given one pound.' He beckons in challengers with his free hand.

'The first one's aalways a stooge', Dad tells Mam. 'It's a stunt to get blokes to throw their caps in the ring. Let one win then fleece aal the others.'

More booths with women like dolls dancing and turning cards that spell *Striptease*. They wear short skirts, skinny heels, and fishnet stockings. Everybody in the crowd gawps at the parade.

'Mutton dressed as lamb,' Mam says under her breath.

'Please Dad,' I take my chance, 'will you buy me a dolly, one of those tied to a stick?'

'Haway then, and that's it. That's the last. Ah've spent a bliddy fortune on yeese lot the day.'

The doll sparkles in layers of blue net, dusted with silver dots and stars. I imagine tying her to the dressing table mirror so she can have a twin to dance with.

At dusk we trudge away, back the way we came, across the

moor. I am high up, being piggy-backed, and my legs bounce off Dad's chest. Teresa jumps up behind to nip my bot, and call me a big baby for not using my own legs.

'What ye been feeding this one, kidda? She weighs a ton.' Dad laughs.

'She can't weigh all that much.' Mam answers. 'Hardly Two-Ton-Tessie.'

'What? A sack of coal's not this heavy. De ye wanna take ower for a bit?'

'Come on, here's the bus.' Joey unplugs his stick of mint rock, and yells at the top of his lungs. 'Here's the number eight, run for it!'

I wake with a start, my toes running on the spot, then once the twitches stop I drop back off. There's Dad on stage wearing a blue dressing coat and gold trunks. Mam is next to him in a green metallic skirt with cupcake pleats, shining like a toffee wrapper. She has a glitzy cowgirl hat, and silver stars on her white cowgirl boots. There is a hole in her fishnets but no one notices. Her bright red lipstick is smiling at Dad, and he is smiling back. He holds up bandaged hands to salute the crowd. Joey puts me up on his shoulders to see. Meena and Teresa laugh at the huge gathering. The sun is shining, glittering off Mam and Dad's heads as if they are king and queen of the shows. Everyone claps and cheers. Then all at once Dad leans in towards Mam.

'Haway, kidda,' he whispers. 'Ah'm getting a bit sick of this lot, let's gan and get worselves a cup of tea.'

'Good idea, Joe,' she slips her arm through his and says. 'I'm ready for a sit.'

Meena

———— ● ● ● ————

Vince is a dreamboat. As far as my new brother-in-law is concerned nothing is too much trouble, and he is being especially lovely to me.

Mam is very polite, and Dad is, to his face. But there are so many daggers in Vince's back it's a wonder he's not staggering about. Dad says he can spot a conman a mile off and Mam says Philomena is being blinded by flattery. Then they both mutter a lot of things I can't pick up. Having a stranger turn into a relative overnight is making the whole family behave very odd.

Vince can say as many flattering things to me as he likes. He takes time to listen to everything I say and is very smiley and patient and polite. At breakfast he picks up the box of cornflakes, asks if I would like some, then pours mine first. He calls me ducky instead of hinny or pet. People from Newcastle only call ducks *duck*. Our Meena says it's because he comes from a town called Stoke-on-Trent.

'Where's Stoke-on-Trent, Vince?'

He is helping me cut pictures from the back of the Kelloggs box.

'The Potteries, duck,' he says.

I picture a romantic place full of crockery: painted cups and flowery plates.

'Vince, will you help me stick some cards in the Brooke

Bond album when we've finished doing this?'

'Of course, ducky, yes.'

Vince wears drainpipes and has blonde hair he plasters with oil to make a big quiff. Our Joey never gets his to look that good. Philomena thinks Vince is the best thing since sliced bread and I do as well. He pays me more attention than I have ever, ever had. I never thought about having any other brother apart from Joey, but I couldn't have found a better one, even if I'd had it planned. Our Joey could learn a lot from him about how to treat a little sister.

When Meena squeezes past with her bump she stops to smile at us, and puts her hand on Vince's shoulder. He grins and winks, then gives her a sharp slap on the bot and makes her jump. If I had done that she would be furious, but she doesn't seem to mind in the least. She has placed a tight silver bracelet over the tattoo to stop Mam from frowning every time she sees it on the inside of her wrist. The tattoo looks likes a Billy Stamper sticker that's slipped because all the letters have come out blurred. It spells VINCE in capitals but if I didn't know it said VINCE I would think it was just a blob of black ink with no word.

Since Vince came to live in our house, I have been going red a lot. Every time he talks to me I feel my face get hot.

'Kissing the boys again?'

'No.'

He laughs at the gaps between my teeth, as if missing

teeth are the most hilarious thing he has ever seen. After two weeks I stop smiling. I try not to open my mouth and avoid any more big talks with him. I don't want any more talks with him at all.

'You know what kissing the boys does, ducks?'

'No.' I suck in my mouth so my lips don't show.

'Makes your teeth fall out.' He nips my cheek, wobbles it, then winks.

I press my lips tight and won't speak. I have never kissed a boy, not ever, except for that one time when Michael Cunningham grabbed me in the cloakroom and rubbed his fat face on my cheek.

'Come on, big smile, ducky.' Vince comes right up to my nose and grins. Then turns the sides of his mouth down: 'Only playing with you, kid.'

Soon all his interest in sticking Brook Bond cards and cutting out Kellogg's Cornflakes boxes has stopped. It's Friday night and Mam is in bed convalescing after another operation, this time to take her gall bladder out. She will soon have so many missing bits she'll be as light as a feather. Like last time, there has to be lots of rest and nobody running in and out pestering. After tea, Dad makes for the pub, warning us before he goes she is not to be disturbed. He would never stay in now, not while Vince is living under his roof, scoffing all his food.

With Mam and Dad both out the way my brother-in-law

grows.

'Come on, time you were off to bed. I'm taking control.'

'But it's Wagon Train.'

Me and Teresa and Joey are all settled in front of the telly, and I don't know why he is picking on me.

'You're not watching it tonight.'

'But I always watch Wagon Train,' I tell him.

'Not tonight.'

Vince has been buttering him like a chicken so I know there is no chance of Joey speaking up.

'Mam lets me watch it. Mam let's me watch anything I like.'

I even watched Quatermass and the Pit so I think I can watch Wagon Train without a fuss.

'Your Mum's not here, ducks. She has to have rest. Teresa can stay up because she's older. You're off to bed.'

Teresa smiles from the corner chair, folding her arms and staying silent.

'Vince, let her watch it for God's sake.' Meena calls over from the big hill of her stomach. At least someone is talking sense.

'Shut up. She has to learn.'

Then it starts, back and forward like a tennis match. Me: *staying up*, Vince: *off to bed*. Everyone else sits and stares at the TV as if they have lost the power to speak. Suddenly my eyes start to spout and my legs spark. A surge of hate flies me up the stairs two at a time. Vince is on my heels with Meena behind trying to calm me down. What ever happens they don't want to disturb Mam.

I grab the big scissors from the dressing table drawer and grip them hard.

'I'm going to stab him.' My voice is shaky but loud.

Meena is out of breath and freezes to the spot.

'Stab! Stab! Stab!' I lunge at him from the top stair.

'Stop it Bernadette.' She says.

'I *am* watching Wagon Train and he can't stop me.' I raise the scissors and swish them through the air above my head.

'Calm down, Bernadette, don't be daft.' Somehow Philomena gets in between us with her big bump.

I feel as fierce as a bull, stick the scissors in his chest, turning and screwing them until his gizzards fall out in one big red slop. I try really, really hard. I am as big and strong as an ox, but he goes for my wrist and twists and twists and wrestles me to the floor and grabs and grabs until the scissors drop.

'I hate you! I hate you!' I scream and sob.

'Alright,' he says, taking a deep, slow breath. 'You can watch bloody Wagon Train.'

I make so much noise through the rest of the programme Joey has to turn it up as loud as it will go to drown me out. My insides feel like an earthquake struck and the shuddering and juddering and sighing take ages to stop.

Cakes

— ● ● ● —

As soon as Mam is on the mend she makes Meena and Vince go to St Michael's church to get married again. Getting married in a registry office doesn't count; and Mam has found out Vince is not even baptised, so he is a heathen, as she suspected. This is a *stumbling block* overcome by him promising to bring the baby up as Catholic. Mam says it is a solemn oath and he will have to do it. Dad says pigs might fly and you can drag a horse to water but you can't make it drink.

Mam is keeping the ceremony low key, but it's more like top secret. At the service there is no congregation, no flowers, no dressing up, no wedding food, and no cake. Our Meena's belly is sticking out so far I doubt anything else would fit in it.

If she had a film for her camera I could take lovely pictures but Meena has no interest in photographs of her in a smock. This is the first wedding I have been to and I thought everyone would be happy and throw confetti and smile a lot.

'You have to give them somewhere to live Joe.'

Mam and Dad are in their room talking. Without seeing their faces, hearing properly is difficult. But I don't peer through the gap in case Mam is nude again, or worse still, Dad; horrible thoughts I push out, pulling my earlobes wide as trumpets so as not to miss the gist.

'Another idle bugger who'll not work nor want. She's

wasting her time with him, kidda, mark my word.'

'No doubt, but she's our daughter, Joe. You'll have to find them a room. They can't stay on here indefinitely.' Mam sounds like she's really fed up. I hear her bedsprings squeak. She must be standing up. I get ready to sneak off fast.

'Aye, alreet.' That's Dad's voice, sounding fed up as well. 'Ah'll sort it oot. There's a room coming up in Malvern Street. It's the biggest room available. Beggars cannit be choosers, they'll have to put up with it.'

I have to act surprised at the news that Dad is giving them a room and Meena and Vince are moving out. Dad never takes in tenants with children but he has to make an exception because it's his daughter and it will be his grandchild. I think about the lady in the basement with the bird and the big jar of sweets. It's ages since the day Dad took me round all his houses collecting rents and I met the Latvian couple with the big heap of coal in the corner of their room.

Meena moving to her own place is the most exciting news since finding out I was going to be an auntie. I will be the youngest auntie by miles of anybody. All the aunties I know are proper grown ups.

By the time they leave our house and go to live in Malvern Street, our Meena is nearly due and fed up with wearing smocks and flatties. The day they move out me and Teresa stretch out in front of the telly to watch Wacky Jacky. It feels like everybody has been sitting up straight for weeks and now all of a sudden we have loads of space to collapse back down and lie flat.

The first thing Meena's does is go to Robinson's Pet Shop and buy a black kitten. Dusty has big yellow eyes that stand out against her black fur. She scampers round, across, in front and behind my sister, until Meena completely forgets what's supposed to be lucky and what isn't. Once Dusty settles in, Meena stops being so bothered about a lot of her superstitions. Within weeks the cat is trained to go outside and I keep my fingers crossed she doesn't find her way down into the basement and sniff out the talking bird.

My nephew is born in Dilston Hall, the same place Philomena was born during the war. In the war, babies had to be born in the country in case a bomb dropped in town and killed them all. Going to see the new baby takes up a whole day. When we get there Meena is in bed and the baby is beside her in a cot. He is wrapped in a blue blanket and she is dressed in a blue nightie to match. She hasn't picked a name yet but says Vince wants to call him John. Philomena looks so happy. I can't wait for her to come home. She will be just up the street and I will be able to be a proper auntie and help her bring the baby up.

Now Philomena is married she can do exactly as she pleases. She can go to Davies' bread shop for pasties every day and even buy herself six fresh cream cakes if she likes. She can buy magazines from the paper shop, and sweets and chocolate from Maynards and nobody can tell her she can't.

On the long walk to Diana Street Clinic I help Meena push the pram. On the way, people stop us to look at the baby, touching his hand with silver, then putting the coins under his mattress for luck. In the waiting room Meena talks to a woman who weighs John, then she collects free tins of Oster Milk and bottles of orange juice and we walk back home.

The orange juice is pure and bitter, but diluted and mixed with a couple of spoons of sugar we soon get used to the taste. There are milk tokens too, to exchange for fresh milk. After a couple of weeks Meena has nearly as much milk in her cupboards as the Co-op does in it's whole pile of crates.

I see our Meena a lot. The baby is great to hold and cuddle and has smooth soft cheeks that I don't even have the urge to nip or pinch or squeeze.

I don't mention my outings with Vince; keeping him company while he goes on job hunts or for interviews. Mam doesn't stop me going to see Meena and the baby but has no idea of the trips. She hardly visits Malvern Street, and Dad dislikes Vince.

Since the night of the scissors Vince has never once told me what to do, and is happy to take me on jaunts. I had never been to a Labour Exchange or a paint shop or an industrial estate or a factory floor. So many places I had never seen before. Meena always stays in to look after John. With the cat and the baby to care for I don't think she would want to come along.

When it starts to pour we take shelter in Marks and

Sparks, then run down Prudhoe Chare where Vince goes to sign on the dole. Once the rain dies off we walk to a pub on Clayton Street. Climbing the stairs I am excited and scared. I have never been in a pub before, and worry I might get yelled at. Vince says it's OK because we are going to the lounge, not the bar. The room has stained red carpet and red smelly curtains and is full of damp men in wet caps smoking tabs and drinking beer. Vince buys crisps and ham sandwiches, a glass of pop and a pint of beer. He calls the barmaid Chris and she calls him Vince, and me, flower, and when she leans over I can see a big line up the middle of her bare chest. Vince tells me to wait while he writes some horses names on a bit of paper, then disappears to place a bet. When he comes back he rubs his hands together and grins.

'That's it, duck. That's the lucky one. Come four o'clock, I'll be in the money.'

'Can I have more crisps, Vince?'

'No, you've had your lot. Come on.'

Dad says, Vince is a gambler, and all gamblers are losers. What Mam does is fine because that's the Pools, and she only does it once a week. Vince bets on horses all the time, and Dad says the gee-gees are a mug's game. Gambling is against the law so Vince has to go to a lot of trouble to put a bet on a horse, while Mam never hides her pools coupons.

Vince says the gambling rules are about to change but he has to be extra careful because he has been in trouble with the law before. He says real police are not like PC Dixon in Dixon of Dock Green and think nothing of beating people up for the least thing. He says the last time he was a suspect they tied cushions round him before the kicking, so he wouldn't go black and blue.

'Don't look worried, ducks. That's a long time ago.'

'Is it?'

'Ages since. Anyway, now the baby's here there'll be no more of that.' Vince gives a little smile, 'Wait and see, ducky. From now on I'm going straight as a die.'

Play On

I take the stairs two at a time, then stop to knock and catch my breath.

'Wait.' Vince sounds odd.

'I've come to see the baby.' I shout at the door. There is music on and I am not sure they can hear me through the thick wood.

'Just a minute, he's having a feed.' Vince's voice gallops like a horse.

After ages, and ages, he opens the door and lets me in. I feel my head go hot to the brim.

Meena is sitting on a hard chair and is all neat in her tight black skirt and high heels. The baby is on her knee and everything seems completely normal; except there is a funny smell in the air and a greasy line of sweat underneath Vince's quiff.

Feeding a baby must be filthy and something that no one except a husband should see. I look at the cot and the rattle tied on it and try not to notice the messy bed in the corner where Vince and Meena sleep. Mam always makes our beds first thing in the morning and would never leave the sheets crumpled like that. When they stayed with us they slept in singles like Mam and Dad and I'm surprised Dad let them have a double bed in one of his rooms. But since Meena is married I suppose there is nothing he can do.

Miller is Vince's friend and when he calls round our Meena's face turns into a yard of tripe. She is so very nice and polite it's clear she doesn't like him in the slightest.

'Alright, Meena, darlin?' Miller talks with a funny accent, but not like Vince.

'Yes, thank you.' Meena's voice is stiff.

'Mmmm, something smells good.' Miller nods towards the corner where the cooker is.

'Irish stew, if you want it?'

'Save some for me, darlin.' He puts his hand round Meena's waist.

'It's ready now. Almost.'

'Have to go out now, men's work to discuss. See you later on. All right, my lav?' Miller is a Cockney, and says *lav* for *love*. In Geordie language *lav* means the toilet or the bog.

'Where you both going?' Meena's voice goes all high-pitched.

Vince slaps scent on his chin and her face twists. It scalds his skin and makes him wince. Then he clags on Brylcream, working and smoothing his hair, pushing and pulling it up into a quiff.

'Won't be long.' Vince pats Meena on the bum and winks. 'Keep it hot, luv.'

Since Miller came, duck, ducky and ducks have taken a back seat.

'Just going to the pub to discuss some business, see you in a bit.'

Once they leave Meena bursts into tears and I don't know what to say to make her stop. I pick up the cat and stroke her till she purrs then look over at John blowing bubbles in his cot. After a bit it goes quiet, Meena's heaving stops and she takes a big white hanky and blows her nose on it until it's full of snots.

She gets the tea-caddy down and boils some water in pan. I ask if she is alright and she passes me a cup with a couple of big sugars stirred in and says yes, she's fine. I don't know what happened to make everything so bad. Up until now I thought being married and having a baby were two of the best things that could happen in a life.

Ambition

———— ● ◉ ● ————

It happens fast. One minute Vince is promising to go straight and get a job, next thing he is in court being sentenced.

I never heard of breaking and entering, but since Vince became part of the family I am learning loads of legal words and terms. I learn so much I am thinking of becoming a solicitor or a lawyer when I grow up and get a job. Not a police woman though. I would never want to be in the police, not now I know how horrible they are.

Meena cries a lot before and during the case, and a lot more after. Vince has *gone down* for eighteen months but Miller only gets done for *receiving* and is handed a *suspended sentence* because he *squealed*, so doesn't have to go to jail.

I am round at Meena's when Miller calls: *Just dropping by to see how things are.*

'Oh!' Meena doesn't know what to say.

'How are you, my lav? You managing without the old man?' He rubs his palms, rustling them like paper, not hands with blood.

'Fine, thank you.' Meena tries to sound cold. Normally she would offer anybody who comes in a cup of tea but deliberately doesn't.

'Terrible thing, lav. I don't know what happened. If there's anything...' Miller comes right up close to Meena and slides his hand across her back.

'We're alright thank you. And he'll soon be back.'

She moves over to the cot and picks the baby out and cuddles him even though he was sound asleep.

Once he leaves we notice the foul smell wafting up from behind the sink.

'Oh my God! Dusty! you little blighter!'

'What's she done?'

Meena picks the cat up by the scruff of the neck and throws her out.

'I thought she was clean.'

'She was. First time she's done that. Must have been when Miller...' Meena stops, going to find a rag to clean up the mess.

'The sound of his voice must have scared the shit out of the poor little sod.' She picks up a cloth and starts to laugh. Soon we are both roaring away.

Going to Durham on the bus is a long way. The prison has huge lion-head door-knockers with metal manes, and me and Meena and the baby go through a small entrance cut into the huge doors, leading to more doors and lots of questions. The prison guards aren't sure about letting me in but our Meena says Vince is my brother and I really want to see him. I think they have a right cheek saying I am too young. I don't look too young and it is not up to them. Our Meena lets me go anywhere and doesn't think I am too young for anything.

There is a row of booths in the visitors' room with

prisoners facing out from behind grilled glass. The partition lets them see and hear without being able to touch. Vince is not amused about me being there but our Meena invited me and she doesn't care. After a few minutes they stop noticing me and go all soppy and talk about how they miss each other and he says stuff about how good and hard-working he will be when he gets out. Then he vows he will never let her down again and talks about how he will earn an honest living and be a good provider for ever and ever, Amen.

With good behaviour, Vince will get a third of his sentence taken off. So he will be free in less than a year. When he gets out they are going to move to the Potteries and start afresh; which means they'll be taking my nephew away and I won't be able to help bring him up.

While she waits she only has a wireless set for company, but sometimes a station will play an Elvis song she likes. I say she should come home and listen to Diana at ours, but she thinks there's no point in us bringing the record player out just to listen to one song. I tell her I will take care of Paul Anka until she gets some more records and her own record player then I will give it back. She smiles and looks happy with that. I think she has forgiven me now for sitting on her records and destroying all her rock and roll.

When the day finally comes for the rest of us to leave for the country, everyone is busy and I try not to think about my sister and nephew being left behind. We are moving out of town to the house Dad has spent all his money and time building. It has taken years to get everything ready and here we go at last.

We have the biggest removal van ever seen. Our furniture is piled in the back and our mam is up front in the cab with Jupiter in a bag on her lap.

It is so big Mister Towers comes out to gawk at it. He takes off his cap and scratches his head and salutes as it pulls out.

I can hardly wait to start our new life. We are going to the most wonderful place on earth, the most wonderful place in the whole entire universe, and everything is going to be just right.

Part Two

———— •◉• ————

1960-1963

Dellside

Bird

——— ◦ ◉ ◦ ———

Once Mam is squashed up in the removal van, Dad locks up the old house passes on the keys then drives to the new place on his silver-red Triumph. She wouldn't be seen dead riding on the back of the motorbike, no matter how sparkly it is, and even if Dad *had* passed his test. I would jump at the chance but it's against the law to ride pillion under thirteen, so I have ages to wait yet.

Me, Teresa, and Joey are forced to follow on the bus. I measure the long journey in stages. The first part ends at Kenton Bar, past Cowgate where Auntie Agnes's new council house is. Then the bridge at Woolsington Pit, where coal tubs cross on overhead wires, and the real country starts. The third bit is from the airport to Ponteland village; over half-an-hour so far, not much longer to go.

Nearly all the other passengers get off at the village so the three of us spread ourselves over the upstairs seats by the front windows. I glimpse a bright flash as Joey points out a red kite hovering over a field. He is dead chuffed he spotted it. From this vantage point we have great views up a-height, and great views down: a gaggle of geese gabbling in a farmyard, hens pecking the ground. Then through the open window the smell of manure sails in.

'Poo! Dung!' I groan. 'Shut it, quick!'

'*Poo! Dung!*' Teresa says, copying my voice, and hee-hawing with laughter until her nostrils are going in and out like bellows and tears wiggle down her cheeks.

'Very funny,' I say, going in the huff.

'No,' Teresa says, dragging her collapsed body back up on the seat. 'It's just something about...It's the way you said...It's just the word du...du..dung.' And off she goes again.

'Better get used to it out here,' Joey sniggers, dragging the window shut.

'Country smells, that's what Mam calls them.' I hold my nose, squeezing until the sides stick.

The last time I saw the new house the windows still had no glass and the land was all creamy clay, churned and ladled with milky puddles. I am so excited now it's finished and in a few minutes we will be there.

Just imagine. No more squelchy plot, huddling in the shed on Sunday visits while Dad makes tea in tin cups with Nestles condensed milk. Now the trenches have been filled in and the mounds flattened out and we will have a kitchen and a whistling kettle and a toilet, so everyone can have as much tea and as many wees as they like.

By the time we arrive I expect everything to be unpacked but Ma is still in the middle of a pile of cardboard boxes and millions of things wrapped in old newspapers.

'Run off my feet,' she sniffs when she sees us, 'and full of cold.' She yo-yos an old hanky up and down her sleeve to wipe her runny nose. 'What a nuisance.'

'Once ye get used to the country air,' Dad says, 'ye'll be as fit as a lop.'

'Once I get the essentials sorted and can sit down for five minutes.'

'Here, sit yersel doon on there. Ah'll boil the kettle.' Dad turns up the tea-chest she's just emptied and Mam sits on it, wrung out.

Mam and Dad would be lost without tea. Tea is the first thing they think about in the morning and it goes on and on all day. Tea was the last thing Mam packed away before we left Elswick, because she knew it would be the first thing she would want out as soon as she got here.

Joey and Teresa show Jupiter the garden. I can't stop running about. This house and everything thing in it is brilliant. Buttercup lino runs right through the kitchen and breakfasting room: repeat, breakfasting room. We have a breakfasting room with a Formica-topped breakfasting table, and six buttercup yellow breakfasting chairs still covered in cardboard. The chairs have tubular metal legs and plump padded seats, nothing like the old wooden ones. All brand new and modern and light. Mam says the breakfasting room and the kitchen are so bright because they face south and the sun flocks in.

'Come on, will you shift yourself upstairs? I need this space.'

I know she's got a cold but still, Mam is in a right crotchety mood, considering how wonderful everything is.

Me and Teresa help Dad get the cardboard off the new buttercup chairs then bounce from one to the other until we've both sat on all six.

'Give ower with that,' Dad interrupts, holding out two clenched fists. 'Now tell iz, which hand is it in?' I tap the left, Teresa taps the right. He turns over each wrist, uncurling his fingers to show two empty palms, then one hand suddenly whizzes across his left ear and produces a thru'penny bit that he passes before our eyes.

'Ye see.'

'How did you do that, Da?'

'Tell us, Da.'

Dad's conjuring tricks always get the same questions.

'Watch closely this time. The first one to guess how it's done gets the prize.'

'Joe, will you give over tormenting those kids with your nonsense and give me a hand.' That's Ma interfering.

'Hush woman. Ah'm trying to teach these two how to do real magic, show them how to get a head start in life.'

'If you cannit get ahead get a hat, isn't that right, Da?' Teresa says.

'Ye see, this one's getting the knack.'

'Enough you two!' Mam snaps then does three sneezes loud as a trumpet. 'Now go upstairs and sort your bedroom out.'

Dad's conjuring tricks are the same as before but this is a different world.

Jupiter

———— ● ● ● ————

Everything in the old house was a mishmash, here it is all perfect: the furniture, carpets, curtains and covers, all with patterns and colours that match. Mine and Teresa's bedroom is themed in lilac. Teresa says *themed* as if she has thought up a new word.

Our bedroom wallpaper shimmers lilac, and the door and skirting boards are a sheen of lilac gloss. The carpet goes all the way round the walls with no gaps, and hanging from the ceiling is a beautiful lilac light shade that shines like silk.

We bounce on the soft springy mattresses then collapse, gazing at our bedroom from different angles. Our old beds wheezed with dust and had ancient bed heads and cast iron legs. These ones have walnut headboards and castors, so they can be wheeled about. The wood grain squiggles and my eyes start seeing faces when I stare.

'Hey, this looks like Jupiter.'

'The planet or the cat?'

'Cat of course.'

'Where?

'There, see, two big pointy ears.'

'And a wiggly worm, right above your head.' Teresa aims a finger at my forehead and makes her eyes go creepy. 'Look, see it wriggling.'

In the kitchen, Jupiter skits about like a nervy kitten, smelling everything he sees.

'Get out the road you dumb animal.' Mam threatens to give him a wallop for getting under her feet. In a good mood she would sing Stupid Cupid and give his head a stroke, but not today. Not when she is unpacking and putting things away.

> *Hey, hey, set me free,*
> *Stupid Cupid stop picking on me.*

'Hey, when is a cat not a cat?' Joey says.

'Don't know, when is a cat not a cat?'

'When it's a little hoarse.' Joey laughs at his own joke then carts the cat to his bedroom while the hullabaloo carries on.

Joey is totally *unamused* by his rose blossom wallpaper after he: *distinctly asked for something green*. He likes his new bed though, and the squares on the eiderdown. When he unzips his jerkin and frees Jupiter, the cat blinks and blinks until his black bullet pupils shrink to small dots, then he pads along the bed as if it's a minefield and he expects his paws to get blown off.

Hours after the removal van leaves, Mam is still busying about. We're starving and can't believe the only things served out onto the new breakfasting table are a pile of tongue sandwiches and sliced hard boiled eggs.

'Come on get stuck in,' she shouts as if there's not a minute to lose.

'Is there no taties, Ma?'

'Think yourselves lucky you're getting this. There's no way I can make a hot meal today. Not when the nearest shop is three miles away.'

'Three miles! Is the village that far?'

'The mobile shop will be coming tomorrow. We'll be able to get bread and other things we might want.'

'Will it bring sweets?' I might drop dead of happiness right on the spot. 'Can we get anything we like?'

'It has to be paid for just like in a grocery shop.'

'Awh!'

'The shop comes twice a week, and the butcher's van too. Then there's a market garden down the road where we can get eggs and veg.'

'Veg and eggs? Urh.' My excitement goes flat.

'And once a week I'll go to Moores Store in the village and get them to deliver the bulk of what we need: tins and groceries.'

'Can I come and help choose? '

Now we have a breakfasting room and a breakfasting table and breakfasting chairs, when will we ever get the chance to use the new dining room? It's very posh and everything in it is red. There are heavy satin curtains and a carpet that swallows my feet. The wireless is going in here so Mam will be able to sit down and listen to Mrs Dale's Diary instead of hopping from the scullery to the kitchen like she used to.

Lying flat I run my fingers through the thick pile of the carpet and feel the eggs and bread and tea I ate all flobbering about. From this view I can see the chandelier has three bulbs shaded with golden glass globes, the most beautiful lights I have ever seen. Every room, even the passage, Mam now calls the hallway, has a fitted carpet and a radiator. In the old house the fire heated water, kept us warm, and cooked toast. I will miss cooking toast over the fire but *not* trying to keep hold of the metal fork once it got hot. It won't be useful here but was great for pretend fights, so I hope it got packed.

Out front, the garage has yellow doors big enough for a truck to drive through, and a smaller door at the back. After tea, Joey moves some boxes to make space for his push bike. He will need to check the tyres before he can ride it to work at Swans. He says Swans might sound nice but it's just a big freezing shipyard in Wallsend; and Wallsend is where the Romans stopped building Hadrian's Wall and invented long-Johns. Joey knows stacks of history and geography and populations.

His black and white bike has a twenty-one inch frame and racing handles and a cross-bar, and when our Teresa tries to ride it she has to go on tiptoe and can barely reach the ground to dismount.

'Let me have a go.' The size of the bike makes my belly jaggle like jelly, but I beg and beg until Joey lets me go on.

'Haway then, just to shut you up.' The saddle is rock hard, and I get a proper prang between the legs that makes me yell. When Joey drags me off, Mam comes to see what all the wailing is about, and tells Joey off for tormenting me. Once she disappears he says that's the one and only time I ever try his bike, and that's that. It's not fair because our Teresa's come a cropper loads of times and he still lets her go on it.

At bedtime I am so tired my eyeballs feel like lead, but can't resist one last glance through the curtains. It's pitch black with no orange street lights shining through the glass. When we turn out the light and pull our jumpers off the room fills with sparks from our electric heads. There isn't a street lamp anywhere in sight and no sounds except for my sister moaning because I am wandering about.

'Will you get into bed and go to sleep for goodness' sake?'

'But my legs are full of aches. I've got Christmas Eve sciatica, and it's not even Christmas Eve.'

'Shut up and get in. Say your prayers and close your eyes. It'll soon pass.'

'But the aches really nag.'

'This time tomorrow you'll be fine. Sciatica is only from the excitement of moving day.'

'Do you think I should say a Hail Mary or an Our Father?' I kneel and make the sign of the cross.

'You better not bother God the Father unless it's something big. Why not say a Hail Mary and She'll have a word with God the Son when He's not so busy with more important stuff?'

'Teresa?' I let out a big yawn and run my fingers over the

curly pattern of the new candlewick.

'You better put your hands together. And I've told you my new name is Terry. I've stopped using Teresa.'

'Mam still calls you Teresa.'

'That's different.'

I don't know. First it was Tress. Then she decided she didn't like that. Now it's Terry. I can't keep up. What's wrong with Teresa for a name? I'll never get tired of being called Bernadette. After a few seconds listening to my brain wondering about I decide to take her advice and have a short silent pray and ask Mary, Mother of God to let Teresa see sense. A prayer about a nickname isn't serious enough to bother Jesus or His Father or the Holy Ghost.

'Amen.' I make the sign of the cross and jump in between the fresh sheets and cool pillowcase then stick my hand out and follow the fluffy candlewick tracks as they curl round and round. The room is totally soundless and I can hear my fingers walking over the tufts.

'Terry, can...can we?'

'Shh! Night, night. Stop now.'

'Was that a meow? You're gonna get killed off Mam if you've got the cat in there.'

'Mind your own business. I'm not gonna leave him alone on his first night.'

'You'll get fleas.'

'He hasn't got fleas. Now shut up...Oh, and don't let the bed bugs bite.'

'Sweet dreams then.'

'Sweet dreams, Bernadette.'

Apart from the prang between the legs, and the cat being hoarse from crying all the way from Elswick to Darras Hall, and Joey moaning about me going on his bike, and him and Dad *still* not speaking, *even* in the excitement; *this* has been the best ever day of my life.

Eye

———— ● ◉ ● ————

Dad zooms about day and night. Taking the Stamfordham Road route he can get back to see to his houses or collect his rents in twenty minutes. It's all very well for him flying off on his motorbike, but our nearest bus stop is a long walk, and the number five is the only bus, and hardly runs. The village is miles and there are no shops before that, and town seems as distant as the moon.

I find him in the breakfasting room and ask how long it will be before I can start riding pillion. The sooner I start pestering the sooner Dad will get tired and give in. He and Mam are drinking tea at the lovely yellow table and looking at the newspapers. The whole place is warm because of the sun piling through the windows; everything she said about it being a sun-trap was true.

'How many's that she's got noo?' Dad frowns at a picture of the royal family on the front of the Daily Mirror.

'Three,' Mam says.

'Another mooth for the tax payer to feed.'

'Andrew, this one's called. Look at the smile.'

'If Ah had a mooth stuffed with that many silver spoons Ah would grin like that.'

'Second in line he'll be. Anne will have to drop down one being a girl.

'One more hereditary landowner who'll never dee a pick

of work. That's aal we need.'

'They're very astute, the British royal family. Not to be underestimated.'

'Ah knaa, she can drive anaal, the queen. Yee should learn to drive, kidda, buy yersel a little car. Then ye could take this one to school.' He pokes a thumb at me.

Mam pretends not to like Da's idea but I think secretly she does.

'Awh, go on Ma,' I butt in. 'Learn to drive. Plee-ease, plee-ease...'

'Stop it, Bernadette. Joe don't encourage her. Anyway, where would I get the money?'

'Awh, go on Ma, I wouldn't have to get the bus.'

I know she doesn't like me getting the bus on my own so I try to persuade her.

'Bernadette, stop your play-acting.'

'Awh, it's not fair.' I push out my bottom lip.

'Now you've set something off, Joe. And you know very well I *would* learn if it wasn't for this.' Mam touches the pointy blue rim of her glasses on the side where her bad eye is. Normally I don't notice it under the glass. But now she's drawn attention to it I sneak a look at the droopy eyelid.

'*Winds of change*, kidda, that's what auld MacMillan says. Everything's different noo, noo we're oot here.'

'I didn't know you were a fan of the Tories.'

'Baby-starvers, that's what the auld chep used to say.'

'Your father?'

'Aye. Bliddy Tories. The Irish have got the right idea, kidda. Nee time for royalty ower there. Mind, they divvent like Catholics, them royals.'

'The Republic, yes, not the six counties though. They still rule the roost there: the Tories and the Royals.'

'Auld MacMillan though, he gets a few things right.' Dad pushes back his cap and scratches a growth of hair poking his ear. He puts his finger in the hole and wiggles at the wax. 'Think Ah'll have to make time for the barbers the morra. Did ye find the cod liver oil yet?'

'It's on the top shelf in the left hand cupboard.'

'Ah think ah'm gannin a bit deef in this lug, feels bunged up.'

Mam changes back to the subject of cars.

'I *would* make a good driver but they would never let me with this eye.'

'Wey, gan and get it seen tee, man. They can dee wonders these days.'

'An operation?'

'Make sure they dee the right one though.'

Dad is trying to be funny but Mam ignores the joke and carries on.

'I might do just that.' Her good eye lights up. She lifts the knitted cosy off the teapot and lays it flat. The wool is bright blue where the handle goes but tea-stained at the spout.

The blind eye was caused by Mam's da kicking her ma's belly when she was growing inside it. She calls him the *divil himself*, saying he wasn't a father and she will never grace him with the term.

The first time I ever noticed was the day my school friend, Muriel, came for tea. She only got invited because I had been to her house and Mam said I had to invite her back:

'How long has your Mam had a funny eye?'

The minute we finished eating, out she came with it.

'Oh,' I said, trying to sound calm, 'ages.'

A funny eye! Why was I the last to know?

I pictured Muriel announcing it in class: *Bernadette Keenan's mother has a funny eye*. What a laughing stock. What if I get it? I do have to be right up close to things to see properly and I am always at the eye hospital about that. Joey says I'm as blind as a bat and he knows loads about bats and their bad sight.

'Mam, Muriel says you have a funny eye?' I blurted it out as soon as she left.

'Yes,' she said, looking glum. 'Yes, I do.'

'You didn't tell me. How long have you had it?'

'All my life.'

'How did you get it?'

That was the first I remember hearing of her cruel dad or the sightless eye or her mother being kicked.

'He was always knocking my mother about when he came in drunk. My poor mother, God rest her soul. She didn't live long after I was born, and no wonder with that blighter.' Once she started the tale she couldn't stop. 'They didn't give tuppence for me. The midwife said I was a little runt who wouldn't last the night.'

'That's not very nice.'

'I survived though.'

'It's still not a very nice thing to say.'

She stopped listening and drifted away.

'That old goat killed my mother as sure as if he stuck a knife in her.'

I was sorry but relieved. At least her bad eye couldn't be passed on to me. I have enough difficulty seeing the blackboard at school, and with other kids calling me Mr Magoo.

'Can I have a look?'

Close up, the eye looked misty and moist. She took off her spectacles, leaving tiny thumbprint dints on her nose.

'Let *me* see.' I put the blue horn-rims glasses on and looked through. 'Hey, this lens is hazy, but this one's plain glass.'

'Well, there's no point in making a prescription for a blind eye is there?'

'Can you lift it up?'

'What?'

'The droopy lid, can you lift it up?'

'I can't do it automatically because the muscles don't work.'

With the tip of a finger then she hooked the skin up. The worker eye was pale and faded, but the blind eye had stayed deep and dark.

'It's a lovely colour brown,' I remarked.

Rents

The great outdoors. New territories: our vast wild west. Grass verges instead of paths, copper trees and hedges, and weeping willows, and firs dark as night.

There are two bungalows in our street, and one other house, where Janet lives behind a copper beech hedge. Janet has short blonde hair and a blonde Labrador called Finch, and is six months older than me. She wears cream jeans cut-off above her ankles, and rides a small black two-wheeler bike that goes so fast it wobbles.

'Would you like to have a go?' She catches me staring.

'No thanks.' I want to but won't admit I don't know how to balance.

'Why don't you come to my house and have some lemonade? I'm thirsty from peddling uphill.'

Everyone in Janet's family is blonde: her dad, her mam, who she calls Mum, and especially her three-year-old sister, who has eyelashes and hair as white as God. The dog is the colour of Rich Tea and scares me when he races about and jumps. Janet's kitchen is bigger than our lounge and dining room put together. But there is no yellow breakfasting room and all the walls are dull green.

'Mam?' I gallop in the house to no sign of life.

'Mam?' I make my voice loud, but she is nowhere about.

Dad is at the breakfasting table with a red note book and a pencil tucked behind his ear. He sees me coming and lets out a rasper, loud enough to lift his cap.

'Dad, man!'

'What's the marra wi'ye, lad? It's the quiet ones you have to watch out for. Fresh as a rose, that one was.'

I waft the air with my hand as if he's made a right stink.

'What you doing, Da?'

'Bad payers, some of these. He licks the point of his pencil and puts marks beside tenants' names; ticks for up-to-dates, crosses for arrears: 'Watson, Tucker, Metcalf...' A tiny spider scuttles over the page and is whammed. 'Wilkins, Arnold, McCormack...'

'Have you seen Mam?'

'Ah'll have to chase these buggers,' he mumbles, ignoring me, and the small black streak he's made on the corner of the book.

In the plush red dining room Mam is listening to the wireless and sewing curtain hems. The tasselled velour cloth that normally hangs over the table has been pushed aside to make room for the material. In this place there is so much space she can do different jobs in different rooms, as many jobs as she likes.

'*Mam?*'

'*What?*'

'Can I have some jeans?'

'Trousers?'

'Jeans, like Janet's, but better?'

'Oh, we'll have to see. If your Dad ever collects all the rent arrears you might. What was the Fireman's home like?'

The Fireman and his wife live across from us and when they caught me and Teresa nosing, invited us inside their bungalow for a look.

'They've got long hallways, but we couldn't find one secret passage, or trapdoor, or any walls that swing open when you press secret buttons or move books.'

'That's a disappointment.'

'No pets either. Do The Fireman and his wife not have any children?'

'No, I don't think so,' Mam glances up. 'In fact, no, I'm sure they don't. It's a big place for two people sure enough.'

'Will they get any then?'

'Considering their age?' She puts down the sowing needle for a minute and stretches her lips. 'At this stage I think that might put the cat among the pigeons.'

More animals.

On Saturday mornings the Fireman helps me learn to ride Janet's old bike, holding onto the back of the saddle while I balance. I keep looking back to be sure he is still there, still holding me up. It might be a trick, where he lets me fall off when I am least expecting it.

'Don't worry' he says, 'I won't let go.'

Once I learn to ride I go off on my own with Finch, bounding along, his tongue lolling out.

'Finch!' I call him and he comes. And as long as he doesn't bark my heart stays calm. I have three new friends, a blonde ten-year-old tomboy, her two-year-old blonde Labrador, and the Fireman, who is bald.

The accident on Janet's stupid bike means I have almost sliced my knee-cap off and now have nothing to ride until me and Teresa get the new bicycles we've been promised. I can't wait, but hope when mine arrives, Janet never asks for a ride. I keep picturing her dad's frown as he carried her broken bike all the way back to their house after it was mangled. His face was white and flabby as a yard of tripe: like the tripe Mam cooks for her and Dad because no one else will eat it.

One minute I was free-wheeling then a pack of midges flew in my gob. No one explained the front brake is for stopping quick, and I went head over heels into a pile of hot soft dog-dirt. It took Mam ages to clean the wound, and she needed two hands to do it so couldn't hold her nose. My leg was cut to ribbons and wouldn't bend, so I had to lean on Mam and hobble for the bus to get to my new school's fête. By the time we got there we were so late the ket shop had sold out of toffee cakes.

The village school is Protestant so I travel to the nearest Catholic one near town. Mam says I'm lucky because Sacred Heart is a decent school, and the teachers have a good reputation. I do like having a uniform, and they don't give the strap as much as they did in Saint Michael's. I only had it twice but Joey was right: it smarts like blazes and makes your skin itch and burn, like the flames of Hell.

'Let's see what you bought.' Terry nosed in the bags as soon as me and Mam got back from buying my first uniform: grey skirt, red jumper, white shirts, and striped tie.

'Which shops did you go to then?'

'Woolworths for the jumper and socks, Farnons for the skirt, and...Mam where did we get the shirts again?'

'Doesn't matter, you can get that stuff anywhere. The only place that stocks proper uniforms is Raymond Barnes School Outfitters. They do my school but not common ones like yours.'

'Well, I've got a stripy tie like yours.'

'Not mine, mine is exclusive to Saint Anne's.'

'*Saint Anne's*,' I pinched the end of my nose to sound posh. 'Oh bully off!'

Since Terry started going to *Saint Anne's Convent High School for Girls* she has turned into a right snob. Being at a private school that Dad has to pay extra money for means she looks down her big hooter at everyone, especially me.

Dad says his high school was on top of a hill and was free. He says in his day they taught useful things at school: *pull this lug,* he says, and when I do he lets out a massive fart exactly on cue. *Try the other one*, he says to Teresa. But she's too larty-posh and refuses to join in. I reach up and tug the other ear, and he blasts off again. I scream and hold my nose and Teresa does too, secretly admiring his perfect timing.

Even though I've got a bad leg with the biggest scab in the world I am not allowed to take any days off school. I don't really mind because I like my new school and I like my new teacher and I completely love having my own school tie and my own school uniform.

It takes ages to be able to bend my leg again and get a proper lick at my knee. When the crust hardens I pick at the edge where it's pinkest. My mouth waters like meat and I want it to keep growing so there is an endless supply. The thick scab tastes like crispy bits of pork, sweet, like rind. I love the golden taste of it and this is the fattest, saltiest, most succulent one I have ever had.

Jupiter

— ● ● ● —

Mam never farts. Mam would let the top of her head blow off rather than let her backside make a noise. Joey accuses everyone of blowing off except himself and the cat.

'The fox smells his own scent first.' He says if anyone accuses him.

'Arrgh! Is that you or the cat?' I try not to breathe in. 'That is foul.'

Jupiter might not make a noise but he is top suspect for the quiet, lethal ones.

'Inhale through your mouth if you don't like it.'

'What?'

'Breathe through your gob. That way you won't have to smell it.'

Out here in the fresh air a hundred people could let off at once and not make an impression. The back garden is so big and wild Joey soon tires of trying to scythe the mass of tall grass. The effort makes him sweat and he decides to take his shirt off and roll it into a pillow so he can stretch out. Joey's skin is so white it dazzles, and, considering how much he eats, it's amazing how much his rib cage sticks out.

While he weaves through the maze to find a spot to settle in, me and Terry play hide and seek and come across Jupiter batting insects in the bleaching sun; diving to and fro, fresh as a daisy. His fur coat must be as light as air because he never breaks a sweat. Last week he caught a dormouse, the tiniest creature. Joey managed to rescue it and put in a shoe box but it died of shock when it saw his ugly mug come close up.

Distracted by the cat we don't notice Joey disappearing from sight.

'Joey!' Teresa yells.

'Where are you, Joey?'

'Where's he gone?'

Calling is a waste of time, because he won't want to be found and won't give himself away. Joey always says he would like to be as invisible as The Invisible Man. Imagine no one knowing you were on the bus, or in the room, and coming over and sitting on your knee and squashing you, or worse, if you were on the toilet...

'There you are!' Teresa shouts from beside the farmer's trees. 'Found you!'

'How did you spot me?' Joey is chewing a stork of grass and has his hands tucked up under his head.

'I just saw a flash of white,' Teresa says, 'and followed.'

'Har, har. Don't worry, I'll soon be brown if the weather stops like this.' Joey squints up, and I suddenly notice a sprout of gingery-brown hair sticking out of his armpits. I never knew men had hair in there. Disgusting.

'Joey?'

'Mmm?'

'Do you think insects break wind?'

Joey opens one eye and screws it up. Then lies back and slaps his arm where a fly has just landed and started stalking about.

'Never thought about it. Now go away and let me think...'

Once Dad lays the drive to the garage and a path to the front door Mam plans to make proper gardens with flowers and shrubs and a hedge screening off the road. There will be a rose garden and irises with lupins down the sides. I want her to get copper beech, and a lilac tree like Janet has at her place. There can never be enough of the colour lilac, inside or out.

Before we left Frankie said we should get hawthorn hedging and then in the spring we could have gardens full of pink and white blossom. I bet Mam misses talking to Frankie about flowers. She misses the sprouts and cabbages, and we all miss the rhubarb that made delicious pies. Dad still employs Frankie to do repairs on his houses in Elswick, and still complains about the third rate workmanship he supplies. But nobody from our old life would come to see us here, where we live now.

To lay the drive Dad measures and marks everything out with string and wooden stakes and lets me be his labourer, feeding the cement mixer with water and powder as it turns. I love doing it at first, but after a bit I get distracted watching butterflies. These two are bright blue and dip and soar over the path as if they are dancing a jive. Once I've stopped I realise my arms are tired from stretching up and decide I would rather use the shovel to make cement pies.

'Let me mix some of it by hand Dad. Go on.'

'Ye just wanna clart, divvent ye?'

'Arr, go on Da, please, let me have a turn.'

With a bag of dry cement, a shovel and a pail of clean water he shows me how to mix. I learn the ratio of dry to wet, how to turn it in, slice it, lay it down. I am making cakes: mixing, folding, smoothing out lumps. My nose and hair are full of dust, like royal icing.

'Happy as a pig in muck,' Dad says.

He balances planks of wood on bricks and warns me not to go near the drive again until the cement sets.

At the end we add just two decorations: Jupiter's paw print and my initials. This is Hollywood. Me and Jupiter are stars on Sunset Boulevard. He limps away, not realising the honour.

Prisoners of War

The sun is out from first thing in the morning and shines until last thing at night. Once the new bikes arrive we set out to explore everywhere within a radius of five miles. Mine is a gorgeous seventeen-inch metallic lilac. Terry's has a nineteen-inch frame with paintwork the colour of custard. This is our first summer living in the country and I want to make the most of every minute we've got.

Janet's cranky old bicycle has been fixed and takes the front, and me and Terry cruise behind, heading down The Rise to the abandoned prisoner of war camp. We dismount, hauling our bikes over broken stones, clumps of nettles, and hard, spiky grass; setting them by the old watchtower as we clamber inside and climb the rusty iron rungs right to the top. From there we can look out over the whole site, imagining we are commandants with search lights, shouting at the enemy as they attempt to escape.

'Halt. Who goes there?'

'Put your hands up.'

'Stop, or we shoot.'

Once we're back down we dust our orange palms and explore the outbuildings. A few nameplates still cling by the odd nail to doors that flap behind us as we run from one hut to another. In the hut marked *Kitchen* we pretend to stir huge pots, cooking gruel for the German captives.

Back outside we find a weed-strewn pond strung with

frog-spawn like school tapioca and decide to come back every day and watch it transform. We agree to bring clean jam-jars in our saddle bags so we can closely examine it turning into tadpoles, then frogs. Such amazing thrills to look forward to.

This is another world: a deserted prisoner of war camp completely untouched, left over from the last world war, and kept for us to explore. Since we moved, this is by far the best and most exciting place we have discovered.

When we get home I rush into the breakfasting room where Dad has his trouser legs rolled up to the knees and is bathing his feet in the enamel basin he uses for shaving. He is always washing his feet and shaving his chin, but hardly ever uses the bath to have all-over washes in. On the yellow table his corn plasters, talc, and ointments are all set out.

'Bet ye never saw plates of meat better than these?' He lifts a pink foot out of the water and waggles it about.

'Urr, Dad! What are those wiggly lines?' A load of blue podgy worms criss-cross his feet and ankles.

'They're very close veins, they are.'

'Very close?'

'Varicose!' Mam says, coming through with a pot of tea and a clean pair of socks tucked under her arm.

'Varicose veins from years of heavy lifting and carrying,' she says. 'Labourer's legs.'

'Very close, and full of blue blood. Bet yee didn't knaa Ah was related to royalty?'

'Royalty, like a prince?' I say.

'More like the Duke of Northumberland.'

'Here,' Mam says, laying the socks over the back of his chair, 'freshly darned.'

'That's nee way to address Sir Joseph Hotspur Keenan! Did Ah never tell ye that Hotspur was me middle name?'

'You did not.' Mam laughs. 'I thought your people were Irish, going way back?'

'A mix, aye, Limerick, Kilkenny, Northumberland.

Once his feet are dusted and dried and covered with the socks he has cut the tops off *to aid circulation* I tell him about the camp and all the exciting things we found to do down there.

'Only Italians kept in that place,' Dad pushes his feet in and laces up his shoes.

'Not Germans?'

'Nah, it was an open prison. They kept the Hun under lock and key.'

'What's the Hun?'

'That's the Jormans. What they called the Jormans.'

'So, were the Italians enemies as well?'

'Aye, they were classed as enemy, but they didn't need high walls and barbed wire to keep them in. The Italians didn't want away.'

'Why not?'

'Never liked to fight: walked backwards in advance.'

'I don't get...'

'Only knew how to retreat.'

'Eh?'

'They were happy to sit the war out over here, living off the fat of the land.'

'Some of them didn't want to go back,' Mam adds, 'even after the war was finished.'

'Aye, they were put out to work on the land, got well in with the local lasses, some did, settled here after the war. All had an eye for the women, those Aye-ties.'

Mam flashes Dad her *enough about that* look.

'Were they not enemies any more then?'

'Changed sides before the war ended; wanted to finish up with the winners.'

Among his private things that I'm not allowed to go poking around in, Dad keeps a few old photographs: one of himself outside the military hospital he was in after the First World War. He is with a big group of men, some of them lying down on the grass with bandaged heads or arms in slings. Some have crutches beside them and are missing feet or legs. They all wear the same uniform with little round collars like pyjamas. The man sitting next to Dad has his eyes covered and has one hand resting on Dad's shoulder. Maybe he was blinded by the gas. Mam says lots of men were gassed but I had better not ask Dad about that, because it's a taboo subject.

Loony Bin

Setting off, the weather is bone dry but halfway down Foxglove Lane it starts spitting, then properly raining, and before long it's teaming so our feet are slipping off the pedals and we can't steer. We take shelter under a sycamore with big hand-like leaves that make a canopy and stop us getting soaked. Until we came to live here I had no idea there were so many different types of tree.

'Species of trees,' Terry says, spookily reading my mind.

'What?'

'This lane is so long there must be dozens of species of trees and a hundred different greens.'

Since we came here my sister complains she hasn't enough greens in her paintbox and is always having to add black and white to make different shades. Before we moved privet was the only green we knew.

'I don't think it's safe sheltering here in the rain.' Janet pipes in. 'If it starts to thunder we could get struck and killed by lightening.'

Me and Terry share an eye-roll then lean over the damp fence and look at the cows.

'The cows have all moved under the trees,' Terry points. 'See, Janet?'

'But they're cows,' Janet says.

'But cows aren't stupid,' Teresa instructs Janet like a

teacher now. 'They would never stand under there if there was any real danger.'

Once the showers pass the three of us cycle up by the wood, close enough so Janet, the chicken, is bound to be scared. The loony bin is a big stone building with dark creepy grounds and enormous iron gates. We grind to a halt but don't dismount, gripping our handlebars to spy at the long gravel path through the railings. The lunatics must be locked inside. We hope.

'What if they come out and get us?'

'I'm too hot.' A sweat breaks out across Janet's forehead.

'Me too, I'm parched.' Teresa coughs and swallows to unstick her throat.

Since the sun came back out our clothes have got clammy and clamp to our skin like glue.

'I've got some money, let's ride down the village and get ice-pops.' The heat and a quick escape from the lunatics makes me feel generous. And I know Dad will never miss this one measly half-crown I found in his coat.

'The village is miles,' Janet complains, 'and I get wrong if I'm late home.'

'Oh, come on, it's only a few minutes away, and all downhill.' Teresa starts to push off, free-wheeling Callerton Lane, past the golf club, on towards the river, with no thought to the homeward climb. At the paper shop I buy frozen Jubilees, my best discovery of the summer. I bite off one corner of the waxy triangle and let the orange juice melt into my mouth, then rip the top and suck the flavour out until all that's left is a lump of ice. We lie under the weeping willows at the side of the River Pont, resting our bikes beside us on the grass where they trail. I reach over and touch the back of Janet's neck with some ice.

'Ahh!' she jumps with shock.

I roll it over my forehead and along my arms, over all the goose-pimples poking up.

Teresa is daydreaming.

'Imagine having a fridge with an ice maker, an enormous American one like yours, Janet? With an endless supply of ice-lollies, and cool butter and milk, how great would that be?'

'Janet, you are so lucky,' I chip in. 'Your parents must be very rich.'

'Yes, Daddy is, but I don't get to see him when he travels.'

'Small sacrifice,' Teresa says. 'I wish *we* could buy blocks of ice-cream and not worry about them melting. Mam would like it as well. She would never have to fill pans with cold water and float things in it with a prayer.'

'Hey, Teresa, I mean, Terry, why not? Do you think we should ask?'

When we eventually get back, Janet's mother reads her the riot act.

'Where on earth have you been? You were away so long I thought you'd been abducted or molested or murdered...'

Poor Janet doesn't get a word in.

'In future you are restricted to playing in the immediate vicinity. Do you understand me?'

'Yes, Mum. Sorry, Mum.' Janet murmurs.

We squeeze on our handlebars and Teresa gives me an elbow for getting too close to her. Janet's mum might be talking to her daughter but she is looking directly at us, slyly pointing the blame at the bad influence brought in by the city.

My lilac bike can travel anywhere. There is endless space and the ride down to the village is easy. At holiday time we find different routes and explore other villages. Belsay and Stamfordham are only a few miles away. Five miles on wheels is a doddle. With headlamps, reflectors and puncture repair kits in our saddle bags, there will be loads more adventures; with or without Janet.

In Blackberry Week we cycle to Honeysuckle Hill for the best fruit. I dismount to park up but miss sight of the marshy ditch and put both feet straight in:

'Arrh!' My good white socks suck up the black wet. 'I'm soaked.'

'Take them off.' Teresa says. 'Quick, roll them up and put them in your saddle bag.'

Our hands get ripped on hedgerow thorns but we each fill a big bag with ripe berries and I hope Teresa's pies will make up for being scratched and having stone cold plates of meat. Soon we will be back in winter clothes and the lines across my ankles will disappear and my brown summer legs will return to being as white as my feet.

I want to eat fast but have to examine every mouthful of Teresa's blackberry pie in case of creepy-crawlies. Adding Carnation Milk makes a lovely lilac mush, and when our bellies are full we laze on the plush red carpet in our plush red dining room and tune into Radio Luxembourg for Sunday's new pop chart.

Come on let's twist again, like we did last summer.
Come on let's twist again, like we did last year.
Do you remember when...

'The sound's going...Quick...' I twiddle the tuner. The sound comes back. The Twist is fast. We start to dance but I get a stitch. Our Meena used to grip my fingers and stab my hands doing the jive, flipping me this way and that. Twizzle, twizzle, until I was so dizzy I'd flop on the couch. Before her rock-and-roll records got smashed she was always dancing about. I hate remembering that.

The sound goes again and we fall to the floor to get our breath back.

'Here, let me.' Teresa takes the controls and I hum noisily to annoy her, because she is being bossy.

'Age before beauty.'

'Shh! Keep quiet, I'm trying to retune it.'

227

'Hurry up, this one's great.'

'Wait... Got it... Lost it... Got it...Gone!'

The wireless gives high-pitched squeals, and we spend ages fiddling with the knobs to get the right wavelength. All the effort is worth it though, when a song finally comes over loud and clear:

> *I see the lights, I see the lights,*
> *I see the party lights,*
> *the red and blue, and green.*

'Little Stevie Wonder, quick, give me the writing pad and pen, so I can get the words.'

Teresa takes her hand off the dial for a split-second and snatches the paper.

'Too late, it's gone again.'

'Arrh! Man!'

Square Eyes

———— • ◉ • ————

'Have you seen what the cat's doing?'

Coming in from school I catch Jup on his back legs scrabbling at the kitchen door to get through.

'Someone's put a flea in his ear,' Mam says, draining a pan at the sink, her head wafting in a cloud of steam.

When I open the door he races into the breakfasting room and slinks under the buttercup table, blinking like a lunatic, a hundred miles an hour.

'Hey, Mam, he's crying.'

'Don't be a dafty.'

'No, he is. He's crying big blobby tears. Really.'

'Honestly. That animal thinks he's human.'

'Poor Jup,' I drop my satchel and crawl under the table to give him a stroke. 'Arr, look, big juicy teardrops, like a baby. Poor thing.'

While Mam is serving up dinner I find Joey in the garage and relay the news.

'What you on about?'

'Honestly. Mam was cooking onions and Jupiter started crying real tears. It's an *allergy*.'

'Pull the other one.'

'I'm not kidding. Ask Mam if you don't believe me. From now on he has to be kept right away from Irish Stew.'

'Mind you,' Joey sniffs, 'I've never sneezed as much since we moved here either. All this greenery and the smell of all these flowers.'

'Trust you. I knew you wouldn't leave Jupiter alone to have an *allergy* without you having one as well.'

'Me and Jup,' he locks his fingers and smirks, 'we're like that.'

By the time Joey gets in from work, washes his hands and changes out of his boiler suit, he is always dog tired. After dinner he usually goes to his room for a bit. Then, once Dad goes out to the pub he comes down to the lounge and relaxes in front of the telly with us; the cat on his knee normally, and his legs swung over the arm of the chair. Now the nights are closing in, he sets off in the mornings in darkness and comes back at night in darkness, and apart from work, watching telly and saving up is all he does.

Dad never stays in at night whether it's dark or not. Most nights he rides his motorbike to the village where there are three pubs but on rent nights he drinks in town until the bars close. I wish he would stay home and watch telly with the rest of us but he thinks telly is rubbish. And anyway, our Joey and him in the same room all evening would put everyone on edge.

'Joey, how old is Jupiter do you think?'

He looks from the television set to the cat, the cat lifts his face and looks back.

'Says he's six.'

'Har har....But really, is that what he is, six?'

'He was a stray, and he only speaks in Jupinese.'

'He's not old though, is he? Not like Corky was, or Tibby?'

'You're not old are you Jup?' Joey's arm flops down onto the cat's head.

'Says, no, he's still got eight lives left. Now pipe down. I'm watching this.'

I am not bothered about Have Gun Will Travel. The episodes are long and apart from the song I never understand why Joey loves it so much. Maybe it's because he and Paladin both like chess. Joey is teaching me to play, but always wins and takes ages with every turn and makes it a bore.

Paladin, Paladin, where do you roam, Paladin,
Paladin, far, far, far from home...
A knight without armour in a savage land...

'I don't know what you're singing for. You don't even know the words.'

'Yes, I do. Listen...' I start again.

'Shhh! Zip it!.' He goes and turns the telly up. Paladin is the man with the gun, who doesn't like shooting anyone, and Joey won't be distracted.

Unlike Dad, Mam has come round to liking telly and watched every minute of Princess Margaret's wedding when she married Anthony Armstrong-Jones. Captain Townsend was who she really loved but she was forbidden from marrying him because he was divorced.

Mam was engrossed and Dad had to remind her about being Irish, and republican.

'Northern Irish.'

'Irish is Irish: same thing.'

'Not since the British refused to return the six counties. Since they wouldn't I might as well enjoy the benefits of living under colonial rule.'

'Aye, well, at least he's not Catholic. They wouldn't let her marry anybody kicking with the wrang foot.'

'That's true.' Mam wiggled her feet and smiled at the screen as the bride walked down the aisle in her long white dress and veil.

'A one for the women though, Armstrong-Jones.

'Joe! Honestly, how can you know that?'

'Am tellin ye, kidda, he's got a roving eye. Not a snowball's chance in hell of keeping him tied.'

Mam's face disappeared back into the screen and Dad finally left her to it. He has no interest in watching anything apart from the News, and is the only one left in the family who refuses to convert. He says he's sick of seeing the Yanks win World War Two. And if people swallow *that pap*, they will swallow anything; even believing Micky Rooney and Errol

Flynn won the whole thing two-handed.

Apart from silent comedies, the only film I ever saw Dad enjoy was Greta Garbo playing Mata Hari, which he sat through to the bitter end. As soon as it was done he got up and put his coat on, smacked his lips and said *By, but, she was a tidy tart.*

First Winter

———— ● ◉ ● ————

I can't imagine Dad actually fighting in a real war or killing someone else. Mam says that in the trenches some soldiers' hair turned white with shock. Dad's didn't but I wonder if one day it will turn from black to brown like Corky's and Tibby's did before they died; or if it will drop out altogether and make him bald. Worrying about Dad stops me thinking of something nice. I turn to give Jupiter a stroke but he jumps off the bed leaving his shape in the dint. I pat it smooth and brush off his fur, watching it float in a cloud of hairy dust, to the floor.

It dawns on me now that the bayonet our Joey used to play pirates with, standing on his bed, taking it out of its sheath and waving it about, that bayonet must be the same bayonet Dad was made to push into real men's real chests.

It dawns on me now that he must have given it to Joey as a present, the Billy Can as well. So there was a time when Dad and Joey spoke, and Dad gave him gifts. I wish I could remember it, could imagine them getting on.

The cat gallops off downstairs and I saunter through to Joey's room, quietly opening the door. This is the first good root around I've had in here since we moved. Joey is out at work so I am safe to explore. Under the bed there is no sign of the bayonet or the old Billy Can but I find the snow-scene toffee tin full of foreign coins and his collection of marbles, including Sapphire and Emerald, the one Teresa nearly had for a false eye. Old milky is here too, the one called Blind Pew. Instead of weapons there is a stack of Kensitas cigarette coupons neatly piled in batches and tied together with elastic bands. I consider counting but there are thousands and it would take too long. I wonder what he'll spend them on, and think it's a pity he couldn't put them towards the motor scooter he is saving for. The sooner he can afford that the better because cycling all the way to Wallsend on the push bike in this weather is freezing him to death.

Back downstairs Mam is playing war with Dad, saying she's at a loss to know why he hangs on to the flea ridden old coat he keeps thrown over the top of his bed. Dad's Greatcoat is his army coat from the first war, and the effort of dragging it off the bed, the one and only time I did, nearly buckled my legs. It is made of thick khaki and has brass buttons and is no good for playing with, far too long, and itchy and rough. In cold weather he lays it over his bed as an extra blanket. But since we got new eiderdowns Mam says it spoils the look of their bedroom décor, and warns he will cook under it with the central heating. He says extra clothes are the best thing for eliminating cold and she needn't think that just because the house is full of radiators we are keeping them on day and night eating money through the whole winter. Mam looks up to the heavens and shrugs.

'You can take a horse to water,' she says, 'but you can't make it drink.'

I think Dad's Greatcoat is one of his treasures because it kept him snug in the trenches when there was nothing else to wrap up in. These days though, in a modern house, Mam thinks it's of no use to man nor beast, and is the last thing he needs to keep.

All through November and December the kitchen boiler is fed with coke so the central heating keeps the house nice and hot. At Christmas our Meena writes Mam a letter and sends a photograph of her head taken by a professional photographer. She has her hair done and black fish-tails painted on her eyes, and a beauty spot on her chin, that makes her look as glamorous as a film star, Elizabeth Taylor, our Teresa says, or Sophia Loren. The dining room table is all set out and Mam puts her up on the sideboard so she can watch us eating Christmas dinner. After we have finished Dad says that was just the job, then leans back on his dining room chair, crooks his little finger to his mouth and says in a posh voice:

'I have had ample sufficiency thank you very much, and Am full right up to the gunnels.'

Shamrock

———— ● ◉ ● ————

Every school night on my way home I stop at the foot of
The Rise to watch the new lambs skip about on the other side
of the fence. I would stay longer if it wasn't so cold but I'm
starving and even in gloves the tips of my fingers are froze.

For dinner we have chops and gravy, carrots and taties. I
tell everybody about the lambs then try to eat sideways like
the sheep, but chewing from side to side takes ages and I am
too hungry to go slow.

When everyone's finished eating Mam clears the dirty
plates and puts the kettle on for cups of tea.

'Did Ah ever tell ye about the time I was a sheep rustler?'
Dad stretches on his buttercup chair, snaps his braces, and
starts a tale.

'Joe, stop putting notions into the kids' heads'. Mam
comes in from the kitchen with a pack of Rich Tea and full
teapot puffing steam. She pours as Joey collects a few biscuits
from the open packet then picks up his cup and leaves the
room.

'Shush woman, this is educational.' Dad carries on.

'Being a rustler? Does that mean you pinched sheep off a
farm?' Teresa says.

'Wey, there were extenuating circumstances. It was in the
twenties and there was nee work and nowt to eat. To stave off
hunger, people would suck the salt off their own feet.'

'Urgh, stop it Da!'

My lips curl.

'Like Charlie Chaplin in that film, Da?' Teresa jumps back in. 'When he boils boot laces to make a meal?'

'Aye, exactly. Just like him.'

Once Dad starts getting ready to go out I go and find Joey in the lounge, his long legs sprawled out in front of the TV. He always has to take loads of space and can never just sit up properly and be neat.

'Joey?' I flop on the carpet beside the fire and his big feet. 'Did you know that when Dad was your age him and his friends took a sheep and drove it off in a car; and in those days no one needed a license to drive so it wasn't breaking the law.'

'Did you know that most lambs only live to be a few months old before they are slaughtered for meat?'

Joey loves doing this, answering a question with a question.

'And did you know that the chop you ate for your dinner was made of just such a lamb?'

That's two questions and I am not amused by either one.

'Terry?'

'What now?' Teresa is sitting at the dressing table fiddling with her hair.

'Do you think Dad and our Joey liked each other, ever?'

'Dunno.' She droops a curl across her top lip, draping it

like a moustache.

'When our Joey was a little boy?'

'Dunno.' Teresa ponders into the mirror as if she is giving it some thought. 'Our Joey was born early in the war and probably only saw Dad a few times when he was small.'

'Why's that? Dad wasn't a soldier in the second war was he?'

'I know that, you fool, but he worked away and only came home the odd weekend. Ten nights on, two nights off, that was the munitions factory routine.'

'So it must have been like, like not really having a dad?'

'I don't think our Joey, or our Meena, saw him much before they were four of five.'

'Right.' I try to imagine being little and only having Mam.

'Honestly, Bernadette. Work it out.'

'What do you mean?'

'Well, he was *hardly ever* home.'

'I don't...'

'Why do you think there is only one year between Joey and Meena, then such a big gap between her birth date in forty-two, and mine in forty-seven?'

'You mean...Eh?'

'Think about it.'

In the middle of March, Auntie Nora's shamrock arrives in a little box the same as always, and includes a letter informing

Mam of the death of her old schoolteacher Mr Jenner back in Ireland. Mr Jenner taught English and gave Mam a love of Shakespeare and hardly ever gave her the belt because she learned everything he asked of her off by heart. Mam says she loved Mr Jenner even though he was harsh. Maybe that was why she loved him, because he let her off more than everybody else.

I only had the belt once off Dad and can picture him sliding it off and putting me across his knee. I didn't squiggle much at first because I didn't believe he would hurt me until my skirt was raised and I felt the heat of the leather whacking the tops of my legs and wobbling my bot. At first I thought it would be a tap or a slap and then he would laugh and let me go. But it cut and stung and I wriggled like a worm and screamed then slid to the floor. I'd never seen *that* dad before, and can't remember now what I'd done to make Mam so mad that instead of giving me a slap, she waited until he came home and said I had to be taught a proper lesson.

Now Mam complains she is the only one who gives any discipline, because these days Dad only wears braces and I never get hit off him or threatened with the belt, or see the red raw eyes he wore back then.

Joey is always saying I am spoiled and get away with murder and can wrap Mam and Dad round my little finger because I am last in line and treated soft as clarts.

'Teresa?' I must have been in bed for hours but can't rest. My sister is pretending to be asleep and refuses to answer.

'Terry?' I try again, louder, and with the right name.

'What, man!?' She turns over and I feel her eyes glare.

'You know how Dad was a soldier in the war?'

'The first war.'

'The first war, yes. Do you think he ever had to kill anybody with his own bare hands?'

'Like tear their hearts out?' Her voice is drowsy but coming round.

'Or shoot their heads off, or run them through with a bayonet?'

'Bernadette!' Teresa suddenly bounds upright, and the mattress pings. 'Bernadette! We are not having this stupid conversation, now go to sleep and leave me in peace.'

When the tossing and turning finally wears me out, I nod off straight into a dream about Dad standing in a field next to our Joey. Dad is brandishing the bayonet, swinging it over his head and shouting *Aye, Aye me hearties* just like our Joey used to when he unsheathed it to play pirates. At first I think he is going to run Joey through but then realise they are playing Treasure Island and Dad is Long John Silver and Joey is Jim Hawkins. My body sighs and sinks but then Joey transforms into me, and I am in a trench with Dad who is still holding the bayonet, now covered in blood, and he takes out a hanky and wipes the blade and I start to run but can't move, and I look in his eyes and I don't know who he is because his face has changed, and his eyes are red-raw and hard as iron railings.

Spring

———— • ◉ • ————

'Any clues what to get?' I never know what to buy for Dad's birthday and hope Terry has some ideas.

'Dunno. what about a tie?' She's not putting much thought into this.

'I bought him a tie for Christmas, and for his last birthday.'

'Get him a pen then.'

'He's got loads of pens.'

'Not a chatty pen, a nice pen.'

'I can't afford a nice pen. I've only got half-a-crown.'

'Buy him a bath cube.'

'Don't be daft, he doesn't get bathed.'

'Well, I don't know. When we get to the shops you can have a look for something.'

'What star sign is he?'

'Taurus the bull. It's an earth sign.'

'Mmm...Do you know how old he is?'

'Fifty? Sixty?'

'Not sixty?'

'He says fifty, but his passport says sixty...or is it sixty-one?'

My mouth drops. Teresa mimics me.

'Sixty or sixty-one!' Dad has just aged ten years in five seconds.

She counts again.

'Sixty-two actually. Sounds old doesn't it?'

He's ageing by the minute. I can't take it in. My Dad is old. Another thing to worry about. A small black cloud begins to grow. My heart bloats until it feels too big to fit in my chest.

In town, we get off the bus at the Haymarket and Teresa is straight in, pestering.

'Can we look in the record shop, Mam?'

'Later maybe. We've come to buy your dad's birthday presents,' Mam says, 'not to look at records.'

'Can we go up The Monument then?'

If Teresa can go to the record shop I don't see why I can't climb up Grey's Monument. I've always wanted to go to the top.

'Away to blazes with you. I am not climbing any monument thank you very much.'

'Can me and Teresa go up then? You can wait at the bottom.'

'No, you cannot. Not today. You're not getting blown about up there.' She pulls a strand of hair stuck across my face and tucks it behind my ear.

'But I want to get Dad a record.' Teresa refuses to have her nose pushed out. 'Let's go to the record shop.'

'Well, I want to buy him a record as well,' I decide.

'Great minds think alike. Let's go to Windows. Come on Mam, let's?'

Outnumbered, she gives in. We all go to Windows, and Teresa dives downstairs to listen to pop music in one of the booths. I knew she was kidding about buying Dad a record.

'Do you think they'll have Paul Robeson singing Sanders of the River?' I ask. 'Dad loves listening to that.'

'How much did you say you had?' Mam looks at the half crown I hold out and frowns.

On the high stools in Woolworths snack bar we have Pepsi and Mam drinks tea. I take the blue tie out of the bag and give it a stroke.

'It's nice and silky. Do you think he'll like it?'

'Yes pet, just what he needs. It'll go with the navy jumper I've knit. We'll make him look respectable yet, between us.'

'Do I have to pay you back the extra?'

'We'll see.'

I hope she isn't seriously thinking of making me pay her back out of my pocket money.

'Hey!' Teresa sounds like she's had a bright idea. 'Embassy might do a sound-alike Paul Robeson. Why don't we go and have a look?' Her eyes light up like hundred watt bulbs.

'Too late, I've bought my present now.'

'I haven't.' She slides off her stool and heads to the record counter.

On the bus home we eat wine gums and plan new adventures on our bikes.

'Bernadette, do you like the record I got for Dad?'

'Maybe, maybe not.'

'Why not?'

'Because it's Chubby Checker, and I don't think he'll like Chubby Checker or want to do the Peppermint Twist.'

'That's all you know,' she scoffs.

'I think you just bought it for yourself.'

'I did not.' She acts insulted.

'It's not the real Chubby Checker, anyway. It's just somebody who sounds like him.' All Embassy records are copies. I should know, I've already got the sound-alike Cliff.

'So? Dad won't know the difference.'

I take a few secs to think, then a brainwave hits.

'Do you think we should buy him something from the cat?'

'Jupiter?'

'An extra thing?'

'I've got no money left.'

'Neither have I.'

'I know what,' Teresa has a thought. 'Let's put his name on our card.'

'Put love on.'

'Or, no hard feelings?'

'No, put love on, go on. Love from Jupiter. He'll like that.'

Second Summer

───── ● ● ● ─────

'Come on, bread van's here.' Teresa shoves my arm. 'Come on dozy, hurry up.'

Marshall's van pulls up and as soon as he toots we run out to see what Mam buys from his mobile shop. I wish he would start selling sweets, but until he does, I nag for biscuits and cakes instead.

Apart from the butcher's van and Marshall's, there is the shopping Mam does at Moores village store on Fridays: filling a trolley with a long list of groceries, boxed up and delivered next day. Also, there is the market garden on Edge Hill, a short walk away.

Me and Teresa take Mam's note and give it to the elderly brother and sister who are always pottering in their large green house. Mr and Miss Swinburne are bachelor and spinster and go to our church. They give us tomatoes and a lettuce, then we watch them plop six eggs into a thin brown paper bag. On the way out my sister stops to talk to the ducks and hens and notices some of them have big bald patches.

I stay quiet until we get through the gate and up the path.

'Who do you think's done that?'

'Maybe they make eiderdowns as a sideline,' Teresa laughs, 'fill their nights plucking bird feathers?'

'What a horrible thought.'

'No aerial for a television set. They must get bored.'

On Edge Hill Teresa gives me the tomatoes and lettuce then balances the eggs in her arms as if they are the most delicate and precious objects she has ever had to guard.

Back home, we step in to hear Mam direct her thanks to the kitchen. 'Can you put them away for me please?'

'I tried not to let the eggs roll, Mam,' Teresa calls, 'but that road is full of potholes and I think a couple might be cracked.'

She places the thin brown bag on the side and follows Mam's voice to the breakfasting room where she finds her with her right leg up on one of the padded buttercup seats.

'It might be omelette tonight anyway. And don't talk to me about potholes.' Mam winces and tries to smile, pulling her skirt up to show a big tatie in her nylons, and a load of blood forming a lump. On her knee there is huge bump that wasn't there when we left just half-an-hour since.

All weekend Mam is in agony. When the doctor is consulted he says she has a chipped bone protruding from her knee-cap and it may never go back. When Dad sees it he says she had better give up trying to ride a push bike as a bad joke. She looks embarrassed especially when The Fireman calls in to apologise for not being able to keep a hold of the bike, so when she tipped up there was nothing he could do to stop her flying off.

At dinner time Mam hobbles about bringing the food. I eat with one hand and Dad complains about the lamb being auld mutton, so tough it must've given it self up. I like eating with only a fork, it's easier for scooping mashed tatie and I don't want the meat because it's full of fatty streaks like the chewed up bits Dad puts out on the lip of his plate.

If I was an adult I wouldn't bother trying to ride a push bike to get about, not when there is something easier to drive, with an engine. Our Joey's new, red-trim, Italian scooter is a perfect example. That machine is amazing. It has a platform for the driver's feet, so there is no danger of tripping up.

Ever since it came Joey always has the Meppo out, cleaning the cream paintwork first, then polishing the mirrors and the headlight, then shining the chrome. When I ask for a pillion ride, he goes on about not having passed his test and not wanting to get caught with a youngster on the back. He takes great delight in making me fume.

'But you give our Teresa lifts to the village.'

'She's over thirteen. Anyone younger is illegal.'

'It's illegal anyway if you haven't passed. Awh, please Joey, ple-ease, ple-ease, just once and I won't ever ask again.'

It takes ages of pleading, and I have to keep on about how good a driver he is, and how safe, and how brilliant the new scooter looks. But eventually he gives in and lets me on the back.

'Mind, if anybody sees me...'

'I'll keep down.'

'Don't be ridiculous.'

'Nobody will see us Joey, promise.'

'After six-o-clock then, when the traffic's gone quiet. I'll take the L plates off in case we get spotted.'

Joey puts the L plates on a shelf in the garage and pushes the scooter off its stand. We roll quietly down to the bottom of our street, then full throttle, indicate left, along Edgehill, indicate right, down The Rise, indicate right, along Middle Drive, indicate right, up Woodside, indicate right, along Edgehill, indicate left, up our street, onto the drive, straight back into the garage, engine off, onto the stand, L plates retied.

'There now, satisfied?'

'Joey, that was brilliant,' I say, hopping off.

'I just hope nobody clocked us.'

'Nobody saw. Don't worry. But Joey, we didn't really go very far.'

There is nothing like a motor engine to make you realise how long it takes for legs to get you anywhere.

'I wish I could have a scooter. If I had a scooter I would drive for miles and miles, all over the countryside.'

'Save your pocket money up.'

'Awh come on Joey, take me out on it some more?'

'No. Now get out of my way and stop blocking the garage door.'

As soon as he's gone I sit on the scooter and pretend to rev up. I never even notice the wasp land on the back of my hand until I feel the sharp pin of its bum stuck in my skin. I try to shake it off, then scream and shout for help. It's attached itself, and by the time Joey comes back and knocks it off and squashes it, I am shaking with shock.

In the kitchen Mam applies first aid, using the blue bag she keeps for whitening washing, to treat the sting.

'Acid and alkaline,' Teresa arrives, nodding like a doctor.

'You can put your arm down now pet. No need to hold it out like a plank.'

This is the first time I have been stung and it makes me sniff and wince. Teresa says I am lucky it wasn't a bee because bees give up their lives to sting someone so have to make sure it really hurts. She has been stung by both and knows which one is worse.

'Bees go crackers if you upset them,' she says, 'more crackers than wasps. If you saw a bee go crackers you would know all about it. You wouldn't know what had hit you if it was a bee.'

Would know, wouldn't know: make your mind up. She is a right clever clogs and no mistake.

Once it turns dark I curl up in my lovely lilac bed, cradling my wrist and thinking about zooming off with Joey, the low sun flashing leafy honeycombs. I drift off motoring along, the speed of the scooter cutting the air. Squeezing up behind him I clutch my brother's sides, and hug tight, without him having a chance to care.

Runaway

———— ● ● ● ————

Scouring the kitchen for useful items, I take candles, matches, tins of food, and an opener for our long-planned den in the woods. Our Teresa is lying in front of the TV and refuses to shift no matter how much I plead with her.

'But you promised to help make a rain-proof shelter.'

'It was playing. Anyway I don't want to live in the woods now. You go and do it, I can't be bothered. Why don't you go and ask Janet?'

'Some people!'

As if Janet would come without my idle sister to follow. One last ditch effort and that's that.

'Please Terry, you come. There's no point asking Janet, she'll only ask her mother if she's allowed. You know she does whatever she's told, so no way she'll come.'

'Tough luck. Honestly, you make a better door than a window. Get out the way of the television set.'

I scrape across the carpet then lug through to the kitchen for a glass of consolation milk. Mam and Joey are in the breakfasting room with peculiar faces. I stop and wait, Joey is silent while Mam whispers.

'Did you push him in?' She says.

Her right hand is fidgeting with her crucifix and chain, zipping it fast from side to side.

Joey's mouth moves but makes no sound. In the pause

I'm not sure if I should move forwards or back, or stay stock-still and hope not to be seen.

Then Joey bows his head as if it's Confession, and I feel a gush of guilt for listening in.

'Yes,' he lifts his eyes to Mam. 'Yes, I did.'

'All these years,' Mam says, her voice rising a bit. 'All these years, you never said.'

I draw my neck in like a tortoise, creeping backwards down the hall. I have no clue what they are talking about, but milk I decide, is the last thing I want.

Upstairs I take the small blue case from Mam's wardrobe, unwrap the Heinz tins hidden in a cardigan and put them inside with the pop. The tin opener and spoon are already in the stretchy pocket of the lid. I will go alone, go and set up camp as soon as it turns pitch.

My second time of running away is for an adventure, not to stop Dad from murdering the cat. Jupiter has suffered no death threats since that, and even put his paw print on Dad's birthday card. Which goes to prove leaving home can be good. Our Meena left home loads, and now she has a baby and a husband and a new house in Stoke on Trent, where she can do what she likes without asking anybody's consent. Running away worked well for her in the end.

Turning onto Edge Hill I realise this is nothing like the other time. Then I was furious and only scared for the cat.

This is definitely not like that. At Woodside the case feels heavier and I wish I hadn't bothered bringing pop. Still, I will need drinks. I stop to swap hands, look down towards the village. I expect to see lights but everywhere is black.

This is the way our Joey rides his scooter to work. He always takes Woodside while Dad takes The Rise. Both lead to Middle Drive so it's six and two threes, but they never go the same route because if they passed each other on their bikes some outside politeness might make them have to wave or toot, then all the silence at home would be wasted effort.

There are clouds and the houses are so far back from the road the glow from their windows doesn't stretch. In Elswick the houses were right next to the path but here there are long drives and gardens as big as parks. I imagine the hedgerows thick with hedgehogs and mice, and hope nothing runs out over my toes. Cycling as far as Eastern Way only takes a few minutes but legs take ages and ache. Finally turning onto Callerton Lane I trip and drop the torch. The spring and battery both fall out. I rest the case and feel around listening for noise but there is no other soul and no other sound.

Back in the house everything is as quiet as the grave. Not one movement as I tiptoe upstairs and replace the case. Downstairs again I feel exhausted and my cold bones are starved for warmth. I flop at the fireplace hungry for heat.

'Hello, what's on? What you watching?' I pull a cheerful face.

'Shhh! Out the road.' Joey is back to his usual self.

'Mind, will you?' Teresa waves me to one side.

'Shush.' Even Mam has no interest and not the slightest inkling I have been out of the house.

It's hard to believe that every one in this house is so preoccupied no one even noticed I was missing.

My running away was invisible and now I've appeared I am only a pest blocking the view. I know nothing about anyone I am related to, and might as well be a total stranger in this whole flaming family.

Lips

If I say so myself, I am the best in the world at pestering. Joey still hates me riding pillion on his scooter but Dad often picks me up from school on his way home. The motorbike is big, fast and loud and Dad keeps the 'L' and number plates mucky so the lolly pop man at Westerhope wastes his time craning his neck when we speed past. Joey worries he'll get caught breaking the law, but Dad says the law is an ass, and an ass is a stupid horse.

If I had my way I would get lifts every day and never the bus. The number five is always jam-packed after school and if it goes straight past my stop that's an extra half-hour wait in the queue before another one comes and I get another chance.

Today I manage to squeeze on, and better still, our Terry is on too, and has a seat.

'Lucky getting on,' Teresa says.

'I know. Budge up a bit.' I push through, plonking one cheek on the edge of her seat.

'Did you get any twenty-ones?'

'No, not today, did you?'

'I got two in row, here, look.' Teresa takes both bus tickets out of her blazer pocket and I count along the top.

Counting bus tickets adding to twenty-one is one of six things necessary to win our game. There are also ten red cars to count, five beards, three nuns, two poodles, and a priest. Easier said than done.

At dinnertime everyone concentrates on their own plates as usual so no one notices Joey turn grey and stop shovelling until his head collapses and lands in his food with a thump. Amazingly, Dad is the first one to jump up.

'Son, son? Are ye alreet?'

I can't believe my ears. Dad starts to move but before he reaches Joey, Mam is plucking his face from the gravy and wiping his head.

'Joey. Joey?'

I am frozen stiff and my legs are weak as milk.

Joey starts to come round and a bit of colour tip-toes back up his cheeks.

'What is it, for goodness sake?' Mam's apron is smeared with food. 'Are you alright?'

'Yes...I think so,' Joey says. 'A piece of red-hot tatie got stuck in me throat, and I couldn't cough it up and I couldn't swallow it back.'

Mam goes and brings some water and Joey takes a few sips, then she sits down, picks up her knife and fork and we all go back to eating our food.

In bed, me and Teresa whisper about what happened.

'Dad must have got a shock, actually speaking to Joey?'

'I know, I heard him.'

Dad and Joey not speaking happens every day in our house. Speaking never happens.

'I didn't imagine it then? It did happen?'

'It did happen, definitely. Pity Joey was unconscious, he's the only one who missed out.'

Teresa rustles the bedclothes, moving closer to the edge of her mattress.

'Bernadette?'

Her voice lowers to a mutter, and I have to pull out my ear.

'Mmm?'

'Mind, this is a secret,' she pauses for a second...

'Tell me then.'

'Well, when you were little...'

'...When I was little?'

'When you were about four, Mam had another son.'

My mouth drops wide open, smacking the pillow.

'I had no idea.'

'It's right.'

'Where is he?

'He died.'

'What happened?'

'Not sure. It was a boy though, Mam told me that.'

'You mean I had another brother? Would have had?'

'Can you imagine?'

'Imagine how that would have been?'

'Three of them speaking or not speaking,' Teresa mulls it over for a minute. 'I wonder which it would have been?'

'I'm so glad I'm a girl.'

'Me too.'

'I mean, I'm glad I'll never be a man.'

'Being a man? Imagine having to shave and...'

'And only being mad or sad but never allowed to cry any tears?'

I try to think of it: being a soldier like Dad, made to go and fight a war, or having go down a pit, or into a shipyard? Just the thought scares me stiff.

'I used to like dressing up in Dad's stuff, but that was it.' Teresa interrupts my thoughts.

'Dressing up's all right but in real life men give really hard slaps and have to mix with loads of other men, and swear a lot, and be hard as rocks.'

'Dad says our Joey is soft. He says a stint in the army would have done him good.'

'I suppose being soft is the worst thing you can be if you're a man?'

'Dad says they should never have done away with conscription.'

'What's that?'

'*Bring back the birch...hangings too good.*' Teresa rambles off, doing her *man voice* imitations.

We lie still for a bit while I try to take it all in. Another brother? A brother younger than me? So I wouldn't even have been the baby of the family, and would have had someone to boss?

'Teresa?'

'What?' She gives a loud yawn.

'Do you think Dad's jealous?'

'Of?'

'Of Joey?'

'Dad never had a Ma of his own so I suppose he was never even hugged, never mind loved.'

'Is he jealous, because Mam must have hugged Joey at least once, when he was little, before he got to be a man?'

'I don't know, Bernadette. I really don't.'

'Teresa?'

'What?'

'I'm glad you told me about our other brother.'

'Aye, it's a good job you've got me to spill the beans. Mind, I'm telling you, this is top secret.'

'Did he have a name?'

'Died before he was meant to be born, so no, I doubt it.'

I put my finger on my lips, rubbing it all along the top then along the bottom fleshy bit, then back to the middle, and let it rest.

'My lips are sealed,' I say, relishing the feel of it.

Ritual

Teresa is at her school-friend's posh house in Gosforth and I have been invited to a bonfire party in Janet's back garden. I thought I'd been banished forever but Janet's mum smiles and leads me over the squishy turf to a bonfire of fallen branches, dead bushes, logs and leaves. In town, in the lanes, we burned old tables, chairs, mattresses, anything we could seize.

On Guy Fawkes its gets dark early, and once the fire takes, we stand round watching the flames while Janet's mum brings out hot thick soup. I never dreamed Guy Fawkes night could include food and never imagined pea soup would taste good. This is fantastic and afterwards baked potatoes are dished up, fluffy inside but with crispy skins. Baked potato with melted butter makes my mouth sing.

Since I made friends with Janet I've had cheese on toast, potato croquets, proper spaghetti and now, pea soup. In our house we only have breakfast, dinner, tea, and supper. Cheese on toast was my first lunch. Lunch was an entirely new meal.

When the fireworks are brought out so is a tray of orange pop, and a bag full of free sparklers. Janet's dad is home and takes charge of setting off the Catherine wheels, golden cascades, and rockets. Before holding sparklers we put on gloves. No one throws bangers or sets off jumpy-jacks so I never even shake. This outdoor party is cynchie soft, the least scary Guy Fawkes ever, and I come home gorgeously stuffed.

When proper winter comes it looks like a scene off a Christmas toffee tin lid, though I soon get sick of ploughing all the way from Middle Drive after school, where the bus drops me off. This once, I decide to sit on my satchel at the foot of The Rise and wait. Dad will be out on the Triumph and must be due back and will know which bus stop I got off at. I start to freeze in the snow but refuse to give up. He nearly always comes this way and is bound to arrive if I sit here long enough.

My arrival home two hours late has a bad effect on Mam.

'Thank heavens.' She sighs. 'You're a sight for sore eyes, child, and no mistake.'

I jolt about on stiff legs getting told off: her mouth frowning over my snow-caked eyelashes, and the tip of my beetroot nose sniffing in and out like bellows. My books are soaked, and my clothes saturated. The smell of left-over dinner makes my stomach rumble like a snowplough. On top of this, I have to listen to Mam going on and on about *being cut off in this Godforsaken place, miles from anywhere*. Such a fuss. She should have guessed where I would be, and Dad should have come and picked me up, like all those other days. Those other wonderful days when I hoped he would arrive and *he did*, booming round the corner, full throttle, like a knight on a charger to whisk me home.

In town, weather never made that much difference to what we could or couldn't do. Here in the country it means everything.

Last summer was so hot the house was full of moths flying in open doors and windows and Mam had to swim blocks of butter in cold water to stop it turning into liquid. Dad became an expert in killing wasps, one quick swipe with his cap and that was that. Stone dead. Millions were squashed. Unbelievably hot, now unbelievably cold. In town, weather was never an excuse to stay off school but now we're snowed in, and all the men in the street are knee deep, shovelling it into big heaps. The fireman, Dad, even Greg from next door, they are all out the front bent over spades. Janet's dad is away in Trinidad, and Dad says *is useless to the cause*.

Dad comes back in and I hear him complaining about the council and how they haven't supplied enough grit. Mam says if he uses any more salt she is going to run out, and will have none to flavour the food with.

'Cup of tea Joe, to warm you up?'

'Aye, gan on, kidda, stick the kettle on. Where's the bairns? Ah cannit hear nowt.'

I am practising drawing quietly, tracing whatever my sister finishes onto my drawing pad so my girls look almost as good as hers. Tracing is the answer.

Dad sneaks up behind us, sticking his freezing cold hands on the backs of our necks.

'Aaah!' I jump a height. 'Da, man!'

'Aaah!' Teresa shivers and shrugs. 'Look what you've done, you've made me make a mistake.'

'Yeese should be oot in the snow, good for the circulation,

not in here lazing aboot.'

'I don't think so.' Teresa says, looking up at Dad's blue cheeks.'

He wanders through to the dining room sideboard, where he keeps a supply of chocolate hidden among his shaving things, and comes back with one fat curled hand.

'Did yeese two knaa Ah'm ambidextrous?'

'Of course,' Teresa smiles hopefully, while he produces, not chocolate bars, but two silver intertwined pigs-tails he slides apart before our eyes.

'Chinese puzzles, great! Where'd you find *them*?' Teresa forgets the chocolate.

'Dad, Dad, Give me a go, give me a go!' I jump up.

'Wait, till I show ye how it's done. Are ye looking?'

We sit, glued while he unfastens, and refastens the pieces, then throws us the packet with the other puzzles in.

'Here, share them oot between ye. A tenant left them when he vacated his room.'

'Was he Chinese?'

'Foreign, aye. From the mysterious Orient.'

We go through the paired up puzzles but they are impossible to unlock.

'That'll keep ye occupied for a bit.' Dad laughs, going through to the kitchen to warm up on tea.

Having a landlord for a dad means he brings unusual treats that come *free gratis*. On days like these I wish I could stay off school forever, lounging in the warmth of the house, learning how to trace and draw and do puzzles from China, which is at the other side of the world; which is thousands of miles from here and all this incredible snow.

Ambition

The sky is windy and full of smudgy clouds, and even with the light on the garage is dark. I am in there pestering Dad because I am off school with bronchitis and have nothing to do. The scooter and motor bike stand side by side, getting in the way of Dad who is sorting out tools. The scooter has a flat tyre so Joey is riding his push bide to work.

'Will ye get doon off there and gan in the hoose?' Dad snatches Joey's helmet off my head.

'Ow Dad! Good job the strap was loose.' I rub my chin.

'Ah thought ye were supposed to be bad. What ye deein in here messing aboot?'

'I was just pretending to ride. I'm sick of being in the house.'

'Ah've got jobs to dee, ye cannit hang aboot here aal day.' Dad turns Joey's helmet upside-down, examines the straps, then gives a sarcastic laugh. Dad only needs a flat cap to protect his head.

'As much use as a chocolate poker, that,' he smirks, then clanks it back on the seat.

Mam drops the heavy shopping in the kitchen, smoothes her hair, then chases the cat who is brushing her legs. It has taken ages to get back from the village and she is aching for a cup of tea.

271

'You'll get a hoof up the behind, animal, if you don't mind out,' she warns.

'What's the marra, kidda?' Dad stands at the sink washing his hands. 'That knee playing you up again?' He nods towards the lump Mam got when she fell off the push bike, that has never gone down.

'Bus didn't show up, that's twice this week.'

All the trouble Mam took trying to learn to ride, to get out and about on a bike, not be stuck in the house or relying on the bus.

'Drivers divvent like steering them buses in high winds. Get blown aboot too much.'

Once the cups are filled, they sit at the yellow table and Mam tells Dad the village gossip about the boy who drowned in the River Pont last month. It happened in the middle of the day but no one saw him being swept away. The boy drowning has been the talk of the place and makes Mam think we should all learn to swim. But there are no swimming baths except in town so it's just another thing to add to her list of complaints; not being able to do anything, or go anywhere under her own steam.

In the afternoon Dad transfers to the dining table and writes cheques to pay bills and rates. He hates paying the rates any time but the council have sent a letter saying he must demolish the new shed so he is in a bad mood about that as well.

'*Obstructing their view.*' Dad reads it out again.

When the house was being built no one objected to the front shed, but now the couple from next door are complaining the new one to the side is blocking their view.

'Their view of what?' Mam asks.

'Wor back.'

'But it's a wilderness.'

Mam is planting flowers and shrubs at the front, but changing the rest into a garden will take ages and she has barely started on the back.

'Those two have been sitting with a pair of binoculars trained ower here since the day we moved in; waiting their chance to find something to complain aboot.'

'What an odd pair they are. There's no way anything on our land is in their way.'

'Divvent want the likes of us lowering the tone of the neighbourhood *what-what, old chap.*' Dad imitates Greg's snooty voice.

'I knew she was a funny one from the start: Cressida!'

'Well, the cooncil say it has to be demolished' Dad sneers, 'and those cooncil-wallers aalways get their way.'

'Those two stewmers, sat there in that dowdy little bungalow all the time you were putting it up, with not a word to say.' Mam is fuming.

'Aye, that's aboot the size of it. Only when the last slat of wood was nailed in, then they went straight to the cooncil, blabbing aboot the lack of light.'

'They don't even have a window in that side. Sheer cussedness I call it.'

'People like that, kidda. They wouldn't give the likes of us the time of day, can't stand seeing wor sort getting on. Working class getting above their station. Nah! They like to keep it aal for themselves. Working class ambition makes them worry.'

'Could you not appeal against the decision?'

'Waste of time. Cannit win against officialdom. Between themselves and the toffs they've got it aal carved oot'.

'It's so sly, saying nothing to your face then stabbing you in the back like that.' Mam's fingers go round and round, circling each other faster and faster like helicopters about to take off.

'Crackers! Greg and his tart think they're a cut above, *don't you know*. Their sort live in *bangalows* not hooses. Divvent knaa what a hoose is. Not proper toffs either, just toffee-nosed southerners.'

'They've got nerve to talk. Her hair hasn't seen a comb in years, and that beard he's got...'

'Never learned hoo to shave yet, that bugger. Even the fireman noticed his feeble attempt at shovelling snow, said he might as well have used a spoon for aal the elbow grease he put in. Couldn't box his way oot've a paper bag.'

'A stranger to manual labour.'

'Them snooty buggers divvent care what they dee, hinny. Like royalty: one rule for them, another for the rest of us.'

'Stuck up madam she is anyway.'

'Aye, too posh for the likes of yee, kidda. An ugly bint anaal: Ah've seen Lester Piggot ride horses better looking than that.'

This is one of the Big Conversations that takes gallons of tea and makes Dad smoke loads of tabs. I listen hard so as not to miss anything and join in with their sighs.

'Might as well get it ower and done.' When the teapot is empty and their cups drained to the dregs Dad lumps out the back, walking as if his legs are filled with lead and his head is far too heavy for his neck.

'You'll not get all that done in one afternoon, Joe.'

'Ah knaa, but the sooner Ah start to demolish the bliddy thing, the sooner they'll be able to rest, and stop gaping ower here as if there's nowt else of interest to occupy their lives.'

Drowning

A framed picture of Meena and Joey sits on the sideboard. They are dressed in Sunday best with pudding basin haircuts, each clutching a teddy as if it's a matter of life or death. The two of them stare ahead, three eyes looking right into the camera, and one of Meena's off to the side. She hasn't had the squint straightened yet and I can't tell if it's before or after the thing that happened, the thing that can never be talked about.

'It was long before you were born,' Teresa says, 'and Mam was pregnant with me so she was very fat.'

At last.

I cross my legs and tuck my skirt in under my bum and listen with my ears out like trumpets.

'It was our Meena who told me and I had to cross my heart and hope to die, so you can never ask her anything about this, and never breathe a word to anyone else.' Teresa stares and I cross my heart and hope to die.

'Promise?'

'Promise, yes.'

The very next day a letter arrives from Stoke-on-Trent. It includes a picture of my nephew, John, that Mam shows around. The letter goes straight into the sideboard drawer so

I have to wait until there is no one about before sneaking in and reading it.

All day long I think of what Teresa said, keep going through it in my head, over and over and over again. At bedtime I say goodnight to Joey as if everything is the same as before. I snuggle into Ted, but have aches in my legs and it takes ages to drift off. When I finally do I see our Meena sitting on the path outside the old house, she has on the green dress from years ago, and is laying a pack of cards out.

'What you playing?' I ask, as if nothing is unusual.

'Patience,' she says.

'What I haven't got?'

'What you haven't got and also a game. Hey, should I show you a new trick I've learned?'

'Go on, yes.'

Meena's hands start moving the cards fifty to the dozen.

'Cut,' she says, and I do.

'Cut again.' I do it again.

'Say a card,' she says.

'Queen of hearts.'

She taps the pack with her longest nail then turns over the top card.

'There you are.'

It's the queen of hearts.

'Do you remember, Bernadette, when you used to think I was a magician who could make anything happen, just by wishing?'

'Did I?'

'Impossible of course, but I did sense things sometimes.'

'What things?'

'Come on, I know Teresa's told you about what happened.'

'You mean the *incident?*'

'That's it, yes, the *incident.*'

'Well, she did tell me, but only under pain of death if I repeated it.'

'It's okay, Bernadette. Don't look so worried.'

Meena pats the ground and I slide down beside her onto my hunkers.

'I want to explain, that's all, tell you exactly what happened in case she left anything out.'

'Alright.'

I gaze at Meena's face and watch it go into a sort of trance.

'I was five, our Joey six,' she starts. 'It was fiercely hot after lots of rain and the river was torrential.'

'We're going to cool off,' Joey said. 'Come on slow coach, hurry up.'

I wanted to tell Mam we were going out of the street but Joey said *leave it, no time for that.* A band of us saddled up, tally-hoed and galloped to the waterside; hurtling through the desert, shielding our eyes from the blazing sun. Pretending was so much fun. Once we got there we would dismount, tie our thirsty horses up, let them take a drink.

'Cross over now,' Joey called. 'Come on, quick.'

At the last road before the river I ground to a halt.

'Softy!' Joey yelled, speeding up to catch the others, racing off.

In a second they all vanished. I stood dead still, couldn't budge. The sky was clear and silent, no birds, no traffic. Then it happened, the whirlwind whipping up from nowhere, spinning me like a top.

I screamed for our Joey. The stripes on my skirt twirling round my legs, tying them in a knot. I was stuck. There was only me left; caught in the eye of a storm on the calmest of calm days.

As quickly as it came it went. I staggered, turned, steamed home as fast as my legs would go. Back in our street I calmed down, my blood stopped boiling, my heart stopped pounding under my vest.

It was hours before the search party came across the boy's toy drum at the bottom of Skinnerburn steps. His body drifted for ten days before a watchman found him at wharf twenty-three, near Ouseburn Lock; exactly a mile from where he fell in.

When they came to our house the massive policeman with the purple face shouted at our Joey and said he had pushed the boy in. Joey's legs shook like leaves, but he stayed silent and refused to speak. Mam could never make him say anything, not a word. Not one word on the subject all these years.

I wake up with a sweaty neck and damp pyjamas. Teresa says I was talking in my sleep. *Hallucinating* she says.

'Secrets,' she says, hopping from her bed and giving me a hard nip. 'Remember what I said.'

I would try to get her back but can't make myself move. It must be a fever, but I refuse to be unwell. The last time I was ill the doctor made me drink liquid iron through a straw. He said if the mixture touched my teeth they would go black and drop out. I can't go back to the dentist who put me to sleep and told lies about how many extractions he would make.

'Do you have a temperature?'

Teresa looks at me sideways for a minute, as if I am making her worried.

'No, and don't tell Mam on me. And don't make her bring the thermometer.'

'Don't fret, I won't.' She waggles a finger. 'But you better get ready quick. And don't ever forget what I said, or else.'

I nod, and she goes off. My head knows so many secrets now it feels as heavy as a grate.

Bird

———— ● ● ● ————

The garden has started growing again and smells of fresh grass. From a distance it looks like a baby's pink mitten has been dropped on the back path, but close up we make out a tiny bald bird. Teresa cups its floppy head, examining its buttery beak and beady eyes, and even though it has not one feather, decides to save its life. We search in the garage, emptying a small box of nails then lay it inside on a piece of cotton wool.

'Must have been chucked out of its nest.' Joey comes to inspect it without much hope.

We look up at the gutters for signs of a nest or hovering birds.

'Must have fallen from right up there.' My neck cricks from leaning back.

'You don't say, genius. Come on if we're going to rescue it we're going to have to find it some grub.'

'What sort of food do you think it will like?'

I have a horrible hunch.

'Wormy food.'

'Worms! Urgh! No, I'm not doing that.'

'Do you want to save the chick?'

'Ye..yes.'

'All right, let's go, I'll get a knife to slice, you start digging.'

Teresa should think about being a nurse not an artist because she doesn't seem to mind horrible tasks. I won't even touch the bird never mind slice worms for it. And I don't think Mam will be too delighted about using her kitchen knife.

After a couple of days it gives up. Joey pokes Teresa in the ribs and suggests we treat the cat to a delicacy. Teresa is not amused and insists on giving it a decent Christian burial.

'In the name of the Father, and of the Son, and of the Holy Ghost...' After that she's stuck.

She has only done dolls' Christenings before now and has never conducted a funeral.

'Throw a bit of dirt on the box,' Joey says.

I bend down to pick some grit.

'Ashes to ashes, dust to dust,' Teresa resumes.' Remember bird that thou art dust and unto dust thou shalt return.'

It was such a lot of trouble dissecting worms and shoving them down its throat with Mam's eyebrow tweezers. If it wasn't for that one long hair tangling in its tongue and choking it, it might have been all right. Teresa says it was one of mine, but my hair's not that long. It was definitely one of hers.

We tried so hard to keep the bird alive, and now it's dead tears sprout from under my closed eyelids and down my face. There again, I don't know what we would have done if it had survived. How does anyone tame a bird then turn it back into being wild?

Lying on my bed, I picture the old woman who lived in the basement at Malvern Street and kept the talking bird. I wonder what happened to her and her black teeth, and the big jar of sticky sweets, and the bird who had her voice and was locked in a cage.

When I wake, my first thought is of the little boy who drowned in the village, and my second thought is whether I should to learn to swim. My mind leaps from one thing to another: the night I ran away, and the confession I overheard. Joey's secret, kept since he was six. And all the ones I have to keep now, that make me want to burst.

I try to imagine what that would be like, keeping a massive secret locked inside you all your life?

Lip

— ● ◉ ● —

In the silence of the country Dad's motorbike can be heard a mile off and every night I keep an ear out for the sound of him returning from the pub. Tonight he's late and Mam has already told me three times to get away to bed. I am so tired I drift off on the settee but keep making myself wake up to be first to tell him about the bird.

At last, I hear him pulling onto the drive but there is no sound of slamming doors, or locking up, just loud laughs as he comes through to the lounge, then the sight of the Triumph's headlamp plastered with blood and swinging from his hand.

'What did I tell you?' Mam says, as if she's already said something else.

'It's alreet. Calm doon.'

Dad staggers in and Mam rushes over to him. I pick up a cushion and squeeze it under my chin.

'What on earth?...What on earth's happened, Joe?'

'Nowt. Ah'm alreet.'

His body sways but he keeps his feet planted on the lounge carpet, blood leaking on to it like a dripping tap.

'Ah was driving straight then Ah saw this traffic island saying *Keep Left* and Ah suddenly thought, nah! Just for a change Ah'm ganna gan right.'

Mam's mouth opens but she is lost for words.

'Aye, right instead of left, that's what Ah said. Nee use looking at iz like that.'

Dad is very bloody and very drunk, but talks as if he's had brilliant good luck.

'It's a wonder you didn't get yourself killed, lad.' Mam bends him into a chair, and tells him off like a child, as if he's one of us.

'Ah nah. Look at this.' He holds up the headlamp as blue, green and gold wires fall out like snapped veins; the shiny chrome all slimy and greased with red stains.

Mam runs through to the kitchen, brings cotton wool and Dettol and a bowl of warm water to clean his face and chin. She wipes his forehead, eyes, and nose, before noticing his mouth, the cake slice of upper lip torn out.

'What's this? Half your lip's missing.'

'Must've left it somewhere on the road,' Dad tries to grin. 'That'll be breakfast for the crows, kidda. Bord food.' He chuckles like a nut.

I sink back on the couch and try to stop my heart lurching about.

'I have to get you to hospital somehow. That'll have to be stitched up.'

'Aye, Ah'll see to that in the morning, kidda. Ah'm tired. Ah'm gannin up to bed.' All at once his energy goes and he looks wrecked. 'It'll dee for the morra,' he says.

'Might as well save my breath.' Mam takes the bowl of pink slop to pour down the sink while Dad hauls himself to bed, and the open wound has to wait.

The red line down his top lip slowly fades, but Dad's face is not as handsome as it was. There is no spare flesh to fill the space so his lip has to be stretched and pulled aside to be stitched in place.

Once the bike is fixed he says he will stick to a few jars in the village instead of riding from Newcastle in the pitch dark. There is the Blackbird or the Diamond or the Five Stars. And from now on, riding the wrong way round traffic islands is strictly barred.

Mam manages to scrub the blood from the lounge carpet but can't settle now when he's out at night. Up and down off the settee, over to the curtains, fidgeting, peering down the street. Waiting for his return, her hands and feet, twitch, twitch, tap, tap, tap. Whispering away to herself when she thinks she's out of earshot, wondering and worrying until she wears the carpet thin and he eventually turns up:

'Where is he?'

'What's keeping him?'

'Where can he have gotten to?'

'When's he coming back?'

Drowning

— • ● • —

Saturday evening is mild so we take our time to ride to the village. Wearing jeans makes peddling so much easier, and makes me and our Teresa feel free as birds. Trying to hold our skirts in the wind and keep both knees together is a thing of the past. Jeans are genius.

She's Venus in Blue Jeans,
Mona Lisa with a pony tail...

The country air is full of sweet scents, *and* a few others.

'Hold your nose. Urgh, that's rank,' Teresa says.

'Pooh-wah! What a pong.'

'Stop wobbling all over the road, Bernadette.'

'But, I'm holding my nose.'

'Then stop it for God's sake...before you crash!'

The whiff of cow dung is awful but I do as she says.

In the village we park on the stone bridge and peer over the wall. The river is calm and shallow and it's hard to imagine it running fast. Even I couldn't get swept away in that. Not the way it is today.

'Teresa, you know the boy who drowned?'

'Who drowned here?'

'No, not here, the other one, the one our Joey...'

291

'...I told you not to.' Teresa drops to a whisper.

'I know, I know, keep your hair on, I'm not.'

'I mean it, Bernadette, I don't want you ever...'

'...to mention it again, I know, and I won't but can I just ask one question?'

'The last one then,' Teresa glares. 'The last one forever and for all time?'

'Agreed.'

'Go on then.'

'Would you tell me his name?'

'Why do you want to know that?'

'No reason. Just do.'

'Anthony...Tony. He was three years old, the window cleaner's only child.'

'Our window cleaner? Paddy? Paddy who used to give us Spangles?'

'No, not him. Now look, that's all I know, and that's from Meena, second hand. Will you drop it now?'

At that moment some village lads appear and start chatting, asking our Teresa questions and leaving me out. Then as if from nowhere, we spot Dad sauntering across from The Diamond. He stops to say hello, and asks if we are alright.

'Fine.' Teresa says, going pink because Dad is talking to us in front of lads. He eyes them up and down then acts as if they're invisible.

'What time yeese getting off home?'

'Soon.'

'Make sure ye dee. Divvent be hanging aboot here.'

'I said soon, Da.' Teresa's voice dips so the boys won't hear her being told.

'Alreet, make sure ye dee. Ah'm away for one last jar at the Seven Stars.'

Once he's gone the boys point and scoff at Teresa's beetroot cheeks.

On the way home we cycle up Callerton Lane, singing loud all the way:

> *Each night I ask the stars up above,*
> *why must I be a teenager in love?*

In the morning when we come down, Mam is pacing about like a cat on a hot tin roof.

Then we get it, both barrels right in the neck:

Past eleven... sick with worry... damn kids ...end of my tether... had enough.

'He's such a snitch.' Teresa says, once we manage to dodge out of Mam's way.

We are in the dog house but there is no sign of Dad or his big mouth.

'I wouldn't care but I didn't even speak to those lads.' I can't believe this. 'It's only you boys ever want to talk to. Why am I getting blamed?'

'If you didn't follow me about all the time, I wouldn't always have to answer for you as well.'

'Why shouldn't I come?'

'Because I'm fourteen and you are still only ten.'

'So? That's no reason.'

Teresa rolls her eyes and scowls 'I give up,' she says, sounding just like Mam.

From now on we are forbidden to go into the village after dark, and from now on we have to be back in the house for, at the latest, 10 o'clock.

Runaway

— ◦ ◉ ◦ —

Since Teresa is allowed to go to town, and stay at her friend's swanky house, I hardly get a look in at the mirror. These days she is always there first, hogging it, plastering Panstick over her manky chin, or staring at herself and squeezing blackheads and mattery spots that leave yellow streaks on the glass. It's enough to put anybody right off a colour.

Since we went to the pictures to see The Young Ones I've asked her a hundred times to go again but all she says is, *we'll see,* in that lah-de-dah, Jane Eyre voice, as if she is my governess.

Joey couldn't be bribed to go with me because of the first time, when he was *forced* to take me to the Savoy and will never let me forget. He said I showed him up blaring like a siren when Snow White bit the apple and died. But I was only three and it was so sad anybody would have cried.

In desperation I even ask Mam to come, but she's got no interest in Cliff Richard or any of *those boys*. The only film she ever took me to was The Nun's Story, and until they make a film about Ireland, or the Pope, I know she won't go again, and will only want to stay in watching Coronation Street. If I so much as put Cliff on the record player she leaves the room as if her ears have been stabbed:

> *One comb, one key, two nickels, but gee-ee,*
> *where is it, where is my heart?*

I wake up to the sound of a scream and have to lie for a minute trying to figure out where it came from. Teresa is dead to the world so it can't be her, nor me. A dream, that was it: our Meena tipping my pram up again, a big smile as she lets the handle go and I fall to the pavement and crack my head.

I wonder what she is up to today so far away from the smell of sausages and bacon wafting in under our bedroom door. I get up and dress as fast as I can without waking my sister.

'Can I have a raise Dad?' I decide to ask straight after breakfast. Dad is finishing off a fry up so will be in a good mood.

'What ye wanna raise for?'

'To start buying records. I've only got two and can't afford to get any more on the pocket money I get.'

'Give ower, Ah've hardly enough for mesel.'

'Arrh go on, Dad, go on.' I give him my very best begging face.

Dad mops up the last smudge of fat with a heal of bread, tops up his and Mam's teacups, picks up the Daily Mirror and turns his back.

'Hey, kidda, here's something for ye, the farmer says he wants twenty-five quid for those trees at the bottom of wor garden.' He puts the paper back down.

'Twenty-five pounds, for the trees and the land?' Mam rests her cup and starts rubbing her knees round and round as if her fingers are thinking.

My brain gets excited: those trees are huge and great for games, and we could build an official tree house with ropes, and have swings and a hammock; and that avenue between the trees is a perfect short cut and trims five minutes off the walk to the bus stop.

Dad deliberates.

'What will you do?' Mam's hands go faster. And my head whizzes.

'Ah'll consider it. Twenty-five quid though, it's a bit steep.'

'It's a decent strip, Joe.'

'Ah nah, Ah nah, but twenty-five quid's, twenty-five quid. If he'd said twenty…But they're greedy buggers those farmers.'

He looks back at me and puckers his mouth.

'Here,' he says, feeling in his trouser pocket. Here's a few bob, gan and buy yersel a record. And make sure it's nowt too loud.'

I hug his neck then run from breakfast room clutching the warm coins. I have money for a record; and if Mam can talk him into it we will own the trees at the bottom of the back garden. Excellent.

On the morning of the Blaydon Races centenary Mam lets me go to the village on my own. I wear Teresa's cast-offs: a red paisley skirt and matching swirly blouse. I take the footpath, rather than risk the spelky fence, then on the bus get a half to town. Apart from the night I left home unnoticed, this is one of the sneakiest things I have done.

On Northumberland Street I have a great view of the celebrations and parade. Miss Newcastle wears a crown and sits on the top of a float and waves. I follow the procession as it snakes through the city and no one in the crowd looks twice or stops to check my age or ask if I'm alright. I must look like a proper adult and this is better than running away because I don't have to think about staying out all night, or wonder where to sleep. I'll be home in time for tea and no one will notice the difference.

By the time the procession gets to Marlborough Crescent I realise how much of the afternoon has passed and head back for the bus; stopping at a booth to pose for a strip of photographs with a spare half crown I found lying in Dad's coat. Between each shot I make a different face: one smiling, one serious, one with a pout, and one making cross-eyes and holding up the medallion I borrowed from Teresa's drawer. I love its chunkiness, dazzling as it's swings, and only hope I can get it put it back before she notices it's gone missing from her things.

The pictures are still wet when they drop into the slot and I have to blow and blow before folding. On the way home I remind myself a hundred times not to let Teresa see them. If she ever finds out I took her medallion she will confiscate the outfit then flay me alive.

Teresa is nowhere in sight when I get in so I sneak upstairs and take off the medallion. Mam shoots up behind me like grease lightning and before I can return it she looms in with her arms folded.

'So, here you are at last.'

'What do you mean?' I try to sound innocent.

'Where on earth do you think you have been all day, madam?'

'Ju...just in the village.' I try to move away.

'Now you stand still and listen to me my girl.' Mam's arms unfold and grip my shoulders with the strength of Garth.

Oh no, here it comes. I sink onto the bed and the telling off starts.

Eye

I feel queasy from antiseptic fumes floating through Walkergate hospital. Dad has my arm in his and I tell from the squeeze he's glad he kept me off school to accompany him. The nurses looking after Mam are slim and quick, not like the giant at the General where I go for my check-ups:

'Just lean back dear. These drops don't hurt.'

She wears a green dress and has a grip like a vice, and when the sting dies off and my pupils are big as saucers she leads me to Mr Smith who says:

'You should never lose your spectacles unless a magpie comes in the night and steals them off your nose.'

Then Mam says mister this, and mister that, because he is a consultant and a consultant is very high up, and once he gets higher than a doctor he is called mister again.

'I've no idea where she lost them, Mr Smith.' Mam uses her poshest voice.

'Well, we'll give her another pair, courtesy of the National Health Service. Pink or blue, which would you rather have?'

'...Blue, err, Pink...No, blue...No...Yes...Blue.'

Either way I'm not wearing them.

'Blue, it is. Give this to nurse. And make another appointment. Righty ho! Mrs Keenan, make sure she keeps wearing them this time. They're no good in her pocket are they?'

'No, Mr Smith. Thank you.'

'Bring her back in six months.'

Mam loves doctors and hospitals, because she is always in them, and she adores Aneurin Bevan, who made the NHS, and is a true saint.

Once Dad finds our way through the corridors we make straight for a ward where other visitors' bums sag in green canvas chairs. Sister wears a navy dress with a white collar trim and her short dark hair is pinned under a neat white cap. She directs us to a small room at the side where Mam lies, looking tiny and ironed-in under the starched sheets of the big metal bed, both of her eyes bandaged.

At the foot of the bed my heart races and my legs refuse to take another step.

'Is she asleep, Dad?'

'Joe, is that you, Joe?'

'Hello, kidda. What have the stupid buggers done? I thought ye only had one bad eye? Ye look like you've got a part in a war film.'

'Don't you dare come in here and make me laugh. I have to keep perfectly still and not turn my head.'

'That'll keep ye oot of trouble for a bit.'

They have taken a thigh muscle and moved it to Mam's eyelid. If it takes, the lid will lift by itself and not have a droop. Ma will no longer have a funny eye and will be normal like the rest of us.

'Eh don't, Joe, don't!' Mam concentrates on being serious and only moving her mouth.

'They cover both to immobilise them. One follows the other automatically, so I have to have them both bandaged to stop them moving about.'

Dad sits down on the side of the bed to recover from the shock of thinking Mam has gone blind, but Sister spots him through the glass partition and marches straight in and tells him to get off the mattress. His bad knees forget to creak and he springs up like a rubber top.

Me poor Da, still having to obey orders. And me poor Ma, with the use of no eyes.

Outside we both gulp fresh air and sigh and Dad decides that as it's near-by we might as well take a trip to the seaside.

'Haway, we can get the bus from Station Road. Ah'll take ye for a plodge.'

Wallsend is where the shipyards are and where our Joey says Hadrian's Wall comes to a halt. There are huge cranes like big metal birds lining the river, and a massive sign saying Swan Hunters, Shipbuilders, where our Joey works. I realise now just how long his workday journey is.

Dad is in a happy mood so there's no expense spared. In the paper shop he buys me a pencil, a rubber, a sharpener, and a drawing pad. Then, instead of an ice-cream cornet from the kiosk we go inside the Rendezvous Café, its massive windows overlooking waves that bounce in the bracing wind of Whitley Bay promenade.

'Can I have a banana boat?'

'A banana boat? Yee divvent wanna gan oot in one of them, it's high tide, man. Ye might get swept away.'

'Har, har. Please Dad.'

'Alreet,' he brings out a handful of coins and gives them to the woman in the pink overall behind the counter. 'One banana boat, a pot of tea, and a ham sandwich.'

The ice-cream comes in a long diamond-cut dish, and apart from loads of ice-cream it has two whole bananas in it and a pile of fresh cream and golden syrup.

'That's too big for yee. Yee'll never eat aal that. Never...'

'Mmmm...' I admire it for five whole seconds, then plunge in.

'Two bananas! Yee've hit the jackpot. Divvent say nowt to anybody else mind or they'll aal expect two.'

Dad wolfs the ham roll then sits back with his cup of tea and lights a Senior Service.

'Two bananas.' He can't get over it. 'Yer deed lucky, ye.' He shakes his head and grins at me, as if it's beyond belief. 'That's a canny drop of tea anaal, and a canny bit of breed and butter.' The edges of the bread were spongy and soft; even the ham seemed extra pink, not like the shop-bought meat he says tastes like sawdust.

Before the journey home I nag a big bag of sweets. Dad is still feeling generous and I make the most of it. Mam is over the worst and tucked safely inside the green-tiled ward. We walk along the sand, arm in arm with nothing more to worry about. Perfect.

The taste of salt stays for hours and my hair is full of sand and makes my head itch. By bedtime I am so sleepy I can barely be bothered to say prayers, but have a list of thank yous to give so make the effort. I thank God for Mam still being alive, and for my best day out ever, just me and my Dad. I list everyone in my family, and ask God to guard and protect them. Then at the very end, I ask Him to look after the dead, including my unborn brother, and also Anthony, because he was only three-years-old, and was drowned.

Hen

When she was a nun Mam wanted to be a nurse but the reverent mother forced her to teach kids instead. Mam would never watch a programme about schools, but loves anything medical and when she gets home from hospital she watches Doctor Kildare and practices raising her eyelid up and down. She needs to build its muscle strength and wait for the gouge in her thigh to fill out. The only parts of her legs I see normally are between her hem and her shoes and it feels queer when she lifts her skirt and shows me the wound. I'm not sure I should look, but she wants to show me and make me go *Urgh!*

It's miles off being healed, and for a while she has another limp.

She tries hard at first but after a few weeks of effort, gives up. The eyelid returns to its original state and is just as bad as it was in the first place.

When our auntie comes over to visit from Ireland, it cheers Mam right up. I thought she was losing her marbles but now she is off singing, and laughing like a jug:

> *Oh, Mary, this London's a wonderful sight,*
> *The people here are working by day and by night...*

Dad is put on best behaviour and barely complains the entire week. We hardly see him except over meals and cups of tea, and he never once slurps from the saucer.

We go to town and explore all the clothes shops and find a store on Grainger Street where my auntie buys a matching set of buttermilk coat, bag, and shoes, then four ties to take back as presents.

Auntie Nora brings the sun, and our other Auntie, Agnes, who comes up from Cowgate and relates news of Irish dancing championships, and the dresses she makes for my cousins, and the ringlets that they hate, but that make their hair bounce when they do their reels and jigs.

Mam covers the shiny dining table with a fresh white cloth and makes a massive dinner with a huge joint of meat and new potatoes that sets everyone's mouths a-hum.

'You can taste the earth in these potatoes.' Auntie Agnes says; praising the taties because they taste of soil.

Chips, mash and roasts are the only sorts of potatoes I know worth praising.

After we've all finished, Mam and my aunties sit swapping stories.

'Do you know what I'm going to tell you?' Auntie Nora starts...

Me, Teresa and Michael sit on the bench under the kitchen window and eat raspberry jelly and strawberries and Mam brings us a tray of deliciously cold orange juice. Cousin Michael is older than me but younger than Teresa. He is youngest of four boys in his family and the only one Auntie Nora has brought.

He wears flannel trousers and has a school badge stitched on his maroon blazer which looks a bit mad next to his ginger hair.

'Mammy says it looks smart.' He says with his Irish lilt.

'But do you not have any other clothes?' Teresa asks. 'They're no good for exploring in.'

'Sure, it doesn't matter, I'll be grand for exploring.'

This morning he only got two branches up a tree and had to come down again. He and Teresa both tried swinging from it but that pair are much too clever to be any good at trees.

It's good having Michael here but he and Teresa have started having private conversations that leave me out; especially about when she visited Ireland before I was born.

'You lived by the harbour, and kept chickens?'

'You remember alright.' Michael goes pink, so all his freckles stand out.

'I remember the hens. Do you still have them?'

'No. Haven't kept them for long enough. Not for years, not since...' He gives Teresa an odd look. 'That one wee hen Mammy let me have. I cried when you and Auntie Mary came to visit and it was put in the pot.'

'What? What do you mean, cried?'

'Mammy let me keep it as...as a sort of...as a pet.' He says Mammy for Ma, which is babyish but cute.

'That was NOT the chicken we ate!' Teresa's mouth flops. 'Don't tell me we devoured your pet?'

'Mammy said we had to kill it because you were special guests.'

'We ate *your* chicken, *your* pet?'

'I didn't take any of it myself.'

'That explains...I knew you'd been in the huff.' Years later and the penny has dropped.

'Pardon me?' He doesn't understand any Geordie and doesn't get even one word of what Dad says.

'Your hen!' Teresa says, shame-faced.

'I was only a wee thing, sure I was.' Michael apologises.

He leans down and strokes the cat to stop us looking at his beetroot head. Jupiter purrs and weaves in and out of Michael's legs, moulting fur all over his grey school pants.

'Jupiter, here Jupiter.' I dangle my hand then swizzle my finger and thumb to get him to come: 'Psss...sw..sw..sw.. Psss... sw..sw..sw..' I scoop him up and pat him flat onto my knee. After listening to that horror story I don't want our cousin getting any ideas of revenge.

Before bed I sit at the dressing table mirror and make shapes with my mouth, doing my best to copy Michael's Irish twang.

'Would you look at that now, a cat named after a planet? Well, isn't that the be all and end all?'

Holiday

I race down the garden, pull off my sandals and socks then climb over the back fence, making sure no one's in sight. A lemon sun is on the farmer's field and I try to stay inside the tractor lines and not flatten any of the tickly wheat as I run through it.

The excitement of getting ready for next week's holiday to Ireland stops me being still for more than five minutes. Poor Dad has to look after his houses and poor Joey has to go to work, so they are staying home avoiding each other, while me, Teresa, and Mam are away having all the fun.

Before we go, Mam is buying us new clothes. The upper deck of the bus is rocky and she has to be persuaded to climb the stairs. Trees bulge out into the narrow roads, thwacking the windows and muffling our argument.

'Did I say you were? Now, keep your voice down.' Mam wants to look respectable and hates public embarrassment.

'I'm only saying I don't want to be dressed the same as Bernadette. I don't want any identical things.'

Being fourteen has turned Teresa into a right misery guts.

The bus ceiling is low so tall people have to bend to fit into the five-seat rows. It's coated with thick nicotine and someone has smudged rude messages. The seats are bunched together because of the low bridge at Callerton Pit. If it were any higher the roof would rip off and passengers would be decapitated.

In town Teresa chooses a green sleeveless dress and I choose dusky pink to be different. The Roaring Twenties is my favourite TV programme and these are just the style Pinkie wears in it. Mam gets a white summer dress with a green leaf pattern, and a new white hat with a bit of net, and cream summer gloves and cream sandals.

When the day comes we take a train to Carlisle, then another to Stranraer, then a ship to Larne: my first ship, then another train to Newcastle County Down.

Everyone is dog-tired but revives in the sea air. The sea is on our left and the mountains are there, directly in front. We walk to the boarding house and Mam carries the suitcase along Main Street, passing amusements and dodgem cars along the way. They smell rubbery like a dentist's gas mask, even so, I can't wait to come back and have a go.

Mam's relatives organise a family reunion at the cottage where she grew up. The foothills of the Mourne Mountains are in the middle of nowhere and the house is so small I can't imagine how all the people she lived with fitted in.

Auntie Nora brings Michael, and Auntie Agnes travels over from Tyneside the same as us. Everyone is back together. We have tea and cakes, and a load of ham sandwiches; and no chicken whatsoever.

When Dad turns up the day after rent collecting it's a complete surprise, though we should have guessed because he always manages to make it in the end. I am first to spot him sauntering along the seafront, and run ahead to give him a big squeeze. Mam says he likes her to go first, to carry all the cases and sort everything out. But she's just as pleased when he arrives, and he sucks in the rush of salty air and says it's just the job.

At the end of the week we go over the border to County Meath. Dad takes me and our Teresa on a jaunting car and recounts the boyhood accident when he fell off. I remember our Meena saying five of Ireland's top surgeons had taken hours to stitch his leg back in place.

'Nearly lost that peg,' he says tapping his knee as if it's funny. The driver laughs and whips the horse to go faster and I grip the blanket over us and pray like mad, until it stops.

When we come home I see the farmer's wheat has been cut and piled into square stacks. The back field has completely changed. I take my shoes and socks off and climb: one, two, three, jump! My soles are soft and it takes a minute to feel the hard wheat stumps. I push on, but with each leap daggers dig my feet, sharp as broken glass.

'Ow, ow, ow!' I'm out quick fast.

Back on our side of the fence I glare at all the vicious little spikes. My feet feel ripped to shreds but when I lean down to examine my soles thankfully there is no blood in sight.

Mam is busy unpacking, washing, ironing, and putting things away, replaying holiday conversations. When Dad talks to himself he does all the different voices, and doesn't care what anybody thinks. He says talking to himself is the only way he hears any sense. Mam hates being caught in the act, jumping out of her skin when I limp back in the house.

'Stop your antics,' she says, as if I'm the one acting peculiar.

The Nun's Story

Our school play is set in the Revolution and I am playing a French aristocrat. While the rabble jeer I cross the stage with my head held high, then kneel. I have four words to memorise and deliver before submitting to the guillotine. I have a part and four words and have never been so terrified.

Forgive them my Lord, I say haughtily, then cast a defiant look towards the baying crowd, and the waiting basket.

'Forgive them my Lord.' I learn my four words off by heart and also the French national anthem that the whole school sing together at the end; all in honour of Madeleine Sophie Barat, the Sacred Heart's founder.

Olivia is teacher's pet and has the lead, and stacks of words to learn. She is a nun and wears a long black habit exactly the same as our headmistress. Her face is blinkered by a stiff horseshoe frill that pushes her cheeks out like a hamster. I am wearing the apple-green frock donated by Olivia's ballroom-dancing mother. It has layered silk skirts and beaded net and a sequinned bodice that twinkles when I move. My bonnet has satin ribbons to show my aristocratic rank. Dressing like this is worth being nervous for, worth a short life and a horrible death. This outfit could hardly be more perfect.

Forgive them my Lord, whoever they are.

Look at me in this!

'Do you want to come and see my school play Joey?'

I find Joey slouched in front of the television and decide to pester him.

'What is it?'

'It's about the French Revolution and the nun who founded the order of the Sacred Heart. I play a lady and have to say *Forgive them my Lord,* before they cut off my head.'

'Nah! I'm busy.'

'I haven't told you when it is. Anyway, I thought you liked history?'

'I'm an atheist.'

'What's an atheist?'

'An atheist doesn't believe in God, and doesn't have anything to do with religion.'

'Is that why you don't go to church, even at Christmas?'

'No interest.'

'I wish I was an atheist.'

'You're too young.'

'How old do I have to be?

'Twenty-one. I don't know, go and ask Ma. See what she says. I'm watching telly.'

'Awh, come on Joey, you're not even interested in this programme. Haway, show me how to play another game of cards?' Suddenly his head lifts. Got him!

'Well, if you go and find Teresa, I might show the two of you how to play whist.'

'Is it easy to learn, like rummy and pontoon?'

'I'll explain as we go along, but I'm only playing if there are three in the game. It's not worth it for two.'

'Not with marked cards mind?'

'There's no point in playing with marked cards is there? Not since I showed you how to read them.'

'No wonder you always won.'

'I can win anyway, beat you fair and square. Go and find Teresa and we'll have a game.'

Ma is the only one who comes to see the play because it's on a school day and everyone else is busy. She wears her silky cream gloves and keeps twisting the finger ends as if it's her who's nervous and not me, though it's my heart flapping like wings. She says I look very nice and so do loads of people I have never seen before, and forget as soon as they go away. Olivia acts calm and holy like a real budding saint, but I don't think I'm cut out for the stage, because my legs jump about like beans and wobble like jellies. Jelly beans.

After the play we are allowed to come straight home with our parents. I want to keep the make-up on, but Mam makes me wipe it off because we are taking the trolley from Fenham into town, and she refuses to have me out in the street covered in clart.

We go to Farnons to buy underwear then the market for meat, then up to the Haymarket for the number five. Getting on at the terminus means we get two good seats.

I am happy just to sit, and not even bothered that we don't go upstairs until Mam gives me a nudge and smiles at some woman standing over us.

'Offer the lady your seat, Bernadette.'

'Eh?'

'Come on pet, there's a lady standing.'

I am exhausted and have to drag myself up. That's it for me with downstairs. From now on I am going up whether Mam is here or not. There is no standing up there and you never have to give your seat up to an adult, and I don't mind inhaling fumes unless the smoke clouds are really thick.

At supper time Mam makes Ovaltine and brings a plate of Rich Tea, sinking into an armchair with a sigh then plumping up two cushions and tucking them in behind her back.

'Mam?'

She wiggles her slippers around as if it's *her* feet that are tired from standing.

'Mmm?'

'Is Dad an atheist?'

'Of course not,' she says through a mouthful of biscuit, 'what on earth makes you say that?'

'Because he doesn't go to church.'

'That doesn't make him an atheist. He still believes.'

'Does he?'

'Of course he does.'

'Then why did he say you should take Teresa away from the Saint Anne's and send her to the Protestant school in the village?'

'Oh that.' Mam sounds surprised, as if she didn't know I knew. 'Prying ears never hear any good, and always misinterpret.'

'I wasn't prying I just heard him saying it last night when you were having a Big Conver...having a conversation.'

'We were talking about paying Teresa's school fees, if you must know, and he always complains when they're due. Especially this time, because they've gone up again.'

'It's not fair. Why does Teresa have school fees? Why don't you pay school fees for me?'

'Because Teresa goes to a private school, and you don't.' She let's out a big loud breath, straightens her cup and saucer and arches her back a little further onto the cushions. 'Now finish your Ovaltine and stop,' she yawns. 'Your school is good enough.'

Private school: that's another thing Teresa gets that I don't.

'Urgh!' I spit a mouthful back into the cup: the sludge at the bottom I didn't realise I'd reached.

'...Mam?

She's not even listening.

'Mam!' I louden up. 'You know the French revolution?'
'Mmm?'

Her head nods forward then jerks awake.

'Did Marie Antoinette really force the peasants to eat cake?'

End of the World

———— ◦ ◦ ◦ ————

Today's school Mass is extra, and is being said for world peace. Everyone is praying like mad, hoping President Kennedy and Mr Khrushchev will come to their senses and not destroy the world. I am also praying to get revenge on our Teresa, because after months and months she discovered the snaps of me wearing her necklace and has cut them all up. Some people take things far too seriously.

Mam makes a packed breakfast and sends me on my way as usual. A day off seems out of the question, because class Mass is at nine o'clock, and praying for the world is our best bet.

The altar boys push back the blackboard then pull white lacy vestments over their uniforms and light two massive candles. By the teacher's desk, one shakes the incense burner and tinkles the bell before Communion, leaving the other to stick the silver plate under our chins in case any crumbs fall from the Body of Christ. Being an altar boy is a very important job and no girls are allowed to do it. Only a few boys are chosen. Our Joey is too old now, but he never got picked, even years before he was an atheist, which is, to this day, a sore point with Mam. At least me and my sisters couldn't disappoint her in that respect. I hate to think how nervous any of us would have been, trying to say Latin, and being scrutinised by the whole congregation.

After Mass our stomachs wail. The milk monitor passes

bottles round and I sit on my desk and get tucked in to my bait. Soon the classroom stinks of cream and dough and hard boiled eggs.

All the teachers, apart from Mother Lister who is doing yard duty, are in the staff room having their last chat, and their last biscuit, and their last cup of tea. For some reason they want us in the playground when the bombers appear. We try to act normal, play bulldog, tuggy-on-high, and jacks. But every time a plane approaches we hear the sound of death.

One rumbles directly over us and every one stops, as if the whistle has been blown. We all go silent and I start to feel dizzy from looking up. The plane is opening its bomb doors, the nuclear missiles are about to drop.

Time slows.

Time stops.

It's the wrong plane.

Not the bomb plane.

We start up again.

We carry on. My turn to skip:

The wind, the wind, the wind blows high-er,
in comes Bern-ie from the sky-er,
Isn't she beautiful, isn't she sweet?
Tell me the boy that she will meet...

We speed up.

It's after twelve-o-clock.

The time to be blown up has passed.

The whistle goes.

We line up.

Everyone is still alive.

We go back inside.

Mam says she knew President Kennedy would stop the Russians from dropping a bomb on us. She loves President Kennedy and his wife, the First Lady, as if they are saints; always shushing us if they come on the News, or if anyone on the television even mentions them. President Kennedy is a Catholic and his family emigrated from Ireland to America so I think she feels a bit related to him.

Meena

● ● ●

After the letter from Meena arrives, Mam gets some money off Dad, packs a bag and goes off to the Potteries. She shows him the letter but won't let me read it so I have to wait until it goes in the drawer with all the others.

Meena fills four sides of paper with news about Vince cheating, and her having a broken heart. She can't eat or sleep and doesn't know what to do. Then she sends all her love and prayers. This is how soppy my sister has got.

Apart from accidentally killing our Joey's goldfish, and accidentally smashing Meena's records, the most horrible thing I ever did was once squash some blue bottles. I think Vince is a lot more horrible than that. I stick the letter carefully back in the envelope the same way I pulled it out, then close the sideboard drawer as quiet as a mouse.

The difference between Mam going away, and Dad, is that she tells us when and where she goes. Dad just evaporates. Mam says he should be called Houdini, whose tricks he knows a lot about. Dad can make pennies appear from behind his ears and none of us can fathom it out.

Teresa says Vince is an adulterer, and Dad is a bigamist with a French wife. Every time he disappears to Paris he visits them, his other wife and their four children: three boys and one girl. They are our opposite family and all have dark hair and brown eyes and olive skin. I ask her to draw a picture as she imagines them. And she says she might, if and when she has the energy.

When Mam comes back from The Potteries, she says Meena and Vince have been reconciled. I smile and look forward to having proper dinner.

'Been on a wild goose chase, kidda.'

'She's forgiven him and taken him back.' Mam smacks her lips. 'So that's that.'

'Sit yersel doon here and get this,' Dad pours hot tea into his saucer and serves hers into a cup. He blows on the saucer, sips, then leans back and takes off his cap.

'She's pregnant again.'

Everybody stiffens up and stays quiet for a bit.

'Never should've given that bugger the time of day.' Dad lolls his head from side to side.

Mam leans down to take off a shoe, winces and rubs her foot.

Not everything is bad. I can tell Dad is glad to have Mam back and maybe this time I'll get a bonny little niece, and me and our Meena can dress her up in pink. She used to like plaiting my hair with ribbons, and carrying me about. And I used to like watching her back-comb, and making-up, and pressing the beauty spot just so, near the edge of her mouth.

Even after Mam has had three whole days to recover from the trip she still isn't with it.

'Did Philomena say if she wanted a boy or a girl?' I find her gazing out the kitchen window as if something fascinating is in the back garden. When *I* look I can't see anything but drizzle.

'It's not due for months.' Mam snaps back to life.

'But does she want a girl, so she can put ribbons in her hair and buy frilly dresses?'

'Probably, pet, probably. But honestly, I don't know. I forgot to ask about that.'

There are no more letters from our Meena for months. Dad says no news is good news but I think Mam wishes she would keep in touch.

Ambition

My whole class are being driven by coach to the Town Moor, to form a guard of honour for the Bishop. Our teacher says the Vocations Exhibition is even bigger than the Hoppings, with tons of priests, nuns, friars and monks. Mam sews a school badge on my beret then stitches the hole where I twirled the stalk out. I wear my red-checked dress and grey blazer, and pure white socks that make my plum leather shoes look extra smart.

I push into the front line where a photographer from the Chronicle is taking pictures. It all takes ages of standing about and when the bishop does finally comes he just walks up and down smiling and nothing else. Then, before there's a chance to explore it's time to get back on board the coach.

The school trip was a dead loss so at the weekend Mam takes us for a proper look. The Vocations site is massive and we walk for miles. Even Mam has never seen so many religious orders and our Teresa is that impressed she decides on the spot she wants to be a priest.

'I thought you didn't want to be a man?' I can't believe my ears.

'I don't! Well, not like a man who has to do work and look after a wife and children all his life.'

'What's wrong with being a nun? Some of them have

lovely veils. See those pale blue ones?'

'I don't want to be a teacher or a nurse thanks very much.'

When we get home Mam does dinner, then me and our Teresa lounge about for a couple of hours with Jup and Joey, waiting for the Horlicks and biscuits to be brought in.

I tell Joey about Teresa's new ambition and ask if he ever fancied being a priest when he was young.

'I can just picture you in a priest's collar, Joey.'

'Har, har, very funny. Actually I wanted to be a black belt in judo. Do you wanna see some moves?'

'Not from you. You don't know any.'

'That's what you think.'

'Will youse two shut it, I'm watching this.'

'Charming!' I sniff 'Coming from a priest.'

After supper I feel exhausted and for once don't mind going to bed. There is no moon and I can barely make out Teresa's curly lump under the other candlewick. It's gone cold and I tuck my bedspread right in around my neck. I try to imagine my sister in a black trouser suit with a massive crucifix but get a picture of a beret and a smock instead. She is definitely going to be an artist, nothing else.

First thing in the morning Mam pops her head round our bedroom door and starts making a noise.

'Lazy as sin!' She says as if she's miffed, but her voice is mild.

'Do you know what I'm going to tell you, Bernadette?'

Mam leans down and starts shaking the mattress, determined to wake me up.

'Don't you want to know who has their photograph in the newspaper? ...Oh all right then I'll leave you to it. Sleepy head.'

'Whaa...? Let's see! Let's see!' I spring up like a Jack-in-the-box, Teresa moans, still half asleep while I leap about.

'You'll have to come down.'

Two copies of The Journal are on the breakfast table and I am on the front of each one.

'There's me. And there's me. Hey! There I am.'

I am right in the front. There I am in my stitched up beret with no stalk. There I am, famous, waiting to be examined by the bishop.

'That's not yee.' Dad says, looking closely at the page.

'It is! It is!'

'How much did ye get paid for deein this?'

'Nothing.'

'Ye should never dee owt for nowt, especially for the press, not unless they pay a proper fee.'

'Honestly, Dad?'

'Wey, ye wouldn't catch Princess Margaret deein it for nowt, or Tony Armstrong-Jones, or any of those big knobs.'

'Was Princess Margaret there?'

'Take no notice of him pet. He's only having you on. Anyway it's a very nice photograph to be part of.' Mam holds the paper up, pleased as punch.

Rents

When he sees the Chronicle headline Dad's face is like a yard of tripe. Mam sits on the arm of the chair and reads over his shoulder. They read it over and over before the paper drops, and I see *The Kindly Landlord* in big letters right across the top. Our family is in the newspaper twice within a month, but this time it isn't good.

Mam sits stiff as a lamppost. The socks she was busy darning put to one side.

'Is it about you, Dad?'

Dad picks up the matches and lights a tab.

'Ye could say that.' He runs the back of his hand over his lips as if it helps him think.

I wonder if his picture is in, like mine was. I pick it up and examine the words.

'But they call you *kindly*?' I don't know what's so bad.

'Mm...mm.' Mam snatches the paper back for another look. 'That's not how it's meant, Bernadette. It's not meant as a compliment.'

The Kindly Landlord sounds nice but I realise it's not. *Kindly* must be *ironic*: a word Joey told me about. So when the reporter calls Dad kindly he really means mean, the exact opposite.

Mam wipes her sniffly nose on the hem of her apron and says *mud sticks*.

'Ah never should've given them house room,' Dad huffs, 'should've had more sense.'

'You weren't to know, Joe. How could you? The priest coming with a sob story and asking you to take them in.'

'Ah should've known better, but when a priest asks a favour what can ye dee?'

'They pulled the wool over his eyes, right enough.'

'A couple wi' kids living in one room. Never works oot.'

Dad didn't even want to give our Meena and Vince a room when she was pregnant. But she's his daughter and Mam forced him into it.

'Father thought them so plausible though.' Mam's fingers gallop as if she's racing to finish a piece of knitting.

'Easily taken in,' Dad rumbles on. The clergy, washing their hands, passing the problem on; then the blighters refuse to pay, crying to the newspapers when Ah try to get them oot.' He strokes his chin, as if considering a shave.

'Oh, how the worm turns.' Mam starts bringing in the animals.

'Aal this aboot them and *their plight*,' Dad pokes the paper, 'and me, *the greedy landlord*. Ye cannit dee reet for deein wrang man, kidda.'

'Pure play-acting,' Mam nods.

'Wasters, but what can Ah dee when a priest asks? And once the press get their claws in...'

Dad chucks his tab end to the back of the grate. '...Ah'll have to eat crud and say they can stay.'

'Eh, that's not right, Joe, what a pair of bliddy hooks, carrying on like that. Do you think they might be after compensation?'

'Cadgers like that refuse nowt but blows. But they can take a run and jump. They'll not get a penny, no matter what the papers dee.'

'Eee, what a situation. Give a dog a bad name.'

'Aal the press are interested in is selling their rags, hinny.' Dad drops his head and looks at his laces then reaches for another tab. 'They would see ye in the gutter soon as look at ye. It's aal the same to those buggers.' He takes a deep breath, coughs, then lights up again. He sucks so hard the coughing won't stop and the smoke pours down his nose instead of out of his mouth.

'Cup of tea, Joe? Mam smoothes her cheeks with both hands, then squeezes them in her palms. 'Maybe a little tongue sandwich?'

'Aye, gan on, kidda. Ah thowt Ah'd lost me appetite but gan on, Ah'll force something doon. Stick a bit mustard on as well. Aal this carry on's made me taste buds gan on strike.

Rituals

Since we moved to the country we only have to go to church once a week, on Sundays. Not having to go to Benediction is great for me but Mam misses regular visits. Saint Michael's parish was big and always had at least four priests. Saint Matthews only has two and neither of them call in to watch the wrestling, or pester Dad to go to Mass, not the priests or the Brothers or anyone else. Mam doesn't even know the organist, or have any parishioner friends.

Third row, left side, is our regular seat in the small church. Except for strangers everybody sits in the same place week after week. Mam takes her black rosary beads, kneels down, and says a quick decade before Mass. I watch her hands move round and round over the beads and notice all the brown stains on her thumb and fingers, a bit like Dad's but hers are from scraping potatoes not smoking tabs.

Today, extra prayers are being said for a boy knocked down in the village; another child in an accident. I join in, praying for him and his family, and also for the number five bus to show up. Last week we waited an hour-and-a-half and Mam was even more fed up than us because she has dinner to cook when we get home.

The worst part of the wait was the disappointment of the market gardeners pulling away, seconds after the excitement of them pulling up:

'Apologies for not offering you a lift.' Miss Swinburne

337

said, poking the end of her long thin nose over the passenger window. 'But, I'm afraid the space in the back is limited.'

It looked big enough to me. I'm sure we could have squeezed in. After all the money Mam's spent buying their stupid *produce* from their stupid greenhouse and baldy hens. What a pair of old snobs. I bet they only stopped because their car is the colour of sick and unmistakable, and Mam identified Mr Swinburne's creepy eyeballs close up so they couldn't sneak past.

After half a day out of the house, we finally get back and Mam takes off her hat and gloves and disappears into the house to put the kettle on. Dad is in the garage rummaging in a box of tools and mumbling to himself: doing all the different voices in his conversation.

'Alreet?' He braces his chest and stretches. The garden bench he made is lying on its side minus a leg.

'What you doing, Dad?'

'Have to find a six inch nail to fix this bugger.'

'Is that thing falling apart again?' Mam comes through, tying her apron.

'Do you want a cup of tea before I get dinner started?'

'Aye, gan on. Bring it oot here, will ye?'

Once the cups are brought, the work stops. Dad doesn't come to church but likes to hear what the priest talked about.

'The injured child has broken limbs but no brain damage, thank the Lord.' Mam raises her eyes to heaven for a second.

'Looks like the man who knocked him down is getting off as well. Mind he's lucky not to get jail.'

'Taking a drink then driving, that's the temptation living oot here, man.' Dad takes a gulp of tea and goes back to rattling the nails.

'Then you know all about that, Joe, don't you?' Mam gives him a look.

'Ah didn't flatten any kid. Ah was the only one injured.'

'That time, yes.' Mam says. 'You were lucky you didn't get killed, and lucky you didn't kill anybody else. This place is a death trap.'

Mam's face twitches as something rolls and lands with a clink. Dad bends to the dusty floor, grumbling as he goes.

'Ah well, nowt to be done aboot that.' He straightens up, changing the subject.

Teresa saunters off to do homework, which most likely means getting her sketch book out. I hang about in case I miss any more.

'What time you putting the dinner on, kidda, me belly thinks me throat's cut?'

'You and your stomach, Joe. I don't know.'

'Well, somebody's been working round here, while yeese lot've been oot enjoying yersels.'

'At Mass?'

'Aye, that's what Ah said. The three of ye doon at that church, not a care in the world.'

After last Sunday's apple dumplings I could hardly move. We always have pudding on Sunday but today it's only tinned peaches with Carnation milk, and apart from cooking the dinner and opening two tins, Mam hasn't bothered making a single thing; and dropped and smashed one of the best plates.

'If you want fresh fruit' she says 'take one of those pomegranates.'

Pomegranates have sweet juice but I keep stabbing my tongue with the pin and wish there was a better way to get at the ruby segments.

'Ow!'

If I'm not careful I'll have a mouth like a sieve and won't be able to eat anything at all, not just puddings. I chuck the two used halves of peel in the bin and rinse my claggy hands. Mam finishes off the pots and pans while Dad dries and talks. This is all very well but my tongue is swelling up and I have a headache started. And, come to that, I am pig sick of Big Conversations that stop as soon as I walk in the door.

The Loony Bin

First stop Coxlodge. That's what Dad always says about people who are gone in the head. Coxlodge is near Gosforth and that's where the loony bin is, and where we are going to see Mam, who is in it.

I've no idea what happened. I came in from school expecting to find her in the kitchen as usual, but instead of smelling dinner, there was Dad nosing in a bag of taties and scratching his head, with the cat yowling round his feet, half-starved.

'Where's Mam?'

'In hospital. Nowt broken. Divvent worry.'

My face went white as a sheet.

'What happened?'

'Took a bad turn. Divvent panic, she's alreet.'

He started running the cold tap full force over the spuds, a gush of muddy water spouting from the sink. I knew then, that was as much as I would get from him. If only Jupiter could speak.

Dad says Mam is not in the part where the really loonies are. Collingwood Clinic has no locks or bolts, so patients can come out if they really want. It's not like we are going to find her strapped in a straight-jacket he says with a laugh that makes me even more worried.

Going to get check-ups at the eye hospital is easy compared to this. My heart is in a flap and I have to nip myself hard and dig up a smile. Visitors should smile no matter what. I put on my widest grin and quicken up.

The building has no bars on the windows, and, true enough, no one is tied up. In the large room full of high-backed chairs Mam sits in her fur-trimmed slippers, her feet hardly touching the floor. I never knew she was that small before. Sunshine beats through the glass doors onto her salmon pink cardi and the paisley pleats of her dress. I say hello quietly; the room is full of strangers who might be other patients but no one wears a uniform so it's hard to know.

'Priest's been in.' Mam breaks the ice. 'Chaplain to the hospital.'

'Oh, aye?' Dad is quiet as well.

'A young Irishman, gave Communion. He was very nice.'

'Oh, aye?'

'How are you, Joe, you look a bit tired?'

'Am alreet.' Dad is holding his cap and wiping his brow on his sleeve. 'They giving ye enough to eat in here, kidda? Ye look as if ye haven't been fed for a week.'

'Well that's good. I could do with losing a bit weight.' Mam touches her belt then fiddles with the dress material around her knees, scrunching it up then smoothing it out; scrunching it up then smoothing it out again.

'Mam, Mam!' I tug her sleeve.

'What is it?'

'There's somebody over there deliberately spilling tea out on the floor.'

'Don't stare, Bernadette. There are some sorry plights in this place.'

I look down for a minute but most of the people are shufflers and it is hard not to gawp.

'Divvent be lang, kidda. Ah divvent want ye getting in the state of some of these.'

'Joe, honestly. Shush.'

Apart from the ones who are dozing, nearly everyone else in the room is fidgeting or picking. Nobody seems to be able to sit still, including Da and me.

'I hope he's feeding you all well, Bernadette?' Mam is trying to be normal but her voice sounds put on and posh. Like the voice she uses when we go to church or when she talks to people outside the house.

'Yes, it's...erm...it's alright.'

Dad's idea of cooking has always been two things on a plate: a stiff lamb chop and boiled potatoes in their skins. According to him, the skins contain all the vitamins and are the best part. If anyone complains he says: clag it with best butter to harden anything too soft, or soften anything too hard. It might not work but it makes the food more tasty.

'Doesn't touch the sides, kidda. They aal eat like gannets, even the cat.'

'Oh yes!' That reminds me of something to say. 'Jupiter caught a moth and patted it to death. It tried to fly off but...'

The woman in the next chair suddenly stirs and starts to cough. It's hard to have a proper talk like this, surrounded by so many starers, looking suspicious.

'I'll be home soon,' Mam says when time's up.

'Teresa and Joey are visiting tomorrow.' I tell her, leaning down for a peck and trying not to wipe her damp lips off as soon as I straighten up.

'Take care, kidda.' Dad kisses her as well. People are gawping and my face is all hot.

'When will she be better, Da?' I ask on the way out.

'How lang's a piece of string?' It's one of Da's conundrums. He's always asking things like that.

'I mean, how long will she be in?'

'Aboot two weeks. Once they've got the doses sorted, she'll be oot.'

'Good. Proper dinners again. Yum.'

'Yee watch yersel or there'll be nee mere *Gordon Blur* five course banquets served up.' Dad heaves in a big breath, sighs, and lights up. 'Hey look at them.' He squints past the smoke to where two cream butterflies soar, dive and twirl over the grass.

'Ah look, Da, see them darting about?'

'That's lucky, that is.'

'Why, because they've got spots?'

'Nar, because they're not trapped with aal the nut-cases inside this place.'

We crunch along the gravel path and I link his arm out onto the street and down to the bus stop. There's a nippy breeze but my face stays bright pink and sizzles all the way home.

Letters

Since Teresa won first prize in a landscape painting competition all she does is draw loads of boring fields and trees and hardly any lovely girls. On bike rides, when we park up, out come the sketch pad and pencils from her saddle bag, and into her gob goes the stalk of grass to match the moody look. I don't know who she thinks she is.

Mam tells everyone she knows that her middle daughter is a prize-winning artist, even Mr Marshall, who only comes to bring bread and cakes and can't really be that interested. Mam submitted a picture of mine as well but it didn't win anything. Mine was of Jupiter sitting on the back fence looking out over the farmer's field. I copied it from what Teresa calls her *cat studies,* but it was on thick paper so I couldn't trace properly and it wasn't very good.

Amazingly, Auntie Nora's last reply mentioned it too. Her and Mam exchange letters every fortnight so they must get hard up for real news. Mam keeps letters for years and as soon as she gets a new one I sneak it out and have a read through. My Dear Sister, they always start, Your loving sister, they always conclude:

...How wonderful to hear of dear Teresa's success.

That must have given you some pleasure among every thing else. I am very sorry you have been unwell.

You are always doing too much and not taking

enough care of yourself. The situation with Philomena was no doubt a great strain, and Joe's accident, and all the worry over the girls having to travel so far to reach school. What a shame when the house is so grand and everywhere around so picturesque. If only it wasn't such a distance and you weren't so isolated...

God give you guidance my dear sister and I am sure that whatever you and Joseph decide will be for the best...

Decide what? What best? Someone's coming...Quick! I shove the letter back in the envelope as fast as I can and slam the drawer shut, hoping I haven't crumpled it.

Isolated? I look it up in my dictionary, my favourite book. *Like an island, secluded...separated.* I need a while to think, to properly take it in. I will need to read it again.

I find *the artist* in the breakfasting room actually doing some homework. She lifts her head from a text book and yawns, welcoming the chance to take a rest.

'Teresa? Do you ever notice Mam being Irish?'

'What you on about?'

'You know, from the way she talks?'

'Not really. Why do you ask?'

'Well, whenever she gets a letter from Auntie Nora she sounds like her for days after.'

'Hey, I never thought of it but you might be right.'

'And, I heard someone in church tell their kid to pass the plate to *the Irish lady.* '

'Who was it?'

'I don't know. The woman who wears the red hat and the high heels.'

'The one who talks posh?'

'They all talk posh.'

'Good point.'

I wait a few days before having a second read. This time I make sure everyone is out of the house so I have space to think.

I make my mind up to kill two birds with one stone and go to Dad's drawer first. His old tobacco tin is always full to the brim with shillings for his tenants' gas meters and I know he never misses the odd one. I take three to be on the safe side. The school tuck shop's toffee cakes keep going up and I like to have a daily supply to feed my brain.

Mam's drawer pulls open with an annoying screech and I get ready to reach in. Funny. I look and look but everything has been changed. All the letters have gone, every single one. I check underneath in the sideboard cupboard. The door to the cupboard screeches too and I start to worry in case someone comes back and hears. My eyes work fast: there is Mam's knitting, and knitting patterns; her embroidery and two clean folded tablecloths; then the Mass set in case anybody gets sick and the priest has to come and give Communion or the Last Rites. No letters though, not a solitary letter in sight.

Over the next week I search the entire house bit by bit and find nothing but bills and receipts. Finally, I pull Mam's blue case to the floor and kneel, noticing straight away the stretchy pocket inside bulging at the seams. It's them, the letters. I stick my hand in. My heart is going berserk. Out they come, blue envelopes carefully slit open and all tied up in a blue satin bow. Wait a minute. This isn't right. These are not Auntie Nora's letters, and they are not the letters our Meena sent.

These letters are much more interesting than them...

'Teresa?'

'Shush, I'm asleep.'

'Did you know that Mam has a stack of love letters hidden in the lining of the blue case?'

'What?'

That's got her. I can practically feel the draft off her eyelids they are blinking that fast.

'How do you know?' Teresa is up on her elbows, all ears and eyes.

'Seen them. Read them.'

'No way, who are they from? What do they say?'

'From Dad of course. Dated 1940.'

'Before they got married?'

'I suppose...He calls her his *darling girl* and...'

'Stop, I can't stand it. That's revolting.'

'I know.'

'Urgh,' we both say together at the exact same moment.

Simultaneously. No matter how many times I write it down I find the word simultaneously too hard to spell. The dictionary says it's when *two things happen together at the same time. A coincidence*: one thing is lost and another, even better thing, is found.

Lips

———— ● ◉ ● ————

Teresa has her hair cut into a bob and I have mine cut the same. It shows off the scoop neck of my dress and I wear it on Saturday morning to the village. It's breezy and the hem of it billows when I jump off the moving bus then climb the stile, chewing a blade of grass and skipping across the field on the short cut from on the war memorial.

'Wait, I want to talk to you.' From nowhere I hear heavy breath, then a voice gaining ground.

'No, go'way.' A putrid taste floods my mouth as I speed.

'Stop. Wait.' Flushed with running the boy catches up. I have seen him before, on the stone bridge with other village lads. He looks about twelve but when he jumps in front and blocks my path and forces my arms to my sides he has the strength of an ox.

'Kiss!' His face pushes into mine.

'No!'

'Just one kiss and I'll let you go.' He presses my shoulders down, his thick tongue like a wet slug, poking out under his sweaty top lip.

'Get off,' the shakes start. 'Go away! Leave me alone.'

His foot hooks my ankle and I am down in dense grass. My dress is up around my hips and I feel his fat mouth all over my face as I thrash about. If he looks down he will see my knickers and bare skin. My bare skin on display.

I lash and kick like a lunatic. He is still on the ground, but I am up, limping first, then racing fast, back over the stile, and out onto the main road...

Stopping to press the stitch in my side, I heave to breathe, and try to get my heart to calm down. This is what happens when you wear a dress instead of jeans. This is what happens when you wear a dress, even if you have no bumps; even if you are as flat as a pancake.

I worry all night in case he knows where I live, frantically thinking how to avoid the village. Only illness would allow me to miss Sunday Mass so there is no way of being let off that, and I can never tell Mam in case she thinks I gave him encouragement. Worse: she might make me stay in the house until I'm an adult, or never ever let me out without accompaniment. I say nothing except to Teresa then wish I hadn't bothered because she pulls a face as if the details are turning her dinner, and it's all too trivial to be made to feel sick for.

As soon as the nights start to draw in Mam cleans all the windows and changes the light lounge curtains for heavy ones that block the drafts.

'Is it cold, or is it cold?' Teresa climbs into bed shivering, rustling the covers and rubbing her toes.

'Cold. Now shh! I'm trying to get to sleep.' I came to bed ages ago but can't nod off for the clatter all this thinking makes.

'I thought so.' She yawns and stretches. 'Oh, why are weekends so short? Can't believe it's school again tomorrow.'

'Don't know...'

'...What's up, Bernadette?'

'Nothing.'

'Oh, come on, it's not like you to come to bed early. There's something wrong, you can't fool me. I can tell from your voice...'

'...Well'

'God! *You are not* going on about that boy again?'

'Not that...And it wasn't funny by the way. Far from it. And his lips were globby, and sweaty, and...'

'...Alright. I know. I know...'

'...Well'

'Just don't keep on about it.'

We both lie for a bit, keeping quiet.

'Terry?' I give in first.

'Uh-huh?'

'You know this house?'

'Uh-huh.' Her teeth clatter like cutlery.

'Do you think Mam and Dad will stay here? I mean, they wouldn't move away would they, make us have to go and live somewhere else?'

'Whaa? After all the money and years of work it took Dad to build it and...' Teresa's voice stops, as if she's suddenly struck by my identical thought.

'I never want to move. Never.'

'God! Me neither. Bernadette! I can't imagine it, can't imagine not being here. And I don't know about Joey but Jupiter would hate having to move to another place. Mind you, even he had paws like ice picks tonight. It's turned freezing and it's been like a fridge in here today. I've got goose-pimples, and my arms are growing icicles.'

She pats the sleeves of her nightie and I face towards her shape only a small space away in the darkness. As soon as the sound stops everything goes deadly quiet, and the black night brings me my dreams.

Part Three

1963-1964
Westmorland Road

Silverhill

It was a late autumn day with no natural light. When the removal van pulled up at noon and the men started emptying out, Mary put on every bare bulb in the house and left them ablaze for the rest of the afternoon.

Leaving school, Bernadette unfurled Mary's instructions to check the new address. It was her first time there and she had no idea where it was. When she arrived she recognised the tacked up curtains, their pattern lit from behind by a single raw light. Climbing the steep front steps she found the front door open and entered the dim passage.

'Yes, hello...in here.' Mary rushed forward in a dirty apron, her voice and feet echoing. 'Bernadette! I was worried you wouldn't find it.'

'I had to keep reading the note.'

'I would've come to meet you from school, but I've been that busy with shifting.'

'Has our Teresa got here yet?'

'She's upstairs looking at your new bedroom.'

'Teresa? Terry?' On the bare stairs Bernadette's hard heels sounded like hobnail boots.

'Yes, hello, in here.'

'God, everywhere echoes.'

'I know. It'll be better when all the furniture's in and we've got some carpets. What do you think?' Teresa swept her hand lavishly around the large high-ceilinged room.

'No central heating; feels damp as well,' Bernadette shivered. 'And smells like pee.'

'Charming. Don't look at me.'

They moved over together, looking down onto the street, taking separate sides of the two sash windows.

'Do you like the windows? I do.'

'I'm glad you've found *something* good.' Bernadette's spine shuddered.

'Have you seen the houses over there?' Teresa's eyes settled on the derelict terrace across the road. They're in an even worse state than this.'

The two girls stood silently for a while, without the will to speak.

'Mam says they're all getting pulled down and new ones are being built.'

'Just those ones?' Bernadette was alarmed. 'If this house is demolished we'll have to shift again, maybe to somewhere even worse.'

'Doubt that, but don't worry, I already asked. These at the edge of the park aren't part of the council's plans.'

'Windows are mucky.' Bernadette smeared a finger over the inside, leaving one long clean line. 'Could play noughts and crosses on this. Honestly, if we *had* to move back to town, why couldn't it have been to that nice house on Silverhill. I wouldn't have minded living there.'

'Dad was all set to buy it then decided to pull out and get this one instead.'

'Why though? I mean, look at it.' Bernadette smeared the dirt from her fingertip onto the wood frame and turned back to the room. 'There's cracks in the walls and everything.'

'I know...Mam said Dad changed his mind because Silverhill is next to a cemetery, and Dad hates being anywhere that reminds him of death.'

'*And,* Silverhill was more than two thousand pounds, compared to this being just a few hundred quid?'

Mary had only seen the place once herself, giving it a quick glance over with Joe, and had erased its shabby state from her mind. The kitchen was no more than a draughty extension of the long passage that ran from front to back. It had no door and only a few bits of old lino peeling round the edges of the floor. The door to the yard didn't even make contact with its frame, and the wind was already whistling through. Once Joe rolled his motorbike in from the back lane and parked it, most of the space in the small yard was taken, and it was a squeeze to get to the coal house or for him to reach the rusty outside toilet. No one, except Joe, was inclined to use it.

'Hey, that toilet will dee for me. That can be my exclusive, private netty.'

'You're welcome to it.' Mary was unwrapping crockery and trying to find cupboard space. 'I don't think there's any danger of anybody else wanting to use that.'

'Save iz some of those auld newspapers, kidda.' Joe was intent on being jovial. 'Ah'll stick them on a spike in there. They'll dee me champion. Wiping yer backside is aal those rags are good for.'

'This place is going to take a bit of fixing up mind. The little window in the larder's broke as well.'

'That's nowt that, man, I'll stick a bit of ply wood ower it the morra. It'll hold. Ah'll sort oot a pane of glass and a bit putty.'

'Don't forget, please.'

'Hey, is that the teacups Ah hear rattling? Haway man, kidda, leave aal that till later. Stick the kettle on and we'll have a cuppa.'

'It doesn't seem two minutes since we did aal this.' The tinder was damp and Joe struggled to get the fire to take hold. Once he got it away though Mary began to thaw.

'We've certainly been through this routine a few times now, Joe. A dozen or more moves we must have made in our married life. Déjà vu.'

'Noo gan steady. Ah nah yeeve been to France but there's nee need for language like that.' Joe raised her a tired smile soon replaced by an enormous yawn. It had been a heavy day and they were both pleased to sit by the hearth and rest their aching bones.

'I've never felt warm since I got up this morning at six o'clock, even though I've never stopped.'

'First sign of auld age that, kidda.'

'Here, take your cup of tea and put this biscuit in your mouth.'

Joe took the Rich Tea and dunked, swallowing it whole before it fell to mush.

'Yee'll be able to get yersel ower to that church and get a few prayers in now. It should be close enough fer ye.'

'Hardly a stone's throw. That's one good thing.'

Living a distance from church had made Mary's prayer life difficult. Now she found herself directly across the road from the same church they had left three years before. The wrestling priest had moved on but others had come in his place. Mary would have visits from the curates again. She would be back in the parish network.

Folding the Universe

From the girls' bedroom window the old church was just about visible. Bernadette craned her neck to look at the round tower, circled with what looked to her like thin upright lavatory brushes. She remembered how afraid she always felt approaching the grotesque faces above the cold stone work: the winged fish and dragon-backed cats, monstrous beaks twisting above the arched doorway.

Some things she never forgot, like the day she was picked out from school to help fold copies of The Universe. She wondered if the old caretaker, Mr Murphy would still be there, huffing and puffing, his face and clothes crumpled as well-worn sheets:

'Come here and I'll show you what to do.' His breath was wheezy and his chin white, as he headed noisily from the presbytery down the aisle, Bernadette and two classmates sliding out of the pew and tiptoeing towards him. The vivid clang of the iron gates, the gloomy porch, and the dark wooden table where the newspapers were stacked. All these things had stayed with her.

'Take hold of a paper now, and lay it straight, like so.' He watched the children closely. 'Now, fold it three times like this.'

They stood in a line, folding the papers; the other two doing it right first time, going faster and faster, making the Universe into two neat piles.

'Not like that' He glared at Bernadette. 'Like this. Try

again.'

She rubbed a cardi sleeve across her eyes.

'You stupid child! Hopeless. Leave them down now!' His shouting rang out over a row of head-scarved mutterers chanting the Rosary.

'Go back into school and ask Miss Beckett to send another child.'

Bernadette Keenan could not fold The Universe, and soon everyone in school would know. The sound of her blaring went up to the roof, until all at once her mother magically appeared from the group of chanting women, and tried to quieten her down.

'Shush,' Mary said, wiping Bernadette with a hankie that only brought more noise and tears and gulping of snot. It was then Mr Murphy turned soft and kind and the adults moved to one side and talked and smiled.

'His bark is worse than his bite,' Mary had said, taking her youngest by the hand and hurrying her out. 'Dear me, I've never known a child make such a fuss. What's so bad it makes you convulse?'

The enormous sighs took ages to die and made it impossible for Bernadette to reply or ask what that big word meant. From then on she never wanted to be noticed, or chosen again; not picked to fold the Universe, or for anything that made her gasp for air.

Funny how they all found themselves back here in Elswick again. Here, back in the same parish but this time even closer to the priests, and the threat of Benediction.

Attics

———— ◦ ◉ ◦ ————

Mary and Joe took the smaller back bedroom on the first floor, and put the girls in the big room at the front. Joey was given the attic directly above his parents, where he was glad to be out of the way. There were carpets for the main staircase but no spare for the flight to the attic which creaked loudly on every second step. Sneaking in or out would be difficult for Joey, but so would creeping up on him.

'Knock!'

'Knock?' Bernadette didn't see why she should.

'*Go on*, knock.' Teresa nudged her.

Just before they moved, Joey complained that someone entered his room without permission and went through his things and Teresa was keen to reassure him it was not behaviour she would stoop to.

Begrudgingly, Bernadette took the hint and knocked softly on her brother's door.

'Come in,' Joey said in feigned surprise, having heard them on the very first tread. 'Enter.'

'Har, har, Prince Joey.' Bernadette mocked.

'No titles thanks, I'm not a royalist.'

'What are you then? No, don't answer that.'

'Republican: a socialist actually. I've just been reading about...'

'Wow!' Teresa gawped at the gloomy mottled walls and

the tiny black mouth of the fireplace.

'What do you think?' Joey leaned back on his bed looking rather pleased.

His sisters dropped onto the single mattress simultaneously and scrutinised the ancient-looking walls.

'It's alright, bit dark.' Teresa tried to inject some perk into her voice.

'Might paint the cupboard white. What d'you reckon?'

The girls watched him sorting his folded clothes into his old familiar cupboard.

'That'll make a big difference.' Bernadette said.

'Ouch! Sarky.' Teresa pushed her sister sideways towards the foot of the bed.

'Well, living here will be much easier for work. One bus gets me all the way to Hawthorns.'

'Swans?'

'Hawthorns.'

'Oh aye, forgot you got the sack.'

'*Laid off*,' Joey stressed. 'Like most apprentices once they've served their time. Anyway it's better at Hawthorns, get proper pay at last.'

'Have you looked in the other attic?'

'Empty as your skull.' Joey tapped Bernadette's head.

'Owcha!'

'Come on,' Teresa said, 'Let's have a peep.'

The three of them got up and went through to the front.

'What the hell's this room been used for?' Teresa's face swivelled.

'Not much by the looks of it.'

Piles of yellowed papers scrunched under their feet, raising dust. They bent to check inside the low wall cupboards then stretched to the high dormer window to peek out.

'Would you not rather sleep here in the front?' Teresa asked. 'It's a bit lighter than yours.'

'Nah, the back'll do me. It would take too much clearing up, and I'd keep banging me head on the slopes. Have you seen how much the roof slants?' Joey reached a hand and tapped the light bulb, setting it swinging to and fro.

'I wonder if Ma would let us use this room for a den?' Bernadette's eyes lit up.

'She might do. I don't see it being used for anything else.'

'Let's start work on it then. We'll get some pictures stuck up.'

'Who of?' Teresa put a finger to her lip and started thinking.

'Well, there's enough room, we can have film stars, singers, groups, anybody we like.'

'It would be an improvement. Do you fancy putting any pictures up Joey?' Teresa knew he wouldn't be interested but still asked.

'Nah, not unless you could find a good one of Brenda Lee.'

'Brenda Lee! *No*, not still her?'

Joey smiled coyly, revealing the chip in his front tooth.

As they turned to leave Teresa noticed scratches on the inside of the door.

'Hey, animals clawing?' She pointed.

'Must've kept something locked in here.' Joey screwed his mouth.

'Dogs?' Bernadette flinched. 'The only dog I've ever liked was Finch. All other dogs make my heart race like the clappers.

'Well, certainly not a cat.' Teresa noted the height of the marks.' Not unless it had ladders.'

'A cheetah maybe.' Joey scoffed.

'Or an Alsatian. Remember Stan-the-Stiff-Legged-Pole?'

'Keeping the dead dog and getting carted off to the loony bin? Who could forget?

'Come on,' Joey said, 'let's get out of here.'

Bird

———— ● ◉ ● ————

By the time Mary got all the beds made up it was past midnight. Everyone had to stay up and wait even though they were exhausted. Finally ironed in between clean sheets, Teresa and Bernadette stretched, yawned, prayed then wished each other goodnight.

'Why you whispering?'

'Dunno, why are you?'

'Somebody might be listening.'

'Hey, you never know.'

They began to unwind, relaxing just a bit.

'Bernadette?'

'What?'

'Do you realise, we are back living on the same street where we were born?'

'*So we are!* I forgot about that.'

'We were born in 182, this is 256. That means we've come precisely 37 doors.'

'37?'

'182 off 256 is 74, halved for evens is 37.'

'Not counting the park or the picture house or...'

'...Not counting anything but houses.'

'So, we haven't come very far then?'

'It seems further.'

'I know it does.' Bernadette joined in with the yawns. 'Goodnight Teresa.'

'Goodnight Bernadette, and don't dare say anything about bed bugs in this house.'

They dropped off for a while but both came round to a scraping sound at the exact same moment.

'Bernadette, did you hear something?'

It was very dim and they had no idea what time it was.

'Yes, what was it?'

'Don't know.'

'Do you think something is in the front attic, living in the cupboards?'

'Dunno. It was so dark in there I couldn't see right in.'

'It's something being dragged...Did you hear that?'

'I thought something was moving round in there,' Teresa stiffened, 'eyes shimmering right at the back. Maybe a bird got in and made a home for itself?'

'Might have.'

'That would be logical at least.'

'Nothing would surprise me in this place.'

'Should we wake Joey and go and have a look?'

'No. He wouldn't be amused.'

'No. You're right. Let's not. Anyway my muscles are frozen stiff.'

They lay in silence for what seemed like an age, trying to be very still, ears on high alert.

'Bernadette?'

'Mmm?'

'What you thinking?'

'I'm thinking how much I loved living in the country, and how much I hate it here.'

'God, this is miserable.'

'Do you think they told any of our relatives?'

'What, how we've moved back down in the world? Definitely not. They didn't even tell *us* until last week.'

'And I had to find my way here from a note.'

'As if that wasn't a hint.'

'What you implying?' Bernadette picked up her teddy and threw it at Teresa's bed.'

'Hey, thanks. An extra pillow, just what I needed. Goodnight.' Teresa squashed the old battered toy under her head.

'Poor Ted.' An icy blast hit Bernadette's legs as she leapt over to retrieve him. 'I'm wearing socks tomorrow night.'

'Put some on now.'

'I would if I knew where anything was.'

'Stick your toes under Ted.'

'I'm not doing that. Poor old Ted.'

'About time you grew out of teddy bears anyway.'

'Wha! Ted! No way. We need each other now more than ever.' Bernadette pulled him close.

'I've got the cat to keep me warm.'

'That was sneaky.' Bernadette tugged her ears but couldn't hear any purring.

'Is Jupiter alright? Is he still breathing?'

'He's fine, just exhausted from the move, a bit depressed.'

'Depressed?'

'Yes, animals can get depressed you know. Mam's not the only one.'

Bernadette couldn't make her brain think of anything to add and soon the talking petered out. They both tossed and turned and thought and thought, trying to imagine how they would ever live it down: the humiliating move from their beautiful new detached house in the countryside back to an old terraced bomb-site on the dark side of town.

Rituals

———— ● ◉ ● ————

The smell of frying bacon wafted under the door rousing the girls' hungry stomachs.

'What time is it?' Bernadette stretched and yawned.

'I think it's late. We must've slept in.'

'It's Saturday. Hooray! At least we don't have to go to school.'

It was their first chance to examine the bedroom in daylight: an imposing marble fireplace at the chimney breast, and an ornate ceiling rose centring a network of cobwebs.

'There better not be any spiders living in here with us.'

They exchanged nervous looks then threw back the covers, jumped up and started getting dressed.

'You starving? I am.'

'Haway, I'll race you down.'

'Here's your breakfast.' Mary sniffled. 'I'm just nipping over to church to check the list of services.'

She put the pot of tea and bacon toasties down in front of them and fastened her coat. Children's Favourites was on the wireless and the fire was on. The place had been sorted with a table and some dining chairs and didn't feel so bad with a bit of music, some hot food, and a few licks of warmth.

'Oh yeah, one of my favourites. Turn it up.' Teresa attempted to eat and sing along at the same time: *'Thinkin' bout things like a walk in the park...thinkin' bout things...a kiss in the dark....things...things we used to do...'*

'Will you shut your mouth when you're chewing?' Bernadette pulled a disgusted face.

'Har, like you've got room to talk?'

'Now that's enough out of you two. Turn that down please, and no arguments while I'm out.'

'Where's Dad?' Bernadette noticed the used plate with a trickle of egg yolk stuck hard. He must have been in a hurry not to have mopped that up.

'Cleaning the yard.' Mary sniffed and wiped her nose, fastened her headscarf in a loose knot and tucked in a stray wave. 'Says he'll brighten those outside walls with a coat of whitewash.'

'Where's Joey?'

'Still in his room. Goodness knows when he'll emerge. Look, I have to go, I said I'd see Mrs Towers over there.'

'Mrs Towers! Mrs Towers from Warrington Road?' Teresa never expected to see the Towers family again.

'Poor woman's had a lot to cope with since Mister passed. God rest his soul.' Mary crossed herself, quick as a flash.

'Mister *died?*'

'Heart attack. Only the day after your da had seen him on the corner of Elswick Road.'

The food and tea slid down nicely and there wasn't another word until it was demolished and they were sure their mother had gone.

'He might've *seen* Mister Towers, but I bet Da sneaked past quiet as a dormouse.' Teresa let out a muffled laugh.

'Couldn't stand the man could he?' Bernadette said. 'Would cross the street if he saw him first.'

'Hates nosey parkers, and Mister Towers was the super-deluxe star of nosey parkers.'

'He'll be sorry now.' Bernadette stood at the grimy glass of the window and peered out at her dad.

'Doubt that,' Teresa said, sounding smug.

'Teresa? Do you think Mam'll try to make us go to Benediction again?'

'Would you go?'

'No. Would you?'

'No.'

'Not even for a Milky Bar?'

'Not even for a Milky Bar.'

'Milky Bar and a packet of Opal Fruits?'

'Mmm...Yeah, OK. Then, I might.'

Returning to Elswick meant short bus rides again: a five minute wait, and a five minute ride to town. No more hanging around for hours on end. Teresa flung back her arms and smiled. She was looking forward to hearing the latest releases in Windows' soundproof booths, and had arranged to meet two school friends.

'Can I come?'

'No.'

'Why not? I love record shops.'

'Cos I'm meeting friends.'

'You never said.'

'I don't have to tell you everything I do.'

'You stuck up...' Bernadette mumbled but loud enough to be heard.

'Sticks and stones may break my bones but your words can never hurt me.'

'Do what you like.'

'I will.'

'Do then!'

'A nod's as good as a wink.'

'Arrr, get knotted!' Bernadette plopped onto the cold windowsill and poked the cat. Jupiter looked confused, as if he couldn't work out where his cosy life went: his toasty spot on top of the kitchen boiler.

Taking the stairs three at a time, Joey flew down from the attic, said hello to the cat then seeing his father was safely occupied outside went through to the kitchen and made himself a pile of jam and bread, golloping it down with a cup of stewed tea. Once fuelled up he headed quickly out before there was a chance of encountering Joe inside the house.

The walk to town was bracing and just what Joey needed.

He hadn't been in the city's West End for ages and wanted to re-establish his bearings. His stride was long and fast, quickly passing the park and the unmistakable stink of the gents' public toilets. At the foot of Beech Grove Road the old Savoy Picture House was boarded up. How many films had he seen there, at a rough count? Too many to estimate. The building was derelict but hanging on, unlike the shops on the other side of the road, where for years he had bought all his sweets and comics.

At the bottom of Warrington Road he stopped and glanced up. It was hard to see 29 from where he stood, but at least Watson's the chemist was intact and remained open. Not everything familiar had been flattened. Crossing the back lanes his young life reappeared: the magnificent bonfires; the rag and bone man with his whipped horse, clip-clopping over the cobbles, bouncing a bunch of bright balloons.

Welcome to Cruddas Park! Joey cricked his neck to take in the full extent of the new all-dominant twenty-storey block looming above; its subterranean pub and shops gobbling people up, sucking them into the darkness. A wind whipped round it, hurling itself over other multi-storey flats and box-houses. As he gazed, an old man was lifted then dropped, with no more power to resist than a paper bag, his head bashed against the steep concrete steps and Joey noticed a woman in a headscarf bending to help him up; her shape and gait reminiscent of Mrs Towers. Mrs Towers the fly-trap, who, once her subject was caught, would squeeze out blood. She had been more than a match for Mister, and he wondered if her husband's death had made her more or less talkative?

Kind and well-intentioned as she was, he would try to avoid her.

At 182, Joey paused, noting the wall he once fell from and broke his arm. He nodded up at the old house where his sisters were born, with its fancy wrought iron and ornate stone now worn and neglected. Nostalgia done, he took the opportunity to lengthen his stride and was soon in town checking Halford's and considering a new push bike. The scooter needed repairs and was too expensive to keep but he wasn't keen on going back to peddles. The bus would do. The number one and number two went right past their door and the two would take him near enough to work. He would get used to it. At the next shop he checked the price of television sets. Now that was something he *would* like, a TV all to himself.

On the way back he found the old joke shop near Marlborough Crescent, thankfully still open for business. He bought a new pack of marked cards; a complicated pattern he could learn from scratch. Once it was memorised he would win every hand poker-faced, not letting on until his sisters were fit to burst with rage. He gave a sideways smirk and stroked his chin. It would be so amusing to see them foxed, yet again.

Jupiter

———— ● ◉ ● ————

'Have you seen the cat?' Teresa asked, pulling a puzzled face.

'I haven't to be honest, pet.' Mary's cold was heavy and made her voice sound rough as sandpaper.

'What's that you're drinking?'

'Andrews Liver Salts. My stomach's off as well.' Mary tipped her head back and poured in the cascading froth.

'Where's Bernadette?'

'Upstairs...I think.' Mary gasped, barely catching enough breath to speak.

'Up to no good, I'll bet.' Teresa dashed off, bursting in on her sister as she blew a mass of rubbings onto the floor.

'Ah-ha! Caught in the act!'

'Eee, where've you scuttled in from? I thought you were out with your friends.'

'Red-handed at last!' Teresa closed in.

Bernadette sat on her bed cross-legged, one arm folded hopefully over the sketch pad.

'My bloody sketch pad, you little thief! Do you realise how expensive that paper is?'

'I only used one page. One measly page. You would never have missed it.'

'Oh my God, you've got my best pencils as well. Let me see...'

'Here, have them. I don't want them...No need to snatch. Ow!'

'So that's why the fuchsia one's so worn down. You've been using all my best colours. I knew your rubbish pictures had my colours in. God, I hate you so much...'

'Charming. If that's the way you feel you can keep them. You mingy thing.' Bernadette sidled off the mattress and out of the room. Moving quietly but fast. She had been on the receiving end of her sister's wrath enough times to know when to admit defeat and flee.

'If I promise never to take them again can we call it quits?' Bernadette was worried by the barrage of threatening looks Teresa threw over tea. The need to call a truce before being isolated with her sister again at bedtime gained urgency.

'Give me one good reason why I should?'

'I know, I know. But I promise on Ted's life, look, you can cut him up and scatter his limbs to the four winds if I do it again.' Bernadette crossed her fingers and held them up: 'Skinchies, Teresa?' She pleaded. 'You can nip me black and blue if I do. Oh, come on Teresa, please, skinchies?'

'Oh...alright, you pest. I shouldn't, but for the sake of peace and nothing else.'

Bernadette's face settled in for the lecture that came as an aftermath: *time you grew up, should know better,* yak, yak, yak.

'By the way, in between wearing down my pencils and using up my book, have you seen the cat?'

'No, but now you come to mention it...' Bernadette welcomed her sister's change of tack. 'I'll come and help you look.'

'That's all the attics and bedrooms searched.'

'And everywhere downstairs.' Teresa flipped the sneck on the cupboard under the stairs, making sure it was shut.

'Do you think he could have got out on to the street?'

'I don't see how. The front and glass doors are closed, and he won't have tried to climb out of the yard, not with broken glass cemented all along the top of the walls.'

'Wait...'

'What?' Teresa's ears sprang out on stalks.

'Did you hear something? A faint meow?'

'There, yes, just now.'

'What the hell...'

They rushed to the front room, the source of the noise.

'Look at the soot!' Bernadette gawped at the cloud settling on the carpet.

'Oh my giddy aunt!'

A pool of black dust covered the hearth.

'That chimney must be full. Look at the state of the fireplace, *and floor.*'

'The fireplace! That's where he is...' Teresa and her sister dropped to their hunkers, both holding their skirts up out of the way.

'There he is. Look, I can see his eyes sparkling.' Teresa peered up into the blackness.

'Give me a squint.' Bernadette elbowed in. 'How did he do that?'

'There's a ledge just there look. He's on the ledge, the bloody idiot.'

'Come on Jup. Down you come.'

'Come on cat. Pss...sww...sww...Come on, you can come down now. Everything's alright.'

Once the cat had been enticed down with a saucer of milk and the thick of the mess had been swept, the girls brought a dish of warm water and set about giving his coat a good clean. Later on, Mary administered Germolene to their scratched and swollen hands. For supper they had cocoa to console themselves.

'Is it unlucky do you think?' Teresa asked. 'A cat being stuck up a chimney I mean?'

'I suppose a superstitious person might say it was.' Mary was the right one to ask. She spent her childhood leaving treats out for leprechauns, and knew all about the tricks of Irish sprites.

'Well, he wasn't stuck, not really.' Bernadette said. 'He only went up there because he was scared. Anyone would hide any place if they were scared.'

'Urr, yuk.' Teresa quickly dropped the teaspoon she had just picked up. 'What on earth's been on that?'

'Oh, I meant to move that,' Mary picked it up. 'That's the spoon your dad was using before he went out to the pub.'

'Using for *what*?'

'Pouring caster oil into his ears.'

'Urgh!' Teresa put a hand over her mouth.

'He's as deaf as a post and I'm sick of telling him to go to the doctors and get them syringed.' Mary yanked a well-used hanky from up her cardigan sleeve, blowing as long and loud as a trumpet. 'Doesn't trust doctors, your dad. Never has. The wax in there must be an inch thick by now. If he waits much longer to dig it out it's going to take a trowel.'

Rituals

———— ● ◉ ● ————

Bernadette and Teresa raced to the second floor and went out onto the flat roof overlooking the park and the grounds of Saint Joseph's Home. The Little Sisters of the Poor looked after old people there and Teresa remembered Meena helping out when she was a Girl Guide.

'Why did she stop?' Bernadette asked.

'Fell in love with Elvis.'

'Ah! Yes, I remember it.'

'And reading tea leaves and stars and getting dolled up. Lost interest in old people.'

'Hey, we can sunbathe up here in the summer. No one will be able to see us.' There was a sheer drop into the yard. Bernadette went to the edge and peered down. The ground looked miles away and made her head woozy. 'As long as we keep away from the edge,' she said, stepping back.

'You'd think it would have a fence or something,' Teresa wobbled. 'It's making me dizzy it's so high up.'

'If the cat gets out here he might fall off.'

'The cat's not that daft, and he's still got a few lives left.' Teresa glared accusingly at her sister.

'Don't look at me. I didn't put him up the chimney. Bet it's cost him a life though.'

'But you did try to put him in the washing machine once.'

'I did not! I picked him up by the tail, that's all. And as

387

soon as I realised he didn't like it I let him go.'

'When he clawed your arm, you mean?'

'I was only five. You've got the memory of an elephant.'

'Asher's cat's a Siamese.'

'Yeah?' Bernadette was sick of hearing about Teresa's well-to-do friend.

'I'm staying at Asher's tonight.'

'In Gosforth?'

'They've got five bedrooms and a study and...'

'...Hey, look.'

Jupiter was on the motorbike in the yard, stretched on the leather seat, staring up at them. Since they moved back to town the machine was hardly being used, and the chrome was starting to rust. It looked out of place stuck in the yard, lonely and unloved.

Propped against their bedroom wall the girls' bikes remained pristine. The brilliant idea of hauling them up the attic stairs and taking photographs on the flat roof happened only once. Mounting them was easy enough, but Bernadette panicked when hers rolled back.

'I told you not to take your feet off the deck.'

'I forgot.'

'If you'd rolled back any further you would've been off. Talk about the cat committing suicide.' Teresa raised her eyebrows.

'It wasn't my idea, it was yours.'

'As long as the pictures come out it'll be worth it.'

'They better had, after all that.'

'At least having the park in the background will make it look as if we're living somewhere nice.'

The view of Saint Joseph's brought back memories of May Processions: the girls in white veils and coronets throwing petals, the boys in new shirts and ties with slicked hair and scrubbed faces.

Bernadette happily recounted looking like a bride, or a nun being Professed, becoming betrothed to Christ: married to God.'

'Mam only got to be a novice,' Teresa said, 'sort of engaged to God, but no ring.'

'She used to love the Little Sisters though, and taking us to processions. I think, if she hadn't married Dad she would've re-enlisted and become one of them.'

'Except, if she hadn't married Dad she would never have come to Newcastle in the first place, would she?'

'Oh Yeah, but other than that I mean. I could see her pushing old people in wheelchairs and singing Queen of the May, and making the sun shine on the procession every year, because that's what nuns do,' Bernadette beamed. 'That's their power.'

'What about afterwards: the slabs of ginger cake and glasses of green pop? Do you remember queuing at the hatch?'

'I never minded lining up for that.'

'And the curly green moustaches, when you thought you looked so perfect, remember that?'

'Arh, you had to go and spoil it.'

Square Eyes

— ● ● ● —

As Joey woke, his lips were still abuzz with cowboy talk. With a six-shooter and buckskins he looked the part. He had been at a watering hole making a camp-fire, settling down with a blanket to rest under the stars.

Walking past the boarded up picture house brought all the old westerns alive: stills of Shane framed outside, him queuing to get in. Joey had seen that film three times when it first came out. He folded his arms under his head and tried to think how long it was since he last went to the cinema but couldn't work it out.

The television set had been installed in one corner of the front room where it caused continual argument. Mary, Joey, Teresa, and Bernadette took nightly turns to choose what they would watch, but apart from Coronation Street and Z Cars Mary was easily swayed. And Bernadette always complained, even when it was Joey's official turn, especially about The Strange World of Gurney Slade. That clinched it. No more screaming matches. Joey went out and bought his own set for his own room and apart from coming down to collect food, spent all his evenings in the attic, which conveniently meant he was never about when the old man came in full of booze.

'But it won't work if it's not plugged into the aerial.'

This was not part of Bernadette's plan. She hated Joey's choices on the family set but never considered he might buy his own. Joey having his own telly brought the likelihood of her being excluded from his room. She dreaded to think of Teresa going upstairs to watch with their brother, leaving her all alone, or just her with their mother. She would have her own way selecting programmes, but that was no fun. Not one iota.

Fate accompli. Too late.

Bernadette bit the top layer off a Liquorice Allsort, letting the concentrated sugar float; it was impossible to decide a favourite flavour. Apart from the coconut ones they were all delicious, and even coconuts were better than none. She sat back trying to count how many she'd already eaten, and how many she still had to go. She scraped the tip of her itchy tongue on her teeth, a lining of fur gathering on her gums. Sitting all on her own with no one to argue with was as boring as she imagined. As she nibbled, shaped and chewed her way through the sweets she pictured Joey's brand-new television, not small as she hoped but with a nineteen inch screen, only two inches smaller than the big set.

At first, Joey determined not to let his youngest sister enter his domain but finally caved in to the relentless nagging.

'Come on, out now. I want to watch this in peace.' Joey had voluntarily let her in, but Bernadette quickly became an irritation.

'I'll take Jupiter back down should I?'

'Leave the cat where he is, he's fine.' Jupiter was sitting at the foot of the bed on Teresa's knee, watching Joey adjust the aerial in an bid to get the picture to stop spinning.

'Joey? What does ventana mean?'

'It's the word for the aerial that sits on top.'

'How much was it?'

'That's for me to know and you to find out.'

'Oh well, you'll be able to watch Fyfe Robertson and Alan Whicker now as much as you like and learn loads of boring stuff.'

'That's right. I certainly will.'

'And, you're not supposed to bring the cat up.' Bernadette couldn't think what else to add.

'Who says?'

'Mam says he's not allowed in the attics.'

'Why not?'

'In case he has an accident.'

'He's not gonna piss himself. Now you better clear off before you get a clout.'

'You wouldn't dare...' Bernadette made for the door, guessing she was pushing her luck. 'I heard you swear, I'm gonna tell.'

Quickly on his feet Joey gave Bernadette a helpful shove towards the stairwell. The cat and Teresa sat back on Joey's bed, both with wide grins.

'Hell's bells! What a pain in the neck.' Joey slammed the door, rattling the hinges. 'Children should be seen and not heard.'

'I'm not a child!' Bernadette screamed back from the landing.

'Away, you baby. Get downstairs now!'

Bernadette's pet lip was big enough to balance a cup. She held it in position, stomping and stamping on every bare tread until she reached the bottom stair, where there was no further point.

Facts of Life

———— ● ● ● ————

Within walking distance Mary found a GP's surgery, registered, and made her first appointment. The doctors were both practising Catholics which was ideal. After a few visits, Mary found she was unimpressed by the lady doctor, but considered her husband accommodating, happy to try her on any variety of drugs and anti-depressants.

From there she took the bus to town, a mere hop of three stops; calling at the Catholic Truth Society shop to buy Bernadette a book explaining the facts of life. She had been delaying the subject, but Bernadette would soon be twelve and it had to be dealt with. She flicked through one called Growing Up which seemed to cover most of what her daughter would need to know. Good enough. There should be no need for much discussion, or embarrassment.

In the chemist she collected her prescription pills and picked up an extra pack of sanitary towels and a new sanitary belt. She would tuck them discreetly underneath Bernadette's pyjamas and vests, so they would be there ready, for when she needed them.

When Mary was that age there was nothing to use but rags, forever washed and rewashed. Immediately she was struck with an image of the tiny cottage where she was raised and the stingy face of the *auld wife* who married her uncle and took over the house. There had been no privacy in her reign; nowhere to hide from the guilt and shame of existence.

Joe pushed his way in beside Mary, who was draining cabbage, picked up the green slab of soap and began washing his black hands at the sink.

'Watch yourself!' She pulled back the steaming pan and propped it on the small draining board. 'Did you get the cistern mended then?'

'Aye. Flushing like new. Nee reappearing turds.'

'Joe, give over.'

'Wey, it's reet. The ones ye dee, kidda, they would scare the Lochness monster, they would.'

'If you don't get out of here...' Mary gave an exasperated sigh.

Joe stretched his back and flexed his knees, wincing with the pain manual work caused these days. He dried his hands on the tea-towel then skedaddled through to the table where Teresa was already hungrily waiting, until she saw the meat.

'What *is that*?'

'Nice bit of rabbit.' Mary put the steaming creature on the table and went to fetch the vegetables.

'I am not eating a rabbit.'

'Get it doon yer.' Joe picked up his knife and fork. 'Divvent knaa what's good for ye.'

'Rabbit was a very welcome meal in wartime.' Mary informed her daughter. 'Don't turn your nose up,' she said, sitting at last.

'It's not wartime and I'm not eating it.' Teresa grimaced.

'Nee wonder she's a spelk.'

'Dad! I am *not* skinny, thank you very much.'

'Leave her Joe. And where's the other two? I don't know.' Mary laced on the pepper and salt and began to chew.

Joey slid in silently as usual, then Bernadette, who, learning what the pink stuff was, copied her sister in refusing the meat. Joey ate what was put on his plate, facing out his father, who noted every bite he consumed.

Teresa contented herself with potatoes and cabbage, leaving her place as soon as she had enough to offset the stomach pangs. There was art homework to finish anyway, and she decided to go upstairs and get on with that. Joey tucked three ginger nuts in his palm and followed her with a cup of tea.

Ambition

———— ⚬ ◉ ⚬ ————

From the day they moved back, a steady stream of callers began arriving on the Keenans' doorstep: hawkers selling sticks, brushes, dusters; or offering to sharpen blunted knives and scissors. A line of tenants and prospective tenants formed, and Joe's old cronies reappeared, taking tea, discussing pubs they recently frequented. Drinking pals were addressed by surname: McAllister and Van Eck, who Bernadette remembered because his name sounded like *heck*, and because he had cheese-coloured teeth and bad breath. Frankie came back with cabbages and chrysanths. Mrs Towers called to chat, chat, chat. Everything was as was, as if the family had never left, had never gone to live somewhere else.

'Cannit beat a bit of broon breed with best butter.' Joe sat back and patted the jumper braced over his expanding chest. Apart from money, if anything was going to put Joe in a good mood it was food.

'Did Ah ever tell ye aboot...?'

'Here we go...' Mary pushed a flop of hair with the back of her wrist then stood to clear the crockery.

'Divvent be hasty, listen and ye might lorn. *Did Ah ever tell ye aboot* the time Ah was a lift attendant?'

'No.' Bernadette genuinely had not heard this one before and sat glued.

'Well then...'

'Come on, Da, what's the punch line?' Teresa said, hurrying him forward.

'Nee punch line. It was nee laughing matter.'

'It's got to be a joke?'

'Nee joke. There Ah was in this la-de-da department store...'

'Bainbridges?'

'Nah, it was in London.'

'London?'

'Aye, London. Noo shush. Anyways, there Ah was, up and doon like a bliddy yo-yo. Up and doon, up and doon Ah went: Fourth floor, first floor, basement. Pulling that bliddy heavy, iron gate open and closed aal morning lang until Ah was as dizzy as a duck. Stuck in a lift pressing buttons, on and on from nine o'clock in the morning when Ah started, till one o'clock in the afternoon, when Ah handed in me cards.'

'What?' Teresa said. Left?'

'Half a day. The shortest job Ah ever had. Me belly was deein summersaults and roaring like a bear, and that was as lang as Ah could stick it oot.'

The Keenans' house was in the middle of a terrace of seven. On one side were the Bells, who had no children, the Doonans who had two, and the Heaneys with eight. The Heaneys' only lad was a fourteen-year-old altar boy with dark hair combed forward like a Beatle. As far as Bernadette was concerned he was a hunk, and for the first time in ages she stopped complaining about going to church.

So plea-ee-ee-ese

Love me do-oo

Alone among a crowd of sisters, Dermot was the only one of the clan who gave Teresa and Bernadette smiles rather than dirty looks. All the Heaneys had Irish names, but all, with the exception of Dermot, hurled snide comments at every chance. When Bernadette passed in new diamond-pattern stockings the younger ones called out *liquorish legs* from behind their hedge. At first Bernadette thought she was being mistaken for her sister then realised the *snobs* being referred to included her. *Stuck up madams...Who do they think they are?* The Keenan sisters were constantly mocked.

Without realising, the Keenan girls had stopped being townies three years before, when they left for Darras Hall. Their dad was still broad, but they had no discernible Geordie accent at all. Like their mother, who never learned to speak Geordie, they were outsiders. It was official: Bernadette was as big a snob as her older sister. She didn't like the unwelcome attention from the Heaney girls but being classed in the same bag as Teresa, was, she considered, the height of success. And no matter what their spiteful cake-holes spat, she knew her diamond stockings were simply the best of the best.

If the neighbours thought she was full of herself, so be it. She would prove their point by sticking her toffee nose right up in the air. She would admire their hunky brother from a distance, and vow to never to speak to them, even if she was sat in the same pew in church.

Love me do-oo

Oh yeah,

Love me do-oo

On the other side lived the Moons, who were foreign, but no one knew where from. They never said and no one asked. Their daughter was Mercy Moon and their dog, Rebel Moon, and their knotty, long-haired cat, Marmaduke Moon. Marmaduke Moon soon sussed the presence of a fellow feline and became a regular visitor at 256, sneaking in to partake of Jupiter's food, entering by the front to avoid the back wall's spiky glass.

Apart from one family who were non-Catholic the only other neighbours were the old couple who wore dark clothes and large black hats. Mr Forster was a brother of Saint Vincent de Paul and though frail, often helped with the collection plates, passing them around during the offertory. His wife cleaned, scraped candle wax from the church's heavy candlesticks, and flicked a duster to keep the holy statues fresh. Not to be outdone in the service of the Lord, Mary and Mrs Towers joined in the effort. They were younger and could exert more elbow grease, a bit more spit and polish for the cause.

In no time at all Mary felt Saint Michael's was once again her second home. All the same jobs were still there waiting to welcome a devout woman like herself. Good Catholic cleaners, dusters and scrapers always in short supply. Arranging the church flowers was a slightly different matter; for the time being, Mary and Mrs Towers could only aspire to attain that role: flower arrangers were a good deal higher up the greasy parish pole.

At home, Mary set a small round plant table by the window in the front room.

'Come here till I show you,' she said, excitedly, when Frankie called in. 'That geranium you brought the other day, it has the most glorious flower.'

'Peach.' Frankie smiled. 'Looks good enough to eat, does that.'

'Speaking of which, how's the vegetable patch? I do miss having the garden.'

Bon Means Good

—— • ◉ • ——

In the front room mirror Joey admired himself in his new double-breasted blazer then combed his hair and tash, returning the grubby comb to his inside pocket. He straightened the hem of his jacket and tugged the back vent.

'You could be Alan Whicker's twin,' Bernadette said.

'Thanks. I'll take that as a compliment.'

'It's not.'

Alan Whicker looked at least forty, Bernadette thought, and she didn't see the appeal. If her brother had to go and copy somebody off the telly he could at least be modern. She was always trying to get him to grow his hair long, and get with it, but he refused to admire anyone trendy, not even one of the Beatles, let alone a Rolling Stone.

'Are you going out?'

Joey turned round and tapped his nose. 'Maybe.'

'You never normally go anywhere at night.'

'Keep your sneck out.'

As she wasn't getting any information Bernadette decided to change tack and soften her tone.

'Joey, does anything about this wallpaper strike you as odd?'

'Aye, it's all split.'

'Not that.' She sat up in the armchair and nodded towards

405

the fireplace.'

'Peeling?'

'No, the pattern!'

Joey looked at the green leaves, twisting stems, and faded flowers.

'I don't notice anything.'

'Look closer, see, all the flowers are up-side-down.' Bernadette sprang onto her knees, using two fingers to point.

'*Crickey Moses!*' Joey raised his eyebrows so his forehead crinkled. 'You're right.'

'Whoever put it up must've been blind; fancy decorating a whole room without realising that.'

'Might have been done on purpose?' The wavy lines on Joey's brow wiggled like waves.

'Why would anybody do that?'

'Hated flowers? Brain wired back to front? Devil worshippers? I don't know.'

'Devil worshippers? People only do that in films, not in real life.'

'How do you know?'

When Joey left, Bernadette found the cat stretched on the back room hearth, peppered in warm ash, and snoring. Until her mother and sister came back she was on her own with only Jupiter for company. Being alone in this house gave her the creeps. She lay down on the grubby mat, closed her eyes and wondered about where Joey might have sidled off to.

Maybe he was having a romance and had gone out to meet his girlfriend. Bernadette had never even seen her brother with any friends, and couldn't imagine him talking to a girl or going on a date. There again, he was secretive. And no one in their house would dare talk about that sort of thing. Especially since Meena's escapades caused so much wailing and gnashing of teeth.

Joey walked briskly down Westgate Hill towards town, bought a ticket at the Essoldo and went in. He had fancied watching Irma La Douce and seeing The Savoy sitting derelict had made him think about the cinema again. He liked the French theme and when he came out fantasised about saving up and going to Paris and bumping into someone who looked like Shirley MacLaine, with a soupçon of Brenda Lee thrown in.

Bernadette always complained about how difficult learning French was, but at technical high she at least had the chance. For Joey, failing the eleven plus had meant going to a secondary mod, then either life on the scrapheap or life in the shipyard.

He knew some phrases: *ouvre la fenêtre, fermer la bouche,* but learning properly, with the right accent, was off the cards.

The walk back was a bit of a climb but Joey was fit and hardly slackened his pace. A passing car backfired, causing his heart to lurch and jab like a fist; setting off a chorus of howling dogs echoing from lock ups and back yards.

On the last corner before the flat stretch home the smell

of frying from the chippy made his body growl. There was no queue and no reason to resist so he called in for a bag of chips.

'Yes please, lots of vinegar and salt.'

'Any batter luv?' The woman in the white overall winked as she asked, making Joey blush.

'Lots, please, can you leave them open, thanks?'

By the time he got the hot parcel he felt starved and could barely wait to get back outside and gollop them down.

'Ow!' They were just out of the fryer and burned his tongue. 'Blast!' He blew on his hand and slowed up. He wanted to relish the flavour and this would make him have to take his time. Between the full moon and the chips he was soon down to a saunter. It had been an enjoyable night, and a good film. *Très bon.* Shirley was so sexy and cute in her black and green and had given him something nice to dream about. He was on his own with warm thoughts, and was in no hurry to get back to the house.

Bird

No one had a clue how it got in, but it was battering itself against the inside of the front room window desperate to escape.

'Why are birds are so...bird-brained?' Teresa was trying to help her mother catch it but as soon as they got near, the bird panicked.

'No sense have they? Come here you stupid thing.' Mary closed in with the tea-towel, ready to throw it over, but it flapped off again, flying around the room several more times before finally flopping on a coat slung over a dining chair.

'Look,' Mary whispered. 'It's stopped.'

'Must be exhausted.'

'You come from that side, Teresa. That's it. Nice and slow now. Be careful.'

Its beating wings terrified Bernadette, who hid in the passage, pacing. What would happen if they hurt it, or its heart burst with fear?

She listened. Silence. A kerfuffle. A strangled cry.
Suddenly Mary ran out towards the front door, her arms outstretched, her hands clamped round the bird pulsing under the cloth.

That evening it rained hard and showed no sign of letting up. Mary brought a rain hat from her coat pocket and stretched it over the one on her head. A hat on a hat.

'Don't fancy going out in that.' Bernadette said, watching her mother unfurl the plastic concertina and tie it under her chin in a double knot. She would rather get soaked than be seen out in anything so daft.

Teresa was off to Gosforth and Mary to evening Mass, then a talk on Norway delivered by a nun. Bernadette had been invited along but watching television appealed more than looking at slides of fjords and mountains of snow. No fun in that at all, as far as she could see.

'Joey?' Bernadette tapped meekly on her brother's door.

'What you after?'

'Are you coming down to watch The Avengers, there's a better picture downstairs?'

'Is he in?'

'Dad? No, everybody's out.'

'Alright then, I'll be down in a minute.'

Joey was glad of the heat, and stood for ages warming his hands over the hearth. He would never admit it but the picture on his set was not half as good as the one connected to the aerial outside.

'How's the jacket?'

'Ma's dabbed it, but it's marked. Bird-shit stains are hard to get out. A spuggy making that much mess? Joey shook his head disbelievingly. 'More like a blasted albatross.'

'Honestly. Your new blazer...'

'Don't know how it was left there. The one and only time I forgot to take my stuff upstairs.'

'Murphy's law: what can go wrong will go wrong.'

'Well done.'

'Or is it Sod's?

'Either, or. I'll wait till it dries but it'll probably have to go to the cleaners,' Joey frowned.

They both liked The Avengers and settled down to watch, Bernadette curled on one armchair, Joey with his legs thrown over the arm of the other. Each of them wrapped in the glow of the screen and the flickering fire.

'Not fancy a bowler hat to go with the tash, Joey?'

'Very amusing.'

'Like John Steed? Would you not fancy looking like him?'

'Not particularly.'

'I wouldn't mind being Cathy Gale.'

'You in leather trousers?'

'I would do judo and talk in a husky voice, and be *so-phist-ic-ated.*' Bernadette tried it out.

'Right.' Joey shrugged.

'Joey?'

'Will you button up?'

'Have you ever thought about a Beatle cut?'

'Not that again.'

'It would make you look much younger.'

'I don't want to look younger.'

Bernadette pictured all four Beatles, then Dermot Healy. All nice. All trendy.

Joey considered his own image: its projection of gravitas. He liked the idea of looking mature and serious, and wondered how long it would take to save up for a sheep skin like Alan Whicker's.

A comfortable silence settled as they each mused away.

'Jo-eey?' Bernadette put on her best grovelling voice.

'Mmmm?'

'Can I try one of your cigarettes?'

'Yes...'

'Can I?' Bernadette swung her legs out, jumped up, and sat straight as a bolt. 'Arr thanks Joey. Today's been a right stress, what with the bird and...'

'...I didn't finish,' Joey interrupted. 'I will give you a cigarette, but not until you are sixteen.'

'Sixteen! What use is that?'

'When you're sixteen, then I'll buy you a pack.'

'Very funny.' She slunk back down, deeply disappointed. 'Seriously, will you not give me a go? I need one to steady my nerves. I bet you would give Mam one if she asked.'

'Ma's got tablets, she doesn't need tabs.'

'My nerves are shot, Joey. Look.' Bernadette stretched out both hands in front of her face and tried making them shake.

'Your nerves will have to wait,' Joey reiterated. 'When you're sixteen I said, and not one day less.'

Drowning

On Remembrance Sunday Joe lined up alongside a swarm of military uniforms and watched the top brass, adorned with ribbons, lay wreaths at Eldon Square cenotaph. Such a dazzle of decorations. The ordinary Tommies Joe fought with were lucky to get a couple of medals.

The service was long and made Joe's feet ache, but there was plenty of time to scrutinize and take it all in. The council leader there too, of course. No show without Punch.

An hour standing rigid in the rain sopped Joe's paper poppy and numbed his toes. He thought of Belgium's quagmires where many lads who missed the bullets were drowned in flooded shell holes. Tam of course, his Scottish pal, on the advance one minute, then lost his foothold and dropped in the sludge. Arms went out, grasped, but he hadn't a snowball's chance.

On every return trip to Ypres, Joe sought Tam's name on the Mennen Gate. Many unmarked, still waited to be found: over fifty thousand unaccounted. Farmers constantly turning up and adding lost skulls, bones, and spoons.

Man's inhumanity to Man
Makes countless thousands mourn.

Tam had been the man for Rabbie Burns, always at the

ready with a fitting quote.

When they played the Last Post, Joe removed his cap and let his head drop. He thought of Tam and all the other unlucky buggers who never came back, or came back maimed. As much as he despised the pomp and all the rules the over-privileged used to benefit themselves, none of this was relevant then, and none of this was the reason why he bowed.

Listening to the remembrance service on the wireless Mary stopped what she was doing for two minutes at exactly eleven o'clock. The joint was roasting in the oven and the warmth from it steamed the window, battered by hail. She rubbed a circle with a tea towel and glanced out, glad Joe had gone to the service on his own and she hadn't been tempted from the house.

'Hey Mam, look what I found.' Teresa hurried through to the sink where her mother was slicing turnip.

'Where did you dig up that old thing?' Mary turned the silver curler in Teresa's palm.

'Poked it from a loose floorboard.'

'It looks ancient.'

'Must've been stuck there for years and years.'

Mary rinsed her hands and returned to preparing Sunday dinner.

'Come on Teresa, leave that and help me lay the table.'

'Mam?'

'What is it?'

'Do you think...' Teresa hesitated. 'Do you think this house is haunted?'

Mary paused and stepped back, looking directly at her daughter.

'What makes you say that?'

'You do, don't you? I can tell from your face.'

'Don't be ridiculous. Come on gather the knives and forks up and help me get these places set. Your dad will be back soon from the remembrance service and he'll want feeding. It's teeming out there and he'll be soaked to the skin.'

Birds

———— ● ◉ ● ————

The nights were drawing in and Mary put in a high wattage bulb so she could see to finish the blue cardigan she was knitting. Jupiter was using the fender as a chin prop, sitting so close to the coals his white bib was stained rust. She put down the needles, poked the fire then sat back to rest her eyes. Teresa and Bernadette were lodged in front of the television set and apart from breathing in and out were motionless.

Their mother took a moment to admire her daughters. She thought about her oldest girl and wondered had she been too strict, too dogmatic in her views? Things had changed so much since the war ended; it was a different world. These two in front of her were far better off, might make something of themselves, get exams, find qualified occupations and catch good husbands. She didn't like Bernadette going to a non-Catholic school but it was decent, those secondary moderns were useless. Joey and Philomena had had no chance of learning anything in those institutions.

As soon as she got home next day, Teresa sensed something was up. For a start, the wireless was off, and when she left in the morning her mother had not had a cold. Following Mary's sniffles into the front room, all became clear: the hanky was out and the new three piece suite had disappeared.

'What happened?'

'They came and took it back to shop.' Mary's voice echoed

in the empty room. 'Your dad won't sign the HP agreement so it had to be returned.'

'Dad made you send it back?'

'Point blank refuses to have it on tick.'

'But I thought *you* had bought it?'

'I had. But your Dad has to sign the contract as well. A married woman can't get hire purchase without the say so of her husband.'

'What! And he wouldn't sign?'

'Says he's not wasting any more money on...' Mary stopped and blew her nose hard. 'It's not like I ever had any debt. I would have paid it back.'

'I can't believe it. I had no idea Dad could do that.'

'If only it hadn't been delivered it wouldn't be so bad. But seeing those men come in and carry it away down the steps in full view of the neighbours...' Mary yanked the hanky from her sleeve again and nipped it over her nostrils to stop the drips.

Teresa was speechless. It had been taken away as if they were paupers. Her friends from Gosforth would imagine things like that only happened in the dark ages. For a moment she wondered if the bird that got in the house had brought them bad luck, then dismissed it. That was something her parents might think; and she didn't want to imitate any more superstitions.

Nonetheless, there was also the matter of the pigeon they found drowned in the outside toilet: Joe's own private netty.

Its wings outstretched over the seat, its velvet head submerged in the dark water of the bowl. Birds were accruing. Omens were everywhere.

In truth, no one except Mary had really liked the furniture, but that was besides the point. Everybody else thought the chairs were hard and the settee too small, but Mary thought it smelled nice and loved the creams and reds, and all the gold and silver threads. She had brought the antimacassars out and bought new cushions to put either end. It was perfect in the front room, the best room in the house. What was the use though? Without legal status she held no sway. She was powerless.

On the lumpy old settee, Mary sewed in the royal blue cardigan sleeves and felt the satisfaction of making. Knitting helped steady her nervous hands, it was a wonderful soother, and for the time she was busy it pushed the business of the three piece suite, and all her other worries, to the back of her mind.

The Thing

Joey pushed his sister out of the way and moved towards the toilet bowl.

'Get out. I was here first.'

'Were not.'

Bernadette pushed back.

'Get out now. I need a piss.'

'*Language.*' Bernadette folded her arms and glued her feet to the lino. This is what came of only having one inside loo.

'Out!' Joey shoved her again, harder, so her socks skidded across the bathroom floor.

Weight for weight she was never going to win but despite the odds refused to give in.

'No, I need to go, so you'll have to wait. I'll tell Mam on you if you don't let me go first.' Bernadette played her trump card and hoped.

'If you don't get out, on the count of five, I'm going anyway.' Joey hovered over the bowl.

'You wouldn't dare.' Bernadette had never seen a man's thing! and could barely disguise her panic.

'...two...three...' His hand moved downward.

Bernadette froze.

'four...five.' His fingers gripped the tip of his trouser zip...

'Ahhh!' Bernadette turned on her heels. 'You...you...you

are disgusting...' She leapt from the room and fled.

Nothing was going right for Bernadette. She pulled open the cutlery drawer and screamed. It was becoming a habit.

'What's in God's name is wrong now?' Mary came as fast as she could but was only in time to see the tails disappear.

'Rats!'

'They're not big enough for rats, Bernadette.'

'Rats or mice. There were hundreds of them all over the knives and forks.'

'They must have come in from the park.'

'The park?'

'They've had the bulldozers and diggers in and must have turned over their nests. They've found their way in here, out the cold.'

'I only opened it to get a spoon, and there they all were: black beady eyes staring at me.'

'Here.' Mary took a teaspoon and handed it to her. 'Come and eat your egg.'

'I'm not touching that it'll be covered in mouse shit!'

'*Language.*' Mary chastised. 'Here, let me have a look. I'll give it a rinse. Now, come on and sit.'

'God, every time I turn round in this place there's something else.'

'No need to blaspheme.'

'I wasn't.' Bernadette rolled her eyes for effect. 'And, did you hear the sounds from the front attic last night?'

'What sounds are you on about now for goodness sake?'

'The same thing as last time: like scratching, and clawing. Like rats coming out of the walls and skirting boards.'

'You and your sister, I don't know. Too much television, and vivid imagination.'

Settling in front of the TV, Bernadette tucked her legs under a cushion. She always liked to curl up but was being fastidious about keeping her feet off the floor.

'Mam! Mam!'

'Not again! What is it this time?' Mary hurried towards the urgent voice. For the second time in one day she found Bernadette in a state of shock. 'What on earth's going on? What is it for goodness sake?' She dried her hands hurriedly on her apron and looked down at her daughter, then over to the television.

'President Kennedy's been shot.'

'Oh my God!' Mary dropped to the arm of the couch and put both hands to her mouth.

Television was amazing, the best invention in Bernadette's life. Shooting the president was terrible but Bernadette heard it first, was first with the news, saw it hit her mother's face, the devastation registering, then her dropping like a sack of potatoes. Bernadette had rarely seen her mother sob, but this set her off for the night, no stopping.

It was the same with the old Pope, except he was ancient and had been expected to die. Bernadette wondered how on earth her parents survived before the invention of television sets. The wireless was alright, but not half as exciting as telly. Bernadette devoted her life to telly. Without it the olden days must have been very, very empty.

Another Thing

The assassination was televised repeatedly: the cavalcade, the waving, the shots; the president's head in his wife's lap as their car sped off. Jackie's blood-soaked suit turning black, reminding Mary, who had tried her best to put this day off, that blood could not be ignored for ever.

The next time she caught Bernadette alone she took the plunge and handed her the little book from the Catholic Truth Society explaining periods and the facts of life.

Joe puffed for breath, heaved a heaped shovelful of coal to the back of the fire, then stood back to watch it reluctantly catch light.

'A pile of auld slack you've been sold there, kidda. How much did you say you'd paid for it?'

Mary ignored the question, fed up with his grumbling about *the slack* Eddie Graham passed off as *best coal*, and the extortionist price he charged.

Joe dug out a lump of dark brown earwax, held it to the light, flicked it to the back of the fire, then tried another tack.

'Putting the age on, mind.'

'Who, Eddie?'

'Aye.'

Eddie Graham was the same coal man they had before they left. He delivered coal ever since they could remember, and was permanently hunched over from the weight of the sacks.

'It's hard to say,' Mary was still considering. 'All I ever see are his eyes, the rest of his face is always black. I don't even know if I would recognise him scrubbed up and in a suit.'

'What the hell's that smell?' Joe flared his nostrils then gaped at the mug of beige liquid his wife was stirring.

'Complan,' she said defensively. 'It's a diet plan.'

Mary removed the box from the table and replaced it on the cupboard shelf. She was piling on the beef and wanted to loose weight. The male doctor said he could give her nothing to help, and it was no good asking the *skinny bisom* he was married to. There was nothing else for it but self-help.

'How much ye paying for that rubbish?'

'It's not rubbish! One cup of this counts as a meal.'

Mary dreaded to think what her husband would say if he knew the cost. It was a little on the expensive side, but all her skirts were digging in at the waist and she wanted to shift at least a few pounds.

'Yer gannin without food for that stuff?'

'I want some weight off.'

'Yer alreet the way ye are.'

'Half a stone would do.'

'Have ye gorra fancy man like?'

'Give over, Joe.' Mary was not amused.

'Ah divvent knaa, lad. Well, dee what ye like but divvent be serving me up any of that muck.'

'As if you would go without a meal.'

Joe gently patted the jumper stretched over his well-fed stomach and accidentally brought up a belch.

'Nowt wrang wi that, keeps the cold oot. Ah divvent see the point in starving yersel. There's plenty gannin hungry in the world, plenty would be grateful for a plate of proper grub.'

'Indeed they would.'

'The Tories would starve ye soon enough, kidda, withoot ye starving yersel on their behalf. Yeeve gotta look after yer health.'

Unlike Mary, Joe had no handy lines of Shakespeare to throw at life's ups and downs, but there were plenty of Robert Burns quotes in his repertoire. Plenty that echoed his own view of the world.

The rank is but the guinea's stamp,
The man's the gowd for a' that.

When her mother came to wake her for school in the morning Bernadette lay paralysed, completely unable to rouse herself. It was a long time since she had watched Quatermass, but she could vividly remember it: mutant spiders, the earth disintegrating. All the horrors she had been so desperate to watch. How determined she had been as a little girl, browbeating her mother until she gave in and let her stay up. The nightmares had gone on for years, and now, out of the

427

blue, they were back.

It took a considerable amount of hot buttery toast and sweet tea to empty the contents of Bernadette's horror-filled head, but except for the vision of spidery legs tacked inside her eyelids whenever she blinked, she managed to eradicate it.

Back in bed that evening the dream came again; the earth slipping and sliding as she fitfully slept. Everything had gone too far, there was nothing anyone could do. Gravel sucked at her feet, pulling her into the gaping ground as it opened up to swallow her.

The Pit.

The Blood.

Why had Teresa not warned her?

The *Thing* in the Pit.

The *Thing* in the Pit was after her blood.

Everything was mixed up.

Why could no one in her family ever talk about stuff?

Blood, and more blood. The entire place was a-flood.

Bon Means Good

Behind the front door, Mary Bent to pick Meena's letter from the mat, sensing it was bad news. Rereading each page confirmed her instinct about Vincent. She felt vindicated and justified. Her eldest daughter had a broken heart and was coming home for good. They had been right about that man. Joe said all along he was a crook and only married Philomena because he thought they had money. Back then it must have looked as if they did. How times had changed.

With the letter tucked into her pocket, Mary donned her coat and headscarf and headed for church. Inside was dank and dark, but consolingly familiar. She lit a candle for Philomena and her children, then knelt before the altar of the Virgin, got out her Rosary beads and said two decades on their behalf.

Sitting back up on the pew she shivered and it dawned on her how cold she was. All that dense church stone; it was worse than being in the house. Only a few candles were lit but a hundred flames would barely have made an impression of heat. She gazed at the flickering lights and sniffed in the smell of melting wax; it was delicious and took her back: every day rising at six to get dressed, then making her way to chapel to pray and sing God's praises. The long thick habit she wore as a novice was very good at keeping out the draft.

Travelling through Paris had been unbearably hot. The steep climb to Sacré Coeur made her sweat. She pictured all the sisters trying to look demure, holding their long skirts just high enough to stop themselves tripping but not so high as to put their ankles on display. On the inside of *those* heavy stone walls the cool air was a relief. That was a day when she was glad of the contrast in temperatures, the chance to cool off in the Basilica's miraculous atmosphere, regain composure, away from the intensity of the French summer haze.

When Asher came for tea it was clear straight away why Teresa was so enthralled. Bernadette wanted to dislike her sister's best friend but found it annoyingly difficult. Asher *was* posh, but disarmingly natural. She was extremely polite, accepting the house as if it were a palace. She shook hands with everyone, as if she, and they, were all adults, then sat on the couch and made herself at home. Not one to miss an opportunity, Jupiter sprang on her knee, ploughing her legs and purring, loud as a motor.

'Asher has one older sister called Astrid, and one called Anya, and a younger brother called Stephan.' Teresa explained Asher's family to Joey and Bernadette as if they were made up characters she could hardly wait to design costumes for. 'Astrid is seventeen, and lives in Sweden.'

'Sweden?' Bernadette had heard of a Swedish Astrid who knew the Beatles. This was unbelievable.

'My grandparents are Swedish.' Asher displayed perfect pearly teeth. 'And my sister is an au pair.'

Au pair! How French! Joey was immediately impressed and taken at once with Asher's cute lisp and shock of straight blonde hair. She looked him directly in the eyes and gave a wide grin, causing his cheeks to go hot pink. He was unused to pretty girls coming into his proximity, let alone paying him attention. Sisters didn't count and no other females ever entered their house, apart from old Mrs Towers nosing about. He smoothed his tash, aware suddenly that a hair might be out of place and of the small triangular chip in his front tooth.

Asher's stack of natural blonde hair and unseasonably tanned face made Bernadette green at the gills. Somehow she had bypassed black-heads and gone straight to smooth peach. There wasn't one blemish anywhere on her skin, and not one dot of make-up visible. Except for the sweaty handshake, Bernadette would have given up hope and conceded she was perfect.

As the nuns liked their girls to be neat and tidy, Teresa and Asher wore ponytails for school. Make-up was strictly prohibited and Teresa went to great pains to blend her Panstick so it wouldn't be seen. Despite the nuns directive she had no intention of leaving home before covering her spotty chin.

Art and French were taught by good teachers, and were the only subjects Teresa made an effort to be on time for. Mother Térèse was actually French, had an authentic accent, and never raised a hand. The art teacher, Mrs Watson was the only laywoman. She was pretty and young, knew all about art, and was married to a man. She never tutted for no reason, or meted out corporal punishment. Most nuns preferred to give a good hard slap rather than the strap. Mother Margaret had the palms of a navvy, and any girls incurring her wrath could expect what they got.

Braised liver and onions were cheap and a favourite with Joe and Mary, but rarely cooked when the girls where around. Teresa had become so parky she would hardly eat meat at all.

'How much?' Joe sat at the table, having barely digested, and tried to take it in.

'They say they've no choice,' Mary braced herself, 'the term fees have to go up again.'

She always fed Joe a good dinner before hitting him with bad news, and sat watching as the satisfied expression from the liver slid from her husband's face.

'Greedy blighters.'

'I know, but what can you do?'

'Take her away and send her somewhere else. Ah divvent see why Ah have to pay for a private education. None of the others got one.'

'We can't take her away now, Joe, she's only got a year or so left.'

'What the hell's she learned in that place that she couldn't learn somewhere else?'

'Well...She's good at art.'

'Art! Bliddy art's not ganna get her neewhere. She needs to learn something that's ganna get her a proper job.'

'Your sister, Matty, she was an art teacher.'

'Aye, Ah nah! Aal the bliddy money that was wasted educating her, and what did she dee with it? Went oot and got married to the first bloke she met and started churning oot bairns.'

'But Gordon is a lovely man.'

'The point is, she could've got married and had kids without being educated. She didn't have to get educated for that. The Auld Chep spent all his bliddy money on her. Ah never saw nowt.'

Without realising, Mary had led him straight to old resentments involving his father: an unwelcome can of worms.

'Here, pass your plate.' She scrapped the leftovers, stood up and whisked them out. The moment had passed. No point in mentioning Teresa's good marks in French.

Spiders and Flies

―――――― ● ● ● ――――――

Teresa closely examined her face. There were girls in her form with worse acne, but then there were girls like Asher, without a pimple. She nipped and squeezed then sat back satisfied, the dressing-table mirror splattered lemon. Her chin was raw and sore but shining like a new pin. She wiped the mirror with her T-embroidered hankie then took the jam jar with the flour and water paste to the top floor and started sticking magazine pages on the den walls. She planned to use Bernadette's pictures for background, layering her favourites on top.

'Hey, what you doing in here?' Teresa was spooked to hear the floorboards creak, then relieved to see her brother, as she hoofed open the door. 'I thought you didn't want to know about the den.'

Joey was at the window peering out.

'I don't. I just came in to see what the spider was up to.'

'Spider! Where?'

'Out here. Come and watch.'

Teresa put down the paste and sidled up, inspecting the web on the other side of the glass.

'What's it doing?'

'Getting fattened up for winter by the look.'

'Let's have a gander?' Teresa pushed her nose up, seeing two paralysed flies bound in the weave of the web:

one trapped horizontally, the other strung vertically above. The breeze outside made the black net dance, rattling their coffined-bodies.

'I never thought I could feel sorry for a fly, but that's awful.' Teresa turned down her lips.

'Live bait.' Joey copied his sister's face.

'They are very late. I thought they would all have hibernated by now, or whatever flies and spiders do.'

'It's like they are literally frozen in time.'

'Where's the spider hiding then?'

'It's waiting until dark, gonna have one big blow out before the winter diet.'

'Flies are idiots.'

'Spiders are brilliant.'

They stood mesmerised by the macabre beauty; caught between the flies' impending death, and spider's appetite.

Under normal circumstances Bernadette would have had plenty to say to her sister for starting to stick up pictures in the den without her, but there was nothing normal about this day. She needed an ally and Teresa was the only choice.

It was bound to happen of course, spying Rose Ritson by the park gates, the difficulty of hiding behind a lamppost, especially since her chest had begun to develop. Bumping into Rose was the last thing Bernadette wanted: the humiliation of that snob gloating over her family's return to Elswick. Though what followed was much worse.

After Bernadette confided, Teresa was sympathetic, unlike last time, even going back with her to the park to look for the abandoned coat. They found it lying like a discarded snakeskin, in the bushes, exactly where it had been wriggled out of, while still in the grip of her assailant's fists.

'Thank God!' Bernadette had been worried sick. How could she ever explain to her mother about the missing coat? Now it was reclaimed and no one else need ever know.

'*Hal-ay-loo-yah*!' Teresa bent to pick it up. 'Come on, let's get out of this dump.'

The undergrowth in this corner of the park was so thick it couldn't be seen from the path. From now on they would both avoid it like the plague and take the long way round.

'Thank God it was my duffel coat and I managed to undo the toggles, no way I could've opened buttons with one hand.' Bernadette's heart spun like a windmill at the thought.

'How old would you say he was?'

'Fifteen? Sixteen? Honestly, I don't know. I was so shocked when he lunged out like a maniac. Greasy, dark, that's what he was. Greasy, and dark, and hot.'

As they lay in bed late that night, the full extent of the truth dawned. This world was full of snakes and spiders. It wasn't safe to go out.

'You know what we've moved into don't you?' Teresa glared from her bed to her sister's.

'Hell?'

'Nearly.'

'*Hades?*' Bernadette squeezed Old Ted tight round his middle and stuck her feet either side of the lukewarm water bottle.

'Our Joey's word?'

'That's what he calls it.'

'Or, as some would say...'

Teresa paused for full effect.

'...a red light district.'

'A what?'

'A place of rapists, thieves, and prostitutes.'

'Oh!'

'You getting the picture?'

Bernadette sank back flummoxed. She noticed a slice of light through the dull grey curtains. Her eyelids snapped wide in the sliver of bright white moon.

The thin sound of his sisters' voices drifted up the attic stairs as Joey trod the bare floorboards towards the front of the house. The sky was clear and the quarter moon shed enough light to be able to make out the destitute web. No trace of the flies or the spider, not one remnant of a midnight feast.

Outside some drunks were arguing. A woman gave a blood-curdling scream. Joey stood back from the exposed window, then, once they had staggered on, looked out again.

Tall orange lights lined the steep roads, mapping the slopes that moved towards the river. From where he stood the waters of the Tyne couldn't be seen but its eternal flow seldom left him.

Ambition

————— ● ● ● —————

When she got back from church Mary put on a brown rinse then watched helpless as her hair turned the colour of a ginger nut. The weight lost with the Complan diet had come straight back on, and she resented all the meals sacrificed for nothing. A fierce amount of new grey and the recent heavy bleeds indicated the arrival of that time of life; not to mention the bleak moods that landed, and unaccountable feelings of loneliness, and being so tired she hardly knew how to move.

'So, the man pulled over and offered you five pounds?'

'*Yes.*'

'For what?'Bernadette scoffed.

It was the second night on the trot that Teresa had had to explain, spelling it out this time in greater detail.

'For sex, you nincompoop, what do you think?'

'With *you?*'

'With anybody. They even tried to get Mrs Towers into a car one night. Kerb-crawlers aren't fussy.'

'Are you joking?'

'Unfortunately, Bernadette, I'm not.'

'God!'

'They follow women along the road, anybody they see, then slow up and offer money. That's it. It happens all the time around here, especially along Rye Hill.'

When Bernadette asked more questions on the third night, Teresa, told her the conversation was over, and she needed to drop the subject. Nothing made sense, but Bernadette guessed she now knew why Teresa had suddenly changed her tune and become sympathetic to her sister's latest assault.

Every time Mary thought of Philomena, she began unconsciously fidgeting, pulling the crucifix round her neck from side to side. For once, Joe was back early from the pub, and the left off conversation, about their eldest daughter, resumed.

'Where the hell they aal ganna gan?'

'You'll have to find somewhere for them.' Mary sipped slowly at a sweet cup of cocoa, willing herself calm.

'Ah've got neewhere. And before ye look at iz like that, they cannit stop here. Nee way they'll fit in this hoose.'

'Well, there's nothing to be done. Philomena's coming home with two little boys, and they're going to need a place to stay.' Mary curled her fingers around the cup and absorbed the warmth. When the drink was nearly done she cast a gloomy look into the dark wet lining. 'God alone knows.'

For a moment the last of the fire's glow absorbed their worn faces, draining them both of speech.

'At any rate, there'll be nee place for any bugger the way things are gannin.' Joe wearily continued.

'It seems funny now,' Mary directed her nose to the local

paper. 'To think we were both taken in by him, that we considered T Dan Smith a decent man.'

'Bliddy Labour politicians, confiscating property, cheating poor people out of money, betraying aal their class.'

'See what he's up to now.' She stabbed a finger at the front page. 'I would have never guessed this for an outcome.'

'That bloke will not stop until there's nowt left of the place.' Joe shook his head at the picture of the council leader's smiling face.

'Mister Newcastle?' Mary pursed her lips.

'They think nowt of demolishing the West End. But they'll not dare touch the big knobs' hooses ower in Gosforth and Jesmond. They'll not raze them to the ground.'

'And to see what they're replacing the old houses with: new slums just thrown up. I wouldn't fancy living that far up off the ground. Have you seen the height of those flats?'

'Probably won't have much choice soon, kidda. The way this cracker-jack's gannin on. There'll be nowt but high rise boxes.' Joe slumped back.

Newcastle City Council were confiscating any Elswick properties that stood in the way of their idea of progress. Several of Joe's were. They had already claimed four and Joe feared all of his property would end up being taken under their compulsory purchase programme.

'What you going to do?'

'Get fleeced! What can Ah dee against the Local Authority? The likes of yee and me'll never cut any ice faced with their greed. You can bet yer life they'll aal be lining their fat pockets.

'How much did you say they were giving you for Malvern Street, sixty pounds?'

'Sixty, aye. Couldn't lie straight in bed, any of them. Smith's cooncil've got it aal stitched up; conniving blighters, greasing each other's palms.'

'That's where naked ambition gets you. Disgraceful.' Mary frowned.

'Condemn the house see, then pay out a few quid for the land. Not one penny for the bricks and mortar. That's how they work it. That's how they operate.'

The newspaper fluttered to the floor of its own accord, as if it had had enough of being discussed. Joe pushed his cap back and gave his forehead a wipe with the back of his hand then threw his dead tab end on the grate.

'Ah divvent knaa how we're ganna gan on.' His legs felt cold and heavy as marble as he stood up. 'There'll be nowt left round here the way its gannin. The West End of Newcastle's done for, hinny.'

'All these high rises. I don't care for them.' Mary leaned down and rubbed the back of her leg.

'What's the marra?'

'Rheumatism.' Mary winced. 'Not to worry, it'll go off.'

'Haway. Enough for one day. Let's hit the hay, kidda.'

'Could use a good sleep.'

'Ye can never dee nowt about the power merchants of this world, man. The likes of yee and me've got nee chance.

Might as well whistle in the wind.'

'That's right.' Mary looked at her watch and tried to haul herself up. 'Him and his cronies. Power corrupts, Joe, it always does.'

'Come on, kid. It's time to turn in.' Joe offered his hand and pulled her to her feet.

'Hey, what ye been deein t' yer hair?'

'Oh, put a bit of colour on. What do you think?' Mary fluffed the back with her hand and went pink in the cheeks.

'Wey aye. It's canny. Ye look like that film star, ye knaa, what's she caaled? Rita Hayworth. Rita Hayworth, aye, hor.'

Cakes

——— ● ◉ ● ———

Mary got up and dressed at six as usual and went downstairs to fill the kettle, lay the fire, and put Joey's bait up. It was very cold and she was glad of the extra cardigan. She had been wide awake since five, after failing to rouse Joe from talking in his sleep. From the first weeks of their marriage she realised he was haunted by Belgium's battlefields, often reliving the horrors. But in his waking hours those experiences were never discussed; his haunting was entirely solitary except when his moans woke Mary up.

While she worked, Joe remained dead to the world, deep in the clutches of war, where those well-worn terrors lurked:

'Dropped me fucking matches when that barrage of shells went off; have you got a light pal?'

'Aye, there ye gan.' The two men lit up and rested their exhausted backs against the wet sandbags lining the fall back trench.

'Thanks Geordie. Tam's the name.' The Scotsman extended his arm.

'Joe Keenan.' Joe took Tam's hand and shook.

They clocked each other's expressions, Tam sussing that under Joe's helmet was a young boy. At least that's what he would have said before the war, but he had seen plenty younger ones lining these dugouts. And he had gleaned enough to know, no one cared how old the fodder was, as long as there was a plentiful supply of it.

'How come you're with the Yorkshires then, Geordie?'

'Made the mistake of taking the weekend off without permission.'

'Went on the run did ya?'

'AWOL, aye, that's what *they* said. But Ah telt them Ah was only having a couple of days away. Aalways intended coming back.' Smoke sputtered from their faces as they violently choked.

'You were looking forward to this? Aye, like hell.'

'What aboot yersel? You're nee Yorkshire man either.'

'Nah! Scotland. Glasgow originally. I've been living doon there for a few years. Married a Yorkshire lass, from Doncaster.

'Did yee volunteer as well?'

'Aye. Had no idea what I was letting meself in for mind.'

'Who did? Ah signed up with the Northumberland Fusiliers but got hoyed in military prison, missed the boat and ended up here with this lot.'

'That was a bad break, pal.'

'Ah naah. Ah've discovered a lot aboot Yorkshire men since being in wi' the West Ridings. A Yorkshire man can peel an orange in his pocket, that's true enough.'

'And they say the Scots are tight. Still, better keep yer voice down, eh Geordie? Even the rats have ears.'

'Stum's me middle name.' Joe lowered his voice, and they both shivered.

'Which prison was that you were in by the way? I know Tyneside a wee bit.'

'Preston, North Shields.'

'Nah, not familiar.' Tam took a few deep draws. 'Hey, have you got any postcards Geordie?'

'Joe paused for a minute then slid a tentative hand inside his tunic and pulled some out.

'Aye, there ye gan, took these off some dead Jormans.' He passed them to Tam like precious objects. Tam glowered.

'Look at the fucking stance of this lot, and the fucking curly moustaches.' Tam smirked.

'Ah nah. Got a right tip in for themselves. Still, their good and dead now. The only good Jorman...'

'...is a dead Jorman.' They duetted, then doubled over exhausted and coughing.

Tam returned the photographs with respect, holding them like delicate petals until they were deposited back in Joe's uniform. Waiting before he placed his pictures into Joe's hands, careful again, not to bend or tear them.

'Here, have a gander at these.' Tam gave a knowing wink. Joe beamed, his grin broadening as he went quickly through them, then again more slowly, then more slowly still.

'Fuck me!' Where'd ye get these?' He said with a whistle.

'Picked 'em up along the way. Some canny lassies there eh?'

'Mata, fuckin, Hari! Now there's a piece Ah wouldn't mind bumping into.'

'Steady on now pal, I'm first in that fucking queue.' Tam quickly snapped them back. 'Well, good luck Geordie. Thanks for the light.'

'Aye, yee anaal.'

Tam turned, hauled his body upright and trudged off just as a whistle sounded. Joe found the butt end of his rifle had buried itself in the mud and nearly set his back trying to pull it out.

Under the bleeding sky that night, Joe warmed himself with thoughts of Mata Hari: women like her with see-through veils and jewelled skin. Hussies, wearing hardly anything. *Mata Hari, now there is one exotic fucking tart.* It reminded him, just for a moment, he was still alive, he still had the remnants of a beating heart.

'Joe, will you wake up and stop that noise.' Mary had pleaded.

'Eh?' Joe's ears were blocked with wax and at first he didn't know he was in his own bed or that the voice in his ear was his wife's.

'Been fighting that blasted war again, Joe?'

'Aye, something like that.' Joe readjusted his pillow, poked inside his ear, then rolled over and nodded off again. Two minutes later his mouth was on the move once more, trembling with incoherent talk.

The disturbed night left Mary under par and she yawned through most of the seven o'clock Mass. Joe was late getting up, and had to hurry off with only one cup of tea and a slice of bread. He had two leaky taps to mend and needed to meet Frankie to show him a loose drainpipe on Belgrave Terrace.

The Keenans' front door was busy as usual with tenants requests for repairs, or loans of a quid or two to tide over the hardest up until dole payments came through. Living in Ponteland the family had never been pestered: geographically the two addresses were only a few miles distant, but in every other respect they were polar opposites.

Mary had no sooner got back from the shops and put her purchases in the cupboard than another knock at the door interrupted.

'Is your dad in luv?'

'You mean Mr Keenan?'

A shabbily dressed man hovered on the front step, hopping nervously from foot to foot then glancing up at Mary's puzzled expression.

'Oh, aye, err, sorry Mrs...'

Mary felt flattered, being mistaken for Joe's daughter rather than his wife. Her hair was nothing like Rita Hayworth's but maybe the colour looked decent, and the Complan diet had not been a complete waste of effort.

When Joe finally got the jobs done and arrived home for lunch Mary lost no time telling him about the caller and how she had been addressed.

'Bob he said his name was.'

'Bliddy auld cadger. A right sponger, that bloke.' Joe coughed up a chunk of lime green phlegm and spat it into the back of the fire; poking the coals until the sizzling stopped. His knees were stiff with cold and his chronic bronchitis was biting hard; hard enough to make him consider giving up the tabs.

'Did you get everything fixed?' Mary asked, feeling deflated.

'Aye, nowt much, a couple of new washers.' Joe slowly rotated his right wrist, feeling the ache in it. The nut on the first tap had been so stiff it had taken all his strength to turn the spanner. Still, the working man doesn't get a fair crack of the whip, he knew that.

'Canny pie, kidda. Steak and kidney?'

'From Davies bread shop. They always did nice pastries, still do.'

'Aye, their meat pies have aalways been tasty.'

'And their cakes.'

'Ah hope it doesn't give iz heartburn.' Joe kneaded his fist into the middle of his chest and let out a loud belch. 'Ah, better oot than in.'

'Here, I got a couple of jam tarts as well. Want one?' Mary's diet had been temporarily abandoned. 'It's too cold to count calories at this time of year.'

'Ah'll probably suffer but, gan on.' Joe took the lemon

curd tart from the extended plate, leaving the raspberry one for his wife.

Being within easy reach of his properties again meant he could go and do whatever work was necessary in the mornings, getting done in time to share a midday snack. The two of them alone in the house for a while, this was one of the things he liked about being back.

'Hey, kidda, de ye remind the day Saint Michael's went on fire?'

'The incendiary bomb? What a night that was.'

'The same raid that blew in the stained glass windows at St Nicholas's Cathedral.'

'You sure it was the same? That one landed on the Quayside but the blast shook the whole town.'

Another conversation about the war began. Not the first war, the one Joe privately re-lived, but the second war, the one they jointly experienced; the war they had shared and survived, come through together. The subject of the second war brought them close and so they talked and talked until the cows came home, until it was too late to do any more work that afternoon, too late to do anything except enjoy each other's company and drink more tea.

Ambition

The fire was lit but the air was freezing. Teresa and Bernadette sat at opposite ends of the couch, folding their legs and sticking their toes under a shared cushion.

They were settled in front of the television and prepared to watch anything that came on. Bilko was mildly funny, but Hancock bored Bernadette numb. Teresa could never admit to not liking what amused her brother, but her mind had also wandered off.

'What do you think happened to the people who lived in the eighth house?' Bernadette asked.

'What you on about?'

'The eighth house that used to be at the end of this row?'

'Arr that? Demolished.' Teresa's muffled voice crept through the neck of her sloppy jumper, stretched from her chin to her raised knees.

'Did it collapse and crush them?' Bernadette rubbed some circulation into the tip of her icy nose. 'From the state of the walls left hanging there you would think so.'

'Don't be daft. They weren't living in it. It was demolished by the council.'

'Why?'

'Joey says the area's riddled with old mines, and the whole place is rotten with subsidence.'

'What does that mean?'

'It means we're sinking into the ground.'

'*We* are!?'

'Have you not noticed the enormous cracks in the walls?'

'Now you come to mention it…Are they getting wider?'

'That crevice is much bigger than it was when we came. I think a canyon's opening up. '

'A canyon, like in America?'

'Not a Grand Canyon but big enough to step in and enter another world.'

'I might like that, but why does it have to be here?'

On his way back from clearing a vacant room the following day Joe passed their elderly neighbours arm in arm, holding each other up. He said a quick 'Aye, aye,' then driven by his love of food and lack of social etiquette, hurried by and into the house.

'What ye making, kidda?' As soon as he got into the passage Joe's nose filled with promise that made his stomach growl.

'Irish stew.' Mary called from the doorless kitchen, where she was in full view.

'Ah thought Ah was getting a whiff of something canny.' Joe went in the back room and slung his jacket, but kept his cap firmly on his head. He rubbed the arms of his thick jumper to aid circulation then raked the fire, topping it with coal before picking up the newspaper and taking position in the easy chair.

'Here they gan again. Aalways talking about one war or another. Politicians twisting words to suit.'

'Da, man!' Teresa was listening to comedy on the wireless and didn't want to be disturbed.

'Tradition! That's a good one.' He continued.

Teresa didn't know he was on about, but he was making an irritating noise and blotting the sound of the wireless out.

'A lot of bad happens in the name of tradition ye knaa.' The running commentary carried on as he read.

He wasn't about to give up, so Teresa turned off the radio and switched her attention.

'Such as?'

'Such as sustaining royalty and aal their hangers on, and playing that bliddy national anthem. Could they not find a better tune than that: God Save the bliddy Queen?'

'I don't like that song either. It's rubbish. And why do people have to get up for someone they've never even met?'

The last time Teresa went to the pictures she got poked in the back for not standing to attention at the start of the film. Something she would never forget.'

'Ye see, even youngsters can work it oot.'

'Keeps us all in our place doesn't it, Da?

'That's reet. They cannit fool aal the people aal the time, but they only need enough, and the rest of us are stymied. Maintaining the status quo, that's what they caal it.'

When Teresa stopped to think, she saw her dad and her

brother held a lot of the same political attitudes. This must have been totally accidental because obviously they never talked to each other, or shared any of their views.

'Da?'

'Aye?' Joe was turning pages, and moving onto other, less offensive, news.

'You know when you used to juggle and flip tennis balls off the muscles in your arms and catch two in one hand, and then flip them up, nearly to the roof?'

'Aye? Not just baals, fruit: oranges, oranges, they were good.'

'Can you still do it?'

'Ah divvent knaa, why?'

'Cos I'm learning to be a juggler and I need you to show me what to do. I'm gonna work Northumberland Street on Saturdays and make a fortune. I'll be so rich you won't have to give me any more pocket money, or pay for my school.'

Joe's face lit up like a belisha beacon.

'Well gan and bring iz a bit of fruit then, or a couple of taties, and Ah'll show ye how to gan on.'

'Great.' Teresa grinned.

'Ah'll even lend ye a cap. Ye'll need a receptacle for collecting aal that cash.'

Jupiter

———— ● ● ● ————

Teresa woke in a sweat: the nightmare hard to climb out of. Vince and Meena were together again and had a third child. Vince had become a professional shoplifter and made Bernadette his assistant. He befriended Joey and introduced him to gambling and nightclubs. Joey liked it, liked the attention, the risk and the drink. He lavished money on his brother-in-law, spent everything it had taken years to save.

In the last scene Bernadette and Vince had been caught and were in the dock. Bernadette was in her fuchsia coat. Joey, to one side, dressed in pauper's rags. The judge peered down at them with x-ray eyes, lifted a black cloth to his head then pointed a long bony finger at Joey, as if condemning him to death.

Teresa blinked quickly to dispel the image. For a minute she didn't know where she was, staring glakily at Bernadette's bed, trying to gather her thoughts. It was morning at last. She heard her brother's feet pounding down the attic stairs. He was up and about, rushing out. She gave a long sigh and stretched. It was morning. All was correct and as it should be. She dived up and got ready for school.

Leaping off the back of slowing buses had become a craze with Bernadette. The trick was to hit the pavement running then gradually wind to a halt. She became good at it, something of an expert, until the day an unseen lamppost

459

cropped up.

It was her first black eye, and though she detested the swollen nose, she could barely leave the mirror for more than five minutes, fascinated by her own distorted face.

'Do you think it's gone down?'

Teresa glanced up from the table for a split-second, mumbled a few inaudible words then put her head back into her book.

'Joey, do *you* think it's gone down?'

Joey was ladling raspberry jam onto half a loaf, piling slices as they were coated. When the plate was stacked with bread he glanced up.

'You look like you've gone twelve rounds in a boxing ring.'

'Do you think so? As bad as that?' Bernadette felt proud.

'Our 'Enry, yeah. You look like him: Henry Cooper.'

'It's really sore.'

'Least you only hurt yourself, no innocent bystanders.'

'Eh?'

'Domino effect: you could have sent a whole queue of people crashing.'

'There was no one else there.'

'No permanent damage then. You'll recover.'

Later on, when he came back down from his room with the empty plate, Joey was decidedly put out.

'Has anyone seen Jupiter?'

'Not since early on.'

'I don't think he's well.'

'How do you mean?' Teresa laid down her sketch pad and raised herself.

'Seemed really listless before and now he's nowhere about.'

Teresa and Joey delved all sources of heat but he was no where to be found inside the house.

Outside there was ice in the yard. At first glance the vomit reminded Teresa of lemon top cakes; pools of bright yellow sick frothed on the concrete next to Jupiter who was stretched out and turning stiff. It was difficult to believe he was dead, because he looked so content, as if absorbing one last drop of winter warmth.

Only when they moved close did they notice spelks of wood lodged like darts at the centre of his deep green eyes. None of them could face the thought of trying picking them out. Afraid to touch death, they left the cat to blindly stare, popping in and out of the back every now and then to see if, like Lazarus, he would miraculously return to life. Eventually they gave up. Mary donated an old white bed sheet which Joey and Teresa worked in under him to make a shroud. A hole in the small front garden was dug, and once Jupiter was tightly bound they laid him to rest. There was no requiem this time, like there had been for the baby bird. No one pretended to be a priest. And all their prayers were said in silence.

In bed that night, the girls consoled themselves with chat.

'He didn't settle did he?'

'Hated this place.'

'I wonder why.' Teresa and Bernadette convulsed, fluctuating between laughter and tears. Their bodies rocked, rattling the bedsteads until a tumble of loose plaster fell noisily behind the papered wall. They waited until it stopped.

'He knew it was haunted. Animals can tell by the atmosphere.' Teresa continued.

'Jupiter could sense ghosts.'

'The old couple next door told Ma that someone died in here.'

'In this room?'

'The attics I think. Maybe they were murdered.'

'Oh my God! I knew it. The way those stairs creak without a footstep. I tell you what, I'm never ever being left in this house on my own again. The whole place is pure evil.'

'Evil in the walls, Bernadette? Do you believe in it? Do you believe a house can be evil?'

'Before we moved here I would have said no, but this house...?'

'Do you?'

'*Do you?*'

'Yes, *I* do.'

'So do I.'

Ten minutes of intense thinking passed with neither

of them any nearer sleep. Bernadette pulled Ted under the covers and squeezed him tight.

'Poor Jupiter.'

'Our Joey's upset.'

'Never cried though.'

'He's a man, men aren't allowed. He is upset though. Jupiter was his cat.'

'Was not.' Bernadette would never concede that.

Lying silently the girls studied the darkness for a time, thankful for one street light's orange beam through the drab curtains. Bernadette was glad to let some tears and snot flow into her throat rather than down her sore nose. The bruising from the lamppost was still coming out around her eyes: satisfying shades of lemon and green, a few streaks of lilac. Lemon, she decided, was not such a nice colour to have as skin.

'It was so quick. He was right as rain a couple of days ago.'

'Joey thinks he was poisoned.' Teresa said with emphasis.

'What! Deliberately?'

'Who knows? Could've been anything.'

'Nobody would deliberately poison a cat...Would they?'

'There's some weird people living across the road. Giddy-guys, Da says.'

'Oh God, don't say that...'

Bernadette let another batch of mucus slide down her tubes.

'I wonder what happens to all the fleas. Do you think they die as well?'

'Nah,' Teresa grinned. 'I saw them all marching along the street looking for Rebel and Marmaduke Moon.' They both sniffed and giggled.

'I didn't want them crawling on me.' Bernadette's spine gave a quiver.

'Not furry enough. You would never do.'

The tears and laughter continued for what seemed like an age. And there they lay, caught on the edge: the dangerous corner between hilarity and raving hysteria; the sharp bend of Devil's Elbow where their dad once rode his motorbike.

Silverhill

———— ● ● ● ————

Overwhelmed by exhaustion Teresa and Bernadette finally began to doze. Bernadette felt she could sleep for a week, a month, even a year. Soon her dream life transported her to the house that should have been theirs. Silverhill, the house intended for them, the house overlooking the graveyard: the house Joe paid search fees for, then changed his mind about buying.

She rose. It was lovely. It was the next best thing to living in the country and everyone was delighted to be here.

Being close to dead people did not bother Bernadette one little bit. These dead people were quiet, and harmless, and made good neighbours. She and Teresa were allotted the front bedroom to save their father from the view of the graves. They didn't mind, because it meant they had the biggest room, and the sun's rays shone in on them all afternoon. Unlike their dad they felt far away from death, and anyway, the cemetery in summer was full of luscious trees and shrubs and blooms, and the gravestones looked good between the grass. The open view was reminiscent of the country, like Dellside but with all the advantages of being next to town. There were local shops and they were only minutes from the city's regular bus route. There was a Roman Catholic Church that Mary could reach in a hop, skip, and jump. Moving to town again, as it turned out, was not so bad after all. Westmorland Road was just a mistake. 256 never happened.

As she peered from the window Bernadette saw Joey stir and waved. He was relaxing beside a rowan tree, lazing there perfectly content, as if he was in a park rather than a cemetery. Stretched out on a newly turfed grave he smiled and returned her greeting. Everything had been put right. Jupiter was alive and full of beans, and moving to Silverhill thrilled everyone in the family, even Joe and Mary. When Philomena finally came back with the kids, Vince would never bother her again. Bernadette would be able to play auntie, and Meena would find a place close by and go to night school to learn new and useful things, like juggling and crochet and magic, or laying bricks.

After a long day of tears Bernadette was pleased to be here, in this place of pleasant dreams. In this place it was possible to believe none of them would wake in Westmorland Road again. And none of them would ever again be haunted.

Acknowledgments

———— ● ● ● ————

Thanks are due to the Royal Literary Fund for financial support, and to Sheila Wakefield for her commitment to this work. Gratitude also goes to Leah Page and Jeremy Campbell for editorial advice, and to Sarah and Rachael Page for additional input.

Front cover painting by Pauline Kenny.